$1/50

## It was do or die...

Grimacing with pain, Bolan sat near the edge of the ravine, staring into its depths. If he lost it here, he lost it all—a sudden drop might finish him.

The soldier inched forward until he was stretched out on the slope of the gully, expelled one pent-up breath before slithering down the bank. He landed in a crumpled heap and lay there waiting for the flares of pain to subside.

Then he crawled through the gully on his hands and knees, ignoring the stones and thorns that tore into his palms.

The Executioner didn't need to look over his shoulder to know that he left a crimson trail behind him in the dust.

D1011865

# MACK BOLAN

## The Executioner

# DON PENDLETON's EXECUTIONER

# MACK BOLAN

## Run to Ground

### A GOLD EAGLE BOOK FROM
## W®RLDWIDE

TORONTO • NEW YORK • LONDON • PARIS
AMSTERDAM • STOCKHOLM • HAMBURG
ATHENS • MILAN • TOKYO • SYDNEY

First edition October 1987

ISBN 0-373-61106-4

Special thanks and acknowledgment to
Mike Newton for his contribution to this work.

Printed in Canada

"It is easy to be brave from a distance."

—Aesop, *Fables*

"Courage is the thing. All goes if courage goes."

—J.M. Barrie

"Sometimes it takes a crisis for a man or woman to discover courage within themselves. Sometimes it takes a trial by hellfire."

—Mack Bolan

To the men and women of the DEA,
who stand a different and more deadly
kind of border watch.

# PROLOGUE

"I'm getting too damned old for this."

"You're twenty-eight."

"That's too damned old."

And he was right. At twenty-eight, with six years on the job, Roy Jessup was already sick of staring at the border, waiting for the wets to make their way across by moonlight. He had not expected high adventure when he joined the Border Patrol straight out of college...not exactly. Still, there had been all those movies: Charlie Bronson, Kris Kristofferson, Jack Nicholson, all fighting major-league corruption in the desert sunshine, running up their score against the smugglers and top *coyotes*, but it only went to prove that life bore no relationship to Hollywood. With six long years in uniform, Roy Jessup had not seen a gram of coke outside of parties, never fired his gun in anger, never stumbled into an adventure ripe and waiting for a tough young stud to bring the house down.

"Hell, you're just a kid," his partner growled.

Compared to Elmo Bradford, maybe it was true. The guy had twenty years in come November, and it showed. At forty-something, he was losing hair, and what he had was going gray so fast that you could almost see the change from one shift to another. When he buckled on his leather, Bradford's gut damn near concealed the pistol belt in front, and Jessup knew for certain that Elmo's blotchy nose and cheeks

were not entirely due to working half his life beneath the
Arizona sun. If Bradford cut himself, the younger man was
sure the wound would bleed one hundred proof.

"I don't feel like a kid," Roy told him sourly. "I gotta
look around for something else."

"What else? You gonna start in on that teaching bit
again?"

Roy Jessup had his elementary teaching credential, kept
it up to date, but he had never seriously thought of using it
since he had done his student teaching in Los Angeles. There
might be better districts, better schools, but at the moment
he was not inclined to take the risk and gamble with his future.

"Jesus," Elmo said, chuckling, "you'll be better here in
the desert, I promise. At least out here you know the enemy, awright? You know the wets just wanna come across,
and after while you know that some of the *coyotes* wouldn't
mind a little midnight one-on-one. But in the schools today, forget about it. Straight-A students flyin' around on
crack and PCP, you know? One of the staff might cut your
throat, you never know."

You never know. But Jessup knew one thing: his time in
uniform was limited. He did not mind the paramilitary reg-
imen, which was relaxed in the extreme along the barren
Arizona border. He did not really mind the hours; it was too
damned hot for working days, and nights held out the only
hope of any action—thus far unfulfilled. He never gave a
second thought to danger, even though he knew that it existed. If the past six years were any indicator, he would die
from boredom on the job before he faced a threat to life and
limb.

That boredom was the worst of it. Night after dreary
night, they sat and watched the nonexistent borderline until their vision blurred and they began to see elusive phan-

toms drifting through the spotty forest of mesquite and cactus. They encountered wets from time to time, though nothing like the traffic other stations handled on the Rio Grande or coming into San Diego. On occasion, they would spot a drug plane minus running lights, skimming low beneath the radar, and they would radio the information back to base, for all the good that did. Without a destination or the aircraft's registration number, they were jerking off, and everybody knew it.

As for Jessup, he was tired of jerking off.

This midnight, they had parked beside a narrow black-top ribbon south of Cowlic, east of Santa Rosa, in the barren no-man's-land of Pima County. At their backs, the Comobabi Mountains hulked against a velvet sky devoid of moonlight. It was as black as sin outside the cruiser, and Roy was about to try the night glasses again when pinprick headlights made their first appearance on the dark horizon.

"Lookee there, now."

Elmo reached across to get the glasses, and Roy let them go, knowing the cars were still too far away for a visual scan. They were still on the Mexican side, heading north, but distance could be deceiving in the desert, and especially after dark.

"How long you figure?"

"Twenty minutes, give or take, unless they turn around."

Roy Jessup felt a prickling sensation on his scalp, and there was sudden gooseflesh crawling on his arms despite the desert's warmth. At midnight, the temperature was close to seventy-five degrees, and twelve short hours earlier it had been one-ten in the shade, if you could find yourself a patch. However, the sudden chill he felt bore no relation to the outside temperature. There was something of anticipation in the feeling, but he recognized that there was something else as well.

And Jessup knew that something else was fear.

Why should he be afraid? How many times had they staked out this highway, or some other lonely stretch of blacktop, stopping border runners for a little hands-on scrutiny? Not often, when you thought about it. Almost never, if you really put your memory to work. So why were four cars—make that five—approaching in a midnight convoy from the south?

Roy ran several reasons through his mind, in search of one to take the chill away. They might be pilots out of Luke, the local Air Force base and testing range, returning from an expedition into Mexico, half-crocked and carrying a dozen different kinds of clap. They might be Papagos, returning to the reservation after sampling southern hospitality. And then again . . .

They might be *narcotraficantes*. Sure, why not? It might be easier, more economical, to fly the shit across, but everybody knew that some of it came overland. He would not have expected such a convoy—it was too conspicuous, for one thing—but on second thought, that might indicate the shipment was too valuable to send across without an escort. That meant guns, and now the fading chill was back full-force.

They had two Smith & Wessons in the car, as well as a 12-gauge riot gun racked underneath the seat. Twelve extra rounds per man, and maybe half a box of double-ought tucked under maps and Kleenex in the glove compartment. If the convoy up ahead was armed in normal *narcotraficante* style, they would have automatic weapons, shotguns, maybe even hand grenades. Two border cops would never stand a chance against that kind of army.

Jessup jerked the leash on his imagination, smiling to himself and banishing the chill with concentrated effort. He was fantasizing now, projecting himself into *The Alamo* when, in fact, they were probably looking at some refugees from *National Lampoon's Vacation*. Frigging tourists, either lost or trying to pull off a fast one, smuggling a little low-grade grass, illegal fireworks, switchblades for the juveys back in Phoenix or Las Vegas. It would be a piece of cake, and best of all, it would provide a bit of interest in an otherwise excruciating shift.

It wasn't twenty minutes. More like ten, and Jessup thought the new arrivals must be really making time. Five cars, for sure, and he could see them with the glasses now, although the glare of headlights kept him from examining the passengers. There would be time enough for that when they were stopped, and Jessup hoped they might have girls along. You couldn't get away with anything on duty, but it never hurt to window shop. Hell, no.

The convoy was a hundred yards away when Elmo put the cruiser into gear and coasted down the sandy bank to park the vehicle on the center stripe of the road. He flicked on the high beams, left the engine running and had his door wide-open before the leader of the convoy saw them and slowed down from sixty-something to a crawl, eventually coasting to a halt no more than twenty feet away.

"Let's take it nice and easy," Elmo muttered, climbing from behind the wheel. Before he straightened up, he had the safety strap unfastened on his swivel holster, just in case.

Roy Jessup did the same, his thumb looped through the gun belt, close enough to quickly draw the Smith & Wesson magnum if he had to. Feeling foolish, knowing his precautions were in vain, he thought about the shotgun underneath the driver's seat, and left it where it was.

The lead car had its four doors open, and Jessup noted that the dome light must have burned out because he still had no clear view of passengers beyond the headlights. Sudden apprehension caught him by the throat as dark men started piling out on either side of the vehicle, but Elmo was the senior officer and he apparently saw nothing wrong with what was happening.

"You fellas musta missed the interstate," his partner said, chuckling, playing with them, knowing they could not have taken such a tiny, piss-ant road by accident. "I'd like to welcome you to the United States. Of course, I'll have to have a look inside your cars, you understand."

They understood, all right, but Elmo clearly didn't, and the darkness prevented him from catching sight of the rising weapons as they locked on target. There was no way he could have missed the muzzle-flashes, but he had no time to think about them as converging streams of autofire from several weapons blew him backward.

Jessup's apprehension turned to all-out fear and he bolted for the car, his mind consumed with visions of the radio, the riot gun, *escape*. If he could put the cruiser in reverse before they shot the tires off or inflicted damage on the engine block, he had a chance. He never gave a second thought to Elmo Bradford, who had obviously been very dead before he hit the ground.

Ten feet or less separated him from the vehicle and he was close enough to taste it when a voice behind him said, "Don't hurt the car." What kind of crazy fucking thing was that to say when you were killing people? Jessup had no time to mull it over because a giant fist slammed home below one shoulder blade, and he was falling, falling, with the echo of another gunshot ringing in his ears.

He tried to move, to reach his service pistol, but his flaccid arms would not respond to orders from his brain. Behind him came the sound of footsteps closing in the darkness, crunching over gravel, clicking on the blacktop. One of them was wearing taps, and he could not believe that anybody went in for that macho bullshit anymore.

Rough hands reached out and turned him over, lighting flares of agony along his spine. Above him, silhouettes like looming towers blotted out the stars.

"He's still alive," one of them said.

Another stooped in close, his stainless-steel automatic pistol filling Jessup's field of vision.

"Wanna bet?"

**1**

His car had given up the ghost at 2:20 a.m., and Bolan had been walking ever since. Three hours, give or take, and yet it felt like days on end. The fading darkness was his only proof of passing time, his movement and the constant pain the only proof that he was still alive.

The highway was a quarter-mile due west and running parallel to Bolan's track. Remaining with the car or following the asphalt ribbon would have been a suicidal gesture, worse than useless, but he kept the highway fixed in mind, just visible in his peripherals. Cars had passed on three occasions, their headlights lancing through the early-morning darkness, and the wounded man had lurched for cover, knowing they would not have picked him out without a spotlight, still unwilling to reveal himself. The highway and its destination were his secrets of survival. They could also get him killed...assuming that Bolan was not dead already.

There was no sign of Rivera or his gunners yet, but they would be along. They couldn't let him go, could not allow the fates or Mother Nature to complete the job they had started earlier tonight. Mack Bolan now knew enough about Rivera's operation to burn his friends on both sides of the border, and before it came to that, he knew, those friends would sacrifice Rivera in a bid to save themselves.

Unless Rivera found a way to plug the leak, and quickly.

It had been hot all day and warm all evening, but the predawn chill was biting at him. It never ceased to puzzle Bolan that the desert, baking like an oven in the daytime, could become a vast refrigerator after nightfall. Shivering, he blamed it on the chill, refusing to accept the thought that the loss of blood had sapped his strength and made him more susceptible to cold. If he allowed himself to dwell on failure, he might fall, and if he fell, the soldier was not convinced that he could rise again.

Nightbirds whistled round him, unintimidated by his presence. Beyond the range of Bolan's night vision, desert animals occasionally scuttled through the sagebrush, making Bolan hesitate, his free hand clutching at the weapon on his hip. Each time it was a false alarm, but he could not allow himself to grow complacent, take the safety of the night for granted. He was alone and badly injured, poorly armed, with hunters on his track. Surviving past the sunrise would be an achievement. Winning any sort of final victory would be a miracle.

The Uzi had been empty, useless weight, and he had left it in the car. The shoulder rigging for his Beretta 93-R had prevented him from keeping pressure on his wound, so Bolan had discarded it as well, although the pistol and its extra magazines now filled the pockets of his trench coat. Underneath the coat, his AutoMag, Big Thunder, rode the warrior's hip on military webbing, perfectly concealed but still accessible at need.

The bullet wound was in his side, and despite the dizziness and pain, he knew he had been lucky. The slug was in-and-out, from front to back, and had avoided bone and vital organs. Two more inches toward the center and it would have ripped open his stomach. Any higher, and the bullet might have shattered ribs, glanced off and into one of Bolan's lungs. He had been lucky, except that he was bleeding profusely and could not keep sufficient pressure on both wounds at once. His injuries might prove fatal if he did not find a medic soon. Rivera might just kill him yet, if he could keep the Executioner in motion, on the run, until he bled to death.

The target of his strike had been Rivera's rancho, thirty rugged miles due west from Nogales, equidistant from the Arizona border. The Sonoran desert was Rivera's best defense, but he did not rely exclusively upon geography. The sprawling rancho boasted barbed-wire fences, mounted sentries, motorized patrols, as well as a ranch house that was fortified like something from the Siegfried Line. The helipad and airstrip were patrolled around the clock by men equipped with automatic weapons, in case the *federales* felt compelled to stage a showcase raid without sufficient warning. If an enemy approached by land, Rivera had the option of escaping in his private jet, which sat protected from the desert sandstorms in a hangar near the airstrip.

Bolan's target had not been the hangar or the fortress ranch house. After icing careless sentries on the north perimeter, he concentrated on the Quonset huts where heroin, cocaine and marijuana were prepared for shipment into the United States. Rivera's chemists and assorted flunkies sometimes worked around the clock to get a shipment ready, but the sheds were dark that night as Bolan had approached to lay his plastic charges, placing the incendiary packs for maximum effect. He would have been content to torch the goods and pick off Rivera another day, and he was prepared to disengage, when fate and refried beans had intervened. A sentry long on flatulence had made an unexpected run for the latrines, encountering a black-clad specter in the process. He was dead before his bowels let go, but not before his dying finger loosed a warning shot and brought down the whole damned army on Bolan's head.

Getting in had been a breeze compared to getting out. Rivera's troops were armed and dangerous, and they were thirty men to Bolan's one. He had already shaved the odds by half a dozen when a rifle bullet knocked him down, but swift elimination of the sniper had not camouflaged the desperation of his plight. Still dazed and losing precious blood, he had been fortunate enough to commandeer a car—Rivera's own Mercedes—for his getaway. The tank was built with personal security in mind, but errant ricochets had found their way beneath the undercarriage, doing mortal damage to the power plant, and after twenty miles or so, the Merc had died. That left approximately another ten miles to the border, and he had spent the past three hours following the highway at a distance, leaking precious blood into the desert sand.

A sudden wave of dizzy nausea brought Bolan to a lurching halt. He fought the blackness that was threatening to overwhelm him, drop him in his tracks. If he collapsed now, it was over. Finished. For a moment he was tempted to surrender, let the darkness carry him away, but that would mean a victory for Bolan's enemies, and while he lived, the soldier would not make it easy for them. No damned way at all. If he was dying, he would tough it out the hard way, make the bastards work for it. Rivera and his people might waste hours trolling the highway, checking roadside service stations, picking over Bolan's bullet-riddled car. He still had time, if only he could focus on his destination.

Before his strike, the Executioner had memorized assorted maps of northern Mexico and southern Arizona, fixing highways, access roads and settlements in mind for future reference. If he was still on course, then he should reach the nearest hamlet soon. It was a tiny desert crossroads, population well below one hundred in the latest census, but the name eluded Bolan momentarily, the memory evoking jumbled images of church and flowers.

Santa Rosa.

He had driven through the town prior to scouting Rivera's stronghold, and the trip had taken barely twenty seconds. He recalled a service station and garage, a diner and a hardware store, a combination pharmacy and post office, a grocery store, a small saloon adjacent to the permanently vacant "motor inn." A scattering of weathered mobile homes and fading stucco houses on the outskirts finished off a classic portrait of the great Southwestern boom town gone to seed.

Was there a doctor in the tiny town? If not, he would be forced to raid the pharmacy for medical supplies, obtain some wheels and hope that he could make it to a larger settlement in time. Before his time ran out. Before Rivera's hit team overtook him on the road.

And if he found a doctor, then what? There were laws regarding gunshot wounds that required an immediate report to the authorities. He could demand the medic's silence, back it up with hardware while his wounds were stitched and cleaned, but he was not prepared to kill a man of medicine to keep him off the telephone. As soon as Bolan left the doctor's office, probably before he had the chance to find a car, the local law would be alerted. He did not remember seeing a jail or sheriff's station, but the town might have a marshal or a deputy in residence. In any case, he would be forced to deal with that eventuality when it presented itself. Anticipation was of value only if it helped a warrior to prepare himself, and at the moment there was nothing for the Executioner to do except continue to walk while he had the strength.

The doctor might not be a problem after all. If Bolan never reached the town, there would be no report to file, no deputies to be avoided. He could lie down here in the desert, surrender to the waves of dizziness that came from loss of blood, and wait to see if final darkness or Rivera's gunners overtook him first.

With iron will, the soldier thrust his morbid thoughts aside and concentrated on the sandy soil in front of him. Another step. One more. Another. It was light enough to see the rocks and cactus clearly now, allowing him to move with greater confidence, and soon the rising sun would start to drive away the chill that penetrated to his very bones. The sun would help, he thought—at least until its heat began to sap his remaining strength.

But that was hours yet, and Bolan knew instinctively that it was not a problem. Long before the desert sun could reach its zenith, he would be in Santa Rosa...or he would be dead.

And, then again, he might be both.

Rivera's gunners might have found his car. They might have pushed ahead to lay an ambush for him at the crossroads, loitering in Santa Rosa for the first appearance of a stranger desperate for blood and medical attention. They would not have any clear description of him, but they wouldn't need one. Santa Rosa was a fly speck on the map; it saw few motorists, and even fewer lone pedestrians from nowhere, boasting bullet wounds and packing pistols. If Rivera's scouts were waiting for him, he would stand out like an alien from Jupiter, and they would have him in a flash. But if he reached the hamlet first there was a chance, however slim, that he could pull it off. With little more than sheer audacity to carry him, he knew that it would be a near thing, either way, but it was not in Bolan's nature to abandon hope. While life and strength remained, the Executioner would not surrender.

Sudden writhing movement in the sand before him stopped the soldier in his tracks. His hand was on the

AutoMag before he recognized the speckled gila monster waddling across his path, a kangaroo rat hanging limply from its bulldog jaws. The lethal reptile flicked a glance in his direction and continued on its way as if the man did not exist, intent upon its meal, survival in a world where there were only predators and prey, with nothing in between.

The chunky lizard posed no threat to Bolan, and he let it go. He was the prey this time, with hungry predators intent on running him to earth and finishing the kill before he had an opportunity to share his information with the world. It was survival of the fittest, but at a level far removed from simple maintenance of any food chain. And at the moment the Executioner was none too fit.

As if to emphasize his weakness, Bolan reached the border of a shallow gully, carved by flash-flood waters sometime in the distant past. No more than six feet deep, it posed an obstacle to Bolan in his present weakened state, and he could feel his energy escaping through his ragged wounds. The gully ran in each direction to the limits of his sight, considerably deeper on his left and closer to the highway on his right. Avoiding it might take him miles out of his way, and Bolan knew he did not have the stamina to strike off in a new direction, leaving Santa Rosa for a stroll around the open desert. He would have to cross the gully, and do it while he had the strength.

With effort and considerable pain, he sat down on the lip of the ravine, legs dangling in space. The bottom of the gully was a six-foot drop from where he sat. He had to gauge the distance, brace himself to take the pain of impact, keep his grip on consciousness no matter what. If Bolan lost it here, he lost it all, and he was not resigned to death yet.

A sudden drop might finish him, and so the soldier wriggled forward slowly, inch by inch, until he was supported on his elbows with his legs and buttocks stretched out on the slope of the ravine. When he was ready, Bolan simply raised his arms and slithered down the bank, his trench coat bunching up around his hips and snagging sagebrush all the way. He landed in a crumpled heap, legs folded under him, and waited for the flares of pain to gradually subside. His touchdown startled several quail from cover and they scattered skyward, beating at the dawn with frantic wings.

Phase one had been the easy part, and Bolan knew it would be harder climbing out than it had been falling in. He waited out the giddy rush that followed in the wake of pain and crossed the bottom of the gully on his hands and knees, ignoring stones and thorns that tore his palms. He did not need to turn and look to know that he had left a crimson trail behind him in the dust.

The gully's northern bank was not as steep—no more than forty-five degrees—and Bolan noted little burrows scattered up and down its face, which he could use as handholds for his climb. The burning pain had momentarily receded to an angry whisper, and he knew that there was no time like the present to begin.

Slowly, hand over hand, Bolan tackled the slope, ignoring fresh alarms of agony that emanated from his wound. New blood was warm and wet against his skin, and he ignored that, too, aware that he would die in the ravine and rot there if he let the pain and blood deter him. Twice he lost his grip and slithered backward, eating sand, and twice he started over. When he finally dragged himself across the lip of the ravine, he was exhausted, and he knew he dared not stop to rest.

So close. He was so close that he could taste it now, and if he lay there, let the weariness devour him, he had no chance at all. His coat was open, and Bolan saw the bright, fresh blood that soaked his skinsuit, further evidence that he was slowly dying, being drained of his lifeblood. There still might be a chance, but only if he stood, continued walking. Only if he made it into Santa Rosa. Soon.

He made it to his feet, somehow defying gravity and the shining motes that swam before his eyes. For several seconds Bolan felt light-headed, and he struggled to resist the sweet, seductive darkness that was waiting for him just behind his eyelids. Gradually the feeling passed and Bolan found that he was still standing. Satisfied with that, he used the highway and the rising sun as reference points for geographic north and started to walk. One foot placed before the other. One step at a time.

It took fifteen minutes for the Executioner to travel ninety yards and top a gentle rise of sandy ground. Below him, still a mile away and dusty-pale as no oasis ought to be, was Santa Rosa. Somewhere in the predawn darkness, he had crossed the border out of Mexico and into the United States. Without a map and compass to assist him, he had never known the difference.

Neither would Rivera, Bolan realized, with so damned much at stake. The niceties of jurisdiction would not faze his enemy this time. The hunters would be coming, could be there ahead of him and waiting at the tiny village, ready for the kill.

It made no difference either way.

The Executioner was walking into Santa Rosa with hellfire lapping at his heels.

## 2

They found the car at 4:15 a.m. The driver's effort to conceal it had been hasty, ineffective, and Rivera's pointmen spotted it where he had coasted off the road, behind a stand of Joshua trees and sage. The convoy slowed, pulled over, six cars now, including the pale-green cruiser they had picked up at the borderline. Their altercation with the patrolmen had slowed them down, but not disastrously, since their quarry was on foot.

On foot and wounded.

Luis Rivera opened the driver's door and peered inside. He did not give a second thought to fingerprints. The car was his, and a "stolen" report would be filed with the *federales* in due time. For now, establishing the name and destination of his enemy was more important. If the gringo bastard managed to escape with what he obviously knew about Rivera's operation in Sonora, he could make sufficient noise to rouse the Mexican authorities, compel them to forget the years of rich *mordida* they had accepted from Rivera as compensation for selective blindness. If Rivera's enemy escaped, if he was free to talk, then it was finished. Loss of merchandise worth millions was enough to put the man on Rivera's hit list, but the drugs could always be replaced. Provided that he was free to make the deal. But he would not survive in prison, even with his wealth to shelter him from harm. His empire would be picked apart by jackals in his absence, and he would be left alone to face the years of isolation, fighting for his life against the animals inside.

It was too much. Rivera pushed the image out of mind and concentrated on the car. The body armor had deflected several dozen rounds, as it was meant to do. The windows had cracked into tiny cubes in back and on the driver's side, but they had held. Rivera smiled and made a mental note to have another set of wheels just like it readied for his use within the week. There might be something they could do about the undercarriage to prevent a ricochet from wreaking havoc underneath the hood as this one obviously had. In any case, the shield around the gas tank had prevented an explosion, stopping several rounds, and there were still a few miles left in the puncture-proof tires.

What interested Rivera most, however, was the blood. Great blotches of it soaked into the cushions of the driver's seat, eliminating any notion that his enemy had slipped away unscathed. Someone had tagged the bastard, and the gunner would receive a bonus if Rivera could identify him. If he was alive.

He had already lost nine men, and while their lives meant nothing to Rivera in the abstract, he considered it a loss of face, a personal affront that must be rectified with blood. A man in his position must not let himself be vulnerable. He must have the wherewithal to stand against an army of his enemies. Humiliation by a single man would be unthinkable, the end of everything that he had worked for all these years.

But now his enemy was wounded *and* on foot. He had already lost a lot of blood, and every step would cost him more. He might already be delirious from pain and shock, condemned to wander aimlessly until the deadly sun finished him. The desert would kill the gringo, given time...but Rivera knew that he could not afford to wait.

He straightened and scanned the dark sandy wastes on each side of the highway, hoping against hope that he might see the bastard, spot his lurching shadow or the huddled corpse he would eventually become. The empty landscape mocked him, its mute rejoinder spelling out what he already knew: that they were dealing with no ordinary man.

This one was special, certainly. No ordinary man had cracked Rivera's security, blown his merchandise sky-high and eliminated nine of his most trusted soldiers before escaping in his Mercedes. It required a special man to drive away—and then to *walk* away—despite his wounds, the shock and loss of blood. He might not last a mile on foot, but while he lived, he was a mortal threat to everything Rivera owned, the empire he had created. While the intruder survived, Rivera was a man on borrowed time.

He had been thinking of the man as a gringo, but Rivera wondered now. The hit man was tall and he was dressed in black, his face obscured by cosmetics. For all Rivera knew, he might have been a black or a tall Chicano. Doubly thankful that the man had taken a bullet, he knew that it would make their manhunt that much easier. Whoever or whatever he might be, the enemy was badly wounded, perhaps mortally, and he would wear that wound as a distinctive badge of his identity. They could not miss him.

Unless the desert swallowed him alive.

If his enemy was rational and strong enough, he would be making for a settlement, a doctor, anyone who might possess the necessary skills to save his life. But if he was delirious he might walk around in circles till he dropped, covering miles with lifeless, zombie strides until his blood and strength gave out. If he had wandered off without a destination in mind, Rivera knew that they might never find him.

Even searches from the air might fail to spot the obvious, and he was on the wrong side of the border for any sort of massive sweep. He must be circumspect, discreet, but thorough.

Above all else, he must be thorough.

Killing those patrolmen at the border had been risky, but Rivera had no choice. Their cruiser might be useful, especially if his enemy should reach the sanctuary of a town. Official trappings could not hurt, and while the uniforms had been a bloody write-off, he still had the car, their weapons, badges. These objects might provide Rivera with an edge, if he was forced to deal with any other Americans in his search. They would not fool a lawman, but with civilians they might be enough to buy some time.

His men were rummaging inside the car, retrieving a submachine gun—empty—from the floorboards on the passenger's side, stripping the glove compartment of registration papers and any other documents. Beneath the dash they found Rivera's nickel-plated automatic pistol still in place in its special holster, undiscovered by the enemy, and one of them handed it to Rivera with a deferential, almost reverent, gesture.

He weighed the weapon in his hand, removed the magazine to verify that it was still loaded and tucked it inside the waistband of his slacks. His enemy had left one weapon empty, missed another, but they could not leap to the conclusion that he was unarmed. He had been carrying explosives at the rancho and he might have other lethal tricks in store for anyone who got too close. Despite his wounds and loss of blood, despite the distance he would have to travel and his loss of the machine gun, he was dangerous. This one would be dangerous until he died.

They were no more than sixty miles from home and yet Rivera felt the chasm widening, experienced the sense of distance that he always felt on entering the States. He was light-years removed from childhood in Nogales, running with the other homeless gutter rats who joined together for survival on the streets. As best Rivera knew, his mother was a prostitute who had been murdered by a gringo when her only son was eight years old. His father was a faceless shadow, never seen and seldom thought of. Rivera had survived without maternal or paternal care, and he had grown up hard, accustomed to the violence of the slums, where life was cheap and love was a commodity on sale.

At nine he had been picking pockets in Nogales, trusting in his size and speed until he grew proficient at the art, acquiring skill enough to dip the fattest wallet without ruffling its owner. Street gangs fought for territory, coveting the districts where the gringos came to spend their dollars, and before he was eleven, Rivera was a grizzled veteran of those wars. At twelve he killed a man—a boy, really, three years his senior—and ascended on the basis of his growing reputation to a leadership position in the gang he ran with. No longer forced to work the streets himself, he had instructed others in the art of picking pockets and began to cultivate a taste for certain minor luxuries.

The members of his gang had always handled pills and marijuana on a small scale—for the tourist trade—but in the early sixties, with the rise of "flower children" in America, Luis had recognized the drug trade's great potential. He had put his troops to work for men who farmed cannabis, had studied them and learned the ropes, until he was prepared to take over the business for himself. It had not been an easy move. There had been bloody work involved, but by the time a certain Dr. Leary had begun to preach the doctrine of "Tune In, Turn On, Drop Out," Rivera had been ready to provide the children of Aquarius with all the marijuana they could handle. In the circles where he traveled, he had been respected and admired for his achievements. He was seventeen years old.

The marijuana trade was still important to Rivera, but his fortune had been tripled by the traffic in cocaine and heroin. The latter poison he refined himself, from poppy fields in the Sierra Madre, but the coke required a loose alliance with suppliers in Bogotá. It was a risky enterprise with Colombians involved—people who were quick to launch a shooting war for no apparent reason—but again Rivera had survived. He was a multimillionaire who purchased politicians and policemen as another man might purchase cigarettes, and now it galled him that he had to do this butcher job himself. If it had not been so important . . .

But it was. The economic loss that he had suffered was sufficient to demand revenge against his enemy, but it was not his prime consideration. He had suffered a loss of face, and while the Oriental concept was an unfamiliar one, no Hispanic male grew up without a sense of pride, machismo, which demanded retribution for an insult. If Rivera let his enemy escape, competitors would think that he was vulnerable, weak. In time they would begin to test him, ripping off consignments, threatening his trade and territory, making inroads with his customers. The fire last night had cost him several million dollars, but it would be nothing in comparison to losses he would suffer if he had to start from scratch, establishing his territories through protracted warfare with the competition. Esquilante in Chihuaha, Lopez in Coahuila, Quintana in Durango: any one of them, or all of them together, would be glad to see him fall. Without Rivera in the picture, there would be more money for the smaller fish, more trade to go around.

Rivera smiled. He was not going anywhere just yet. The jackals might be hungry, snapping at his heels, but he had always managed to outsmart the competition, and he was not finished yet. One man could not defeat him, not when he had dared so much and come so far alone. It was unthinkable.

Possibly the gringo bastard was dead already. If he was, and if Rivera could not find his body in the desert, then the problem would remain unsolved. He might be forced to fabricate an enemy, provide a straw man for display to his competitors, to show results. If worse came to worst, he would not mind the lie. Not if it helped to save his empire, everything he had built and everything he had become.

But, then, the worst of it would be not knowing. If he did not see the body for himself, if he could not reach out and touch the lifeless flesh, how could he ever rest in peace? How could he be certain that the warrior wouldn't come back, this time to kill Rivera in the very heart of his *estancia*, his castle?

Scowling, he admitted to himself that there could be no substitute for certainty. Whatever he might tell his competition, and whoever's corpse he might display for their inspection, *he* would have to know and be convinced that it was settled with this stranger who appeared from nowhere, striking like the wrath of God. Luis Rivera had no faith in anyone or anything outside himself; he was not part of an organized religion, viewing it as a placebo for the peasant class. No Marxist, he was still convinced that fat cats and politicos supported different churches as a method of controlling superstitious millions, falling back upon the name of God whenever man proved frail and fallible. It was a crutch he had never leaned upon.

There were several drug traffickers active along the Mexican-U.S. border and he wondered why the solitary warrior had selected him. He wondered how the man had scouted his defenses, how he knew precisely when the merchandise would be available and where it would be stored. Sufficient mysteries to baffle any man, and Rivera would never know the answers if he didn't find his enemy.

It would be best, of course, if he could take the man alive. Interrogation might be fruitful, and it certainly would entertain the troops. However, the odds were long against securing a prisoner, and if he had to settle for a corpse, he would be satisfied. As long as he found something, *anything*, to prove his enemy was dead beyond a shadow of a doubt.

The gringo's death was not sufficient in itself, however. If he spilled his guts to the authorities before he died, Rivera might have to cope with bad publicity and pressure from the States, outraged denials of complicity from Mexican officials on the pad. It would not matter, in the long run, if the *federales* raided him or not. Publicity itself was fatal, in sufficient quantities, and while the spotlight focused on Rivera, his competitors were free to move against him from the shadows, gobbling up his customers, his territories.

There were precautions to be taken. At home, the cleanup crew would have removed all traces of narcotics from the ranch by now. The bodies of his soldiers would be tucked away for later burial, well hidden in the event of a police search. The damage to his property could be described as accidental, even written off against his fire insurance with a little sleight of hand, but none of that concerned Rivera now.

His enemy was still at large, most likely still alive, and he remained a liability until his head was safely in the bag. As for that head, Luis Rivera would be happy to assist in its removal.

"What is the nearest town?" he asked Camacho, certain that he knew the answer even as he spoke.

"It will be Santa Rosa, *jefe*."

"Take one car north to watch the road beyond, and leave another in the town itself. But be discreet. I want no contact with the enemy until we are prepared."

"It will be done."

"Remain in contact via radio. I will be waiting two miles south of Santa Rosa to receive your news."

"*Sí, jefe.*"

He cast a final glance at the Mercedes.

"Burn the car before you leave. It must appear to be abandoned by a car thief who desired to leave no clues."

Camacho hustled off to do his master's bidding, and Rivera ambled back in the direction of the highway, where his convoy waited. Stone-faced gunners followed him with eyes that showed no trace of human feeling.

They were close. He felt it in his bones as some men feel cold weather in the offing. Soon the prey would fall into his hands and he would make things right again. He would have justice for himself, and for the wrongs he had suffered at a stranger's hands. With any luck at all he would find out who was behind the raid, and his retribution could include the brains behind the gun.

But first he had to find the warrior, run him to ground before the man could report on Rivera's operation. Time was of the essence, and instinct told him that the answer to his problems would be waiting for him when he got to Santa Rosa. Fortunately he was represented in the town. If the stranger tried to hide there, he would know it, and his wrath would fall on anyone who helped his enemies.

Rivera settled back into his padded seat and smiled. It had the makings of a perfect day.

3

Santa Rosa's main street was deserted as Mack Bolan made
his way along the sidewalk, concentrating on each step, determined not to stumble. He looked strange enough already, with a full day's growth of beard, the rumpled, dusty
trench coat covering his skinsuit. He could not afford to
stagger like a wino coming off a bender, drawing more attention to himself from any casual passersby.

As if in answer to his thoughts, an ancient pickup turned
the corner behind him, grumbling along the curbside lane
and gathering momentum, heading out of town. The driver
did not seem to notice Bolan as he passed, but half a block
beyond he did a double take, examining the grimy stranger
in his rearview mirror as he pulled away. Discreetly, trying
not to lose it, Bolan turned to casually inspect a menu
mounted in the diner's plate-glass window.

Santa Rosa was the kind of town that noticed strangers.
Given its location and its size, the soldier could not have
expected otherwise. The farmer, cowboy, or whoever, could
not double back, but he would file the sighting, store it for
future reference, and he would doubtless mention it to
friends throughout the day. "A stranger down on Main
Street? Half-past six? Well, I declare."

And it would rest there, unless some incident revitalized
those memories. Unless some *other* strangers happened to
ask about a tall man, sickly looking, traveling on foot. The

farmer and his cronies might or might not answer, but their silence, if they chose to keep the secret to themselves, might tell the hunters all they had to know.

He wondered how much effort it would take to seal off a town like Santa Rosa from the outside world. The phone lines would be easy, and the traffic shouldn't be much problem either. One or two cars on the road in each direction, letting everybody in, nobody out. It would be safe to assume that the roadblocks would not be swamped with cars. Communication via radio might be another story; if there was a marshal's office or a tow truck operator with a CB, isolating the town would be more difficult. A Mayday message might be broadcast to surrounding towns before the hunters could complete their sweep. There might be opportunities to reach the county sheriff, or the state police.

His mind was drifting, and the warrior brought it roughly back to here and now. His first priority was the location of a medic. Failing that, he had to get inside the pharmacy, stock up on some essentials, and get out again before he was discovered. Bolan had no cash and no prescriptions for the items that he needed; neither could he wait for normal business hours if he planned to make his getaway with minimal endangerment of innocent civilians.

Medical attention, wheels, escape. They were his top priorities, but Bolan liked to hedge his bets. The service station wasn't open, but its pay phone was in working order and he was relieved to find that he could dial the operator without depositing a coin. The nasal voice verified his "Michael Beeler" credit card and took the Southern California number, asking him to hold.

The calling card was perfectly legitimate, aside from the employment of an alias to cover Bolan's tracks. The billings were dispatched each month to a post-office box in Los Angeles, from which they were routinely forwarded to yet another box in San Diego. No one ever called upon the L.A. box, and no one ever would. The semiannual rent was paid by mail, and it existed only for the purpose of receiving monthly bills. A snoopy sort could hang around the post office for months on end and never see a soul approach Box 2035.

The number Bolan had requested was another cutout, shunting calls from a studio apartment in San Ysidro to Johnny Bolan's home and headquarters at Strongbase One, in San Diego. The apartment, rented month-to-month by "Joseph Breen" was vacant except for a card table, telephone and automatic switching device. The remote-controlled passover occurred on the third ring; the fourth would be answered by Johnny, or, if he was out, by a tape that would take the message. Johnny checked in each hour, on the half, when he was not at home. That meant another fifty minutes if they missed connections now, but it was still the best the Executioner could do.

He wanted John to have some grasp of what was happening, in case it went sour in Santa Rosa. He had briefed his brother on the mission generally, but John was not personally involved. It was a one-man show, which had gone suddenly, perhaps disastrously, wrong. But if Mack Bolan was about to buy the farm in Santa Rosa, he would not go out without alerting others to his fate, preparing a surprise for the Rivera forces somewhere down the road.

Three rings. He waited for the fourth and wondered whether he would hear his brother's voice live or the recorded version.

"Yes?"

Relief hit Bolan like a second wind.

"Is this the Blaylock residence?" he asked, allowing Johnny time to scan the oscillator and confirm his voiceprint.

"Yes," the younger Bolan replied, "but Mr. Blaylock isn't in just now. Is there a message?"

"No, I need to speak with him directly."

A muted tone on the line announced completion of the voiceprint scan, and Johnny dropped his tone of stiff formality.

"You're late," he said. "Is something wrong?"

"I ran into a problem on delivery."

"Explain."

"The client's personal security was better than anticipated. I'm a little winded, but I'm pulling out as soon as I can rent a car."

"Where are you?"

"Santa Rosa. It's a pit stop just across the border."

"I can find it."

"No!" The soldier's voice was rigid now, intense. "It's not a family matter. I'll be home before you know it."

"How the hell—"

"Just listen. In case there's some delay, our friend in Wonderland may have an interest in establishing relations with the client. If you haven't seen me by tomorrow, pass the case files on to him for further action."

"Damn it, Mack—"

He saw the scout car coming, recognized it immediately for what it was, and cradled the receiver instantly, cutting off Johnny's protest. Still too far to count the gunners, but it didn't matter. The driver was cruising slowly, taking his time while his passengers rubbernecked, scanning the storefronts and side streets for any sign of life. Two blocks away and closing. Bolan knew that it was time to move.

He ducked behind the service station, moving out as rapidly as possible. He knew they hadn't seen him yet, but they were almost to the end of Main Street, and soon they would begin to section off the side streets, poking into alleyways and yards. He could elude them for a time, but Bolan did not have the strength for a protracted game of cat and mouse. If he was forced to hide for any length of time, he might as well confront them now and get it over with. The end result would be the same.

He paralleled the main drag, pausing frequently to check his backtrack and apply more pressure to his bleeding wounds. It didn't help. No sooner had he staunched the crimson flow than he was forced to move, renewing it again. He was not bleeding quite as much, but it was steady now, his skinsuit saturated to the knee. Another hour would finish him.

There was no time to find the doctor, even if there was one in town, no way to reach the pharmacy without encountering Rivera's gunners on the street. They would be looking for him in the alleys, and Bolan wondered if he should let them find him. He could choose his ground, prepare an ambush, maybe even take them if his head was clear enough, his gun hand steady. But if he missed them with his first rounds . . .

The sign was blurry, but it still attracted his attention, drawing Bolan toward the back porch of an old, renovated house. He climbed the concrete steps, sat back against the railing as he tried to focus on the swimming letters.

### SANTA ROSA CLINIC
### R. KENT, M.D.

Beneath the doctor's name, there was a number to be called in case of emergency. Without a phone, it did the Executioner no good, and he lurched forward, peering through the curtains that covered a window set into the door. No lights, no sign of movement from the dark interior.

He knocked again, then gave up and drew the slim stiletto from a pocket of his skinsuit, stooping painfully to scrutinize the lock. It was an easy one, pot metal and aluminum. He had it open in a moment, took another look along the alley, left and right, then slipped inside.

The former kitchen had been turned into a lab of sorts. He noted microscopes, a centrifuge and sterilizer, stainless-steel sinks and instruments, a cabinet for drugs, an X-ray machine standing in the corner. Bolan did a recon: four examination rooms, a waiting area, a single rest room, all deserted now. There would be hours posted somewhere, but he had no time left. Already fading in and out, the soldier knew that he would have to act now or it would be too late.

He backtracked to the lab and rifled drawers until he found the necessary implements for suturing a wound. The exit hole, in back, would be a bitch, but once he stitched the entry wound, a butterfly bandage might do the trick until he found some wheels and made it to another town, one with a doctor. He couldn't chance an anesthetic—it would knock him out immediately, but the drug stash might contain a stimulant that would help him stay alert while he was on the road.

The light-headedness returned as Bolan struggled to thread the long, curved needle, and he felt the room begin to spin. He reached out for the counter, missed it, tried again, and then his knees were folding. He was losing it, and there was not a damned thing he could do to save himself.

The floor rushed up to meet him like a runaway express train, and the darkness claimed him.

"HELLO? HELLO?"

The line was open, humming for an instant, then the dial tone came back loud and harsh in Johnny Bolan's ear. He didn't bother jiggling the plungers on his telephone. It only worked in movies, anyway, and if he could have raised the operator, what in hell would he have said?

He cradled the receiver, conscious of a sudden chill that raised the short hairs on his neck. Mack's message had been loud and clear: he was on foot and wounded in a town called Santa Rosa near the Mexico-Arizona border. Something had gone wrong with the Rivera strike, and Mack had lost his wheels, had suffered injuries of unknown severity. The very fact that he had mentioned being "winded" was an indicator of his serious condition, but the nature of his wounds, his access to emergency assistance, was a mystery.

Johnny fetched a highway atlas from the bookshelf, paging through the maps until he found a spread for southern Arizona. Santa Rosa was in Pima County, near the border, less than fifty miles from the Rivera stronghold in Sonora. It was 230 miles from San Diego into Gila Bend, if Johnny took the interstate, and after that he would be running two-lane blacktop all the way, through Ajo, Gu Vo, Pisnemo. Extra time, perhaps, but he could push it on the smaller county roads and cut off sixty miles that he would have to cover if he doubled back to Santa Rosa out of Tucson.

Mack had asked him not to come. Correction: Mack had *told* him not to come. But he was always trying to protect "the kid," a designation that he hadn't used to Johnny's face for some time now, but which was always on his mind. The older brother's natural concern was touching, even heartwarming, but it had no place in combat, when his life was on the line.

Some things you did because you had to, no matter what the private risk. When Johnny thought about the times that Mack had laid it on the line for him, the weight that he had carried for the family all these years, the young man knew he could do no less.

He *had* been just a kid when Mack came home from Vietnam to see their parents and their sister buried in the family plot outside of Pittsfield. Johnny was the sole survivor of Sam Bolan's final, desperate act, a murder-suicide that had left the family decimated, brothers stripped of everything and everyone they had loved in life. When Mack had taken up the war against their father's enemies, becoming the most-wanted fugitive in Massachusetts, then in the United States, John Bolan watched the final vestiges of family slip through his fingers, gone, as he had supposed, forever.

Val Querente had been everything a foster mother could ever hope to be. Jack Gray, her future husband and an agent for the FBI, adopted Johnny as his own, but there was no attempt to denigrate his past, the sacrifices his older brother made from day to day. Both Jack and Val had understood—Val most of all, since she had shared the Executioner's original campaign, had seen the man in action, on and off the battle line.

As Johnny Gray, the younger Bolan had enlisted in the military, serving with distinction in Grenada and Beirut. He had been blooded in those killing grounds, returning home to become a paralegal, never dreaming that his life would somehow intersect his brother's everlasting war. But intersect they had, and in the merger of their spirits, the indomitable Bolan will, a new and powerful alliance had been born.

Johnny did not delude himself that he would ever be his brother's equal. He was competent with weapons, trained for combat, seasoned in the fire, but if he lived to be a thousand he would never share the same experience, the seasoning, that made his brother something special. Double tours in Vietnam, backed up by forty-odd campaigns against the Mafia, innumerable clashes with the terrorist elite of Europe, Africa and Asia: all of that combined to make the Executioner a man apart, unique in his commitment and ability to accomplish what he set out to do.

But now he was wounded and on foot in hostile territory with the jackals on his heels. The younger Bolan could no more sit back and let his brother die than he could voluntarily stop breathing. If there was a chance, however slim, he had to make the effort, and he had no time to waste.

Descending to the armory, he chose his gear for the excursion. His main weapon was Interdynamic's KG-99, complete with combat foregrip and conversion to selective fire. Each magazine held thirty-six 9 mm parabellum rounds, and Johnny stowed sufficient extras for a major siege. A secondary backup was the SPAS 12 riot shotgun, awesome in appearance, devastating in its capabilities. Two bandoliers of double-ought and rifled slugs would keep the SPAS spewing death. The younger Bolan's side arm was a Heckler & Koch VP-70, a double-action autoloader packing eighteen parabellum rounds per magazine. Grenades, incendiaries, timers and a satchel of plastique completed Johnny's shopping list, and he was almost ready for the road.

The hardware went into his Jimmy 4 x 4, a custom tank that came complete with CB unit, ramming bumpers and assorted hidden extras that he could call upon at need. The armor plate and V-8 engine cost him something when it came to fuel efficiency, but he could cruise at eighty, with another fifteen in reserve, and dashboard-mounted radar jammers kept the smokies suitably confused. The heavy wheels were registered to Jerod Blake of San Diego, an identity Johnny could corroborate with bogus driver's license, credit cards and social security number.

Rolling out of Strongbase One, he activated the security devices that protected him against intruders in his absence.

It would be a sorry burglar who attempted to invade the Bolan sanctuary; he would live—no point in cluttering the yard with corpses—but for days thereafter, he would wonder if survival was worth the pain.

He caught the eastbound ramp for Highway 8, the interstate he would follow into Gila Bend. A bag of jerky and a thermos of coffee would suffice to keep him fed and wide awake throughout the drive. Six hours, give or take, and he would be in Santa Rosa. With his brother.

If Mack was still alive.

Whichever way it went, Johnny Bolan was coming. If he couldn't help the brother who meant everything to him, he could at least, by God, wreak havoc on his enemies.

And God help anyone who tried to stop him.

**4**

It was a seven-minute drive from home to clinic for Rebecca Kent, M.D. She could have made it faster—had in several cases of emergency—but on a normal morning she preferred to take her time, enjoy the town that had been home, more or less continuously, from her birth. The decade she had spent in Southern California scarcely counted, and she hardly thought about it anymore, except in dreams. Or nightmares.

She had not been born in Santa Rosa, technically. In 1954, the town possessed no clinic, and her father, while a doctor of the highest caliber, would never have countenanced delivering a child—much less his own—in a physician's office. They had barely made it into Tucson, and she had been delivered there, but she would always call herself a child of Santa Rosa.

It was peculiar, when she thought of it, how many times she had been forced to leave the tiny town she loved. In 1960, Santa Rosa's two-room school had somehow covered all the elementary grades, but high school meant a forty-mile commute, to Ajo. She had gotten used to buses in those years, as she had gotten used to turning down prospective dates on grounds of inaccessibility. Her high school years had not been sad, exactly, nor had they been lonely, in the strictest sense. Instead, they had been...dull. In retrospect, Rebecca Kent supposed she must have missed a lot, but she had not been conscious of it at the time, and so she had not suffered terribly.

There had simply been no question of a local college. She was set on medical school, and despite her mother's cautionary words, the very mention of a surgical career had brought a gleam into her father's eyes. He had connections on the staff at UCLA, but in the end she did not need his help. Her grades were more than adequate—a 4.0 in her senior year of high school—and her father's income, while exorbitant by Santa Rosa standards, had been low enough to rate a four-year scholarship. Rebecca Kent had graduated second in her class, and she had taken up her internship at Rampart General Hospital, an institution handling the "county cases": welfare recipients; the indigent; fire fighters and policemen—often with their battered prisoners in tow; drunk drivers and their victims; casualties of war among the countless street gangs; children overdosed on drugs. Before she graduated to the status of a resident at Rampart General, Rebecca Kent had seen more blood and violence than the average beat cop, and she had been learning how to cope with it.

A single night had changed all that and brought her running home to Santa Rosa in despair. Her mother had been gone by then, the victim of a coronary failure in Rebecca's junior year at college. She had never told her father why she had returned, and he had been happy to have his daughter back home, proud to see his daughter taking on the patients that his age and failing health prevented him from serving in the old, accustomed style. When he had finally died, she had kept on with the practice and continued living in the family home, at peace with any ghosts that lingered there. Some things were never meant to change.

She passed the Schultzes' hardware store, saw Vi outside, already sweeping the sidewalk. Rain or shine, she cleaned the sidewalk every day, preparing for the stream of customers that had become a trickle during recent years. The Papagos still dealt with Gib and Vi for tools and seed, a few accounts from local ranches kept them open, but Rebecca wondered how much longer they could keep their heads above the shifting tide.

Santa Rosa was dying. The signs were everywhere for those who took the time to see them. It would not come tomorrow, nor perhaps next year, but it was coming, and Rebecca knew that she would have to make provisions for herself, prepare for the inevitable. She would never be described as wealthy, but she had accumulated cash enough to afford a move, establish her small practice in another town. No cities, mind you; nothing on the scale of San Francisco or Los Angeles, where human beings were reduced, somehow, to predatory creatures of the night. A small town, rather, where the people knew and trusted one another. Where they cared.

But she would never find another Santa Rosa. Never in a million years.

The town itself was nothing special, she supposed. It baked in the summer, and in the winter it was merely warm. The people were a solemn lot, unsmiling when it came to strangers, but if you were local they could spare the time to sit a spell and share the latest gossip, reaffirming ties that held the tiny town together. Most of all, the town had been Rebecca's sanctuary when she needed it the most. It had allowed her to conceal her hurt, her shame, from everyone except herself.

Past Croson's Pharmacy and Stancell's independent service station. OPEC and the larger companies had almost put Bud Stancell under once or twice, but he had stubbornly refused to sell, and anyone who wanted brand-name gasoline at higher prices would just have to drive the extra thirty miles to find it. Bud was opening for business as she passed, and he had time to flash a smile before she turned the corner, nosing down the alley that would bring her in behind the clinic to her "private" entrance.

Rebecca liked Bud Stancell and felt sorry for him, all at once. There had been nothing she could do to help his wife in '81; the burns from a propane explosion had been too extensive, too severe, and she had died before the ambulance was twenty miles from town. Two years later, though, when Bud's son Rick was choking on a piece of chili dog and Bud had run him to the clinic, literally, with the angry, helpless tears still streaming down his face, a tracheotomy had done the trick and saved Rick's life. He was starting quarterback for Ajo's varsity team, and every time Bud spoke his name or saw the boy, pride lit his face up like a neon sign.

There were rewards, yes. The occasional bout of loneliness was worth it, if you waited for the shining moments, when you had the opportunity to make a difference. When your efforts counted, and you knew that you had done your best in the pursuit of something very much worthwhile.

Rebecca Kent was on the porch with key in hand before she saw the door. It stood ajar, perhaps two inches, and she could see brand-new scratches on the locking mechanism from where she stood. She thought of Grant, his badge and uniform, and wished that he was here, beside her now, to throw the door back and step inside with perfect confidence. She could retreat, drive back to Stancell's and report the break-in, but she could not bring herself to leave without examining the damage first.

And if the burglar was inside?

It was preposterous. No one broke into offices in broad daylight, with the business hours clearly posted right out front. Someone—a tramp, some kids, whoever—had al-

ready come and gone under cover of darkness. Seeking
drugs, most likely, or her small reserve of petty cash. There
would be nothing else inside to interest anyone, unless their
aim was vandalism. Sudden anger crowded out her apprehension and she took a bold step forward, fuming at the
thought of strangers pawing through her personal belongings, damaging her medical equipment.

Braced to run at any sign of the intruder, suddenly aware
that she was very much afraid, Rebecca Kent was startled to
discover an unconscious figure stretched out on the floor. A
man, all bruised and dusty, but his trench coat was not
something that a hobo off the freights would wear. Beneath it, he appeared to wear some kind of close-fitting
black garment, but now her eyes were focused on the blood.
So much of it, some crusty brown, as if the wound were
hours old but had refused to close.

She knelt beside him, drew the trench coat back and saw
the holstered weapon on his hip. She dared not touch it,
frightened that it might go off, so she unbuckled the web
belt, slipped it from underneath him and pushed it away out
of reach. The wound was in his side, but she would have to
get him on the table before she could begin an adequate examination. And for that she would require his help.

He was a stranger. She had never seen his face before, and
she would definitely have remembered this one. She had
never seen a pistol like the one he carried, either, and she
wondered if he was some kind of soldier, possibly a spy. It
seemed absurd; there were no secrets to be kept in Santa
Rosa, except perhaps her own.

She cracked a vial of smelling salts and passed it back and
forth beneath his nose. He shuddered, grumbling back to
semiconsciousness, and his ice-blue eyes began to roll. With
soothing words and firm, insistent hands, she got the patient on his feet, one arm around his shoulders. Staggering

beneath his weight, she led him through a narrow door to the adjacent operating room and propped him against the table while she worked the trench coat off his shoulders, down his arms. She tossed the garment toward a chair and missed, surprised by the metallic thud it made on impact with the floor.

She got him on the table, somehow, and he was already fading fast before she had a chance to wash her hands, select the scissors she would need to cut away his blacksuit. The normal antiseptic smell of the clinic was overpowered now by sweat and blood, the stench of violence. Suddenly she realized her hands were trembling.

Who was this man who had intruded on her life? What had he done? What had he suffered? And, above all, did she really want to know?

GRANT VICKERS CHECKED his watch again and knew the diner would not open for another fifteen minutes. Old man Beamer was as regular as clockwork, pulling up behind his greasy spoon at seven on the dot and spending half an hour in the back, preparing for the day. It took him maybe half that long to fire the grill and put the coffee on, but he would no more deviate from lifelong work habits than he would put on purple pants and dance the monkey, or whatever kids were calling all that shit these days. The old man was an institution, and you didn't screw around with institutions. Not in Santa Rosa, anyhow.

In fifteen minutes he could damn near finish off his rounds, and Vickers put the cruiser back in motion, scanning left and right with all the interest of a drowsy fisherman surveying ripples on a pond. In his seven years as constable, he had become convinced that there was no such thing as crime in Santa Rosa. There were "incidents" from time to time, involving drunkenness or family disputes, but even they were few and far between. There were infractions, mostly violations of the traffic ordinances, and he wrote his share of tickets on assorted smart-ass kids, but otherwise the town was as quiet as a grave.

To Vickers, "crime" meant murder, robbery, or rape. The biggies. Getting drunk at Al's on Saturday and pissing in the gutter might be damned unsightly, but it wasn't anything you jailed a neighbor for. If certain good old boys put down a few too many beers and started teeing off on one another, it was Vickers's job to patch things up, make sure that any damages were settled to the dime before he saw them safely home. The teenagers were smart enough by now to do their stealing or whatever up in Ajo, or the other nearby towns, and Vickers felt that he had taught them all a valuable lesson. You don't shit where you eat.

In seven years, Grant Vickers had not fired a shot, though he packed the big Colt Python with him everywhere, just in case. On one occasion he had used his nightstick; he had broken it, in fact, across the skull of an aggressive drifter who had tried to start some trouble with the good old boys. The prick got ninety days, and Grant had been a hero down at Al's until the story went around and everybody had heard it twice, and then it died away like all things did in Santa Rosa. Still, a week of glory might be all that any man could reasonably count in his life, and for the most part he was satisfied.

Oh, sure, he sometimes wondered what it might be like to pull up stakes and try his luck in Phoenix, even in L.A. At thirty-five they might consider him too old for a police recruit, but his experience would have to count for something. There was real crime in Los Angeles, with murders every day and rapes around the goddamned clock, more robberies and sexual assaults than you could shake a stick at. He would really see some action in Los Angeles.

And in the end, it was the prospect of that action that inevitably made his mind up for him. Proud of what he had achieved in Santa Rosa, Vickers knew that he would be just one more body in Los Angeles…and, frankly, he was never certain he could cut it. It was something else again, with real, live criminals who didn't give a shit about your badge or gun. Forget about the pyschos and the heavy syndicate connections; in L.A., the kids alone would chew you up and spit you out. They killed one another by the dozens, and they weren't afraid to drop a uniform or two, if it came down to that.

The bottom line was fear. Grant Vickers would not say as much—would not admit it, even to himself—but he was desperately afraid—of failure as an officer, of death or injury, of being finally revealed as second-rate, inadequate.

And there was money, too. If Grant left Santa Rosa, he would have to ditch his sideline, and he wasn't one to kick a gift horse in the teeth. All things considered, he would have to say that Santa Rosa met his needs precisely.

If there was anything resembling a sore spot, it was Becky Kent. The more he thought about her recently, the more she got beneath his skin. Not that it seemed to do him any good at all. She had gone out with him a couple of times—to Ajo, for a movie, and to Tucson, for a decent sit-down dinner—but she never let him get out of the batter's box, forget about first base. When he had tried to make a move on their second date, she froze and shied away from him as if he hadn't bathed in a month. There was something in her eyes akin to terror that had stopped him in his tracks and made him stutter an apology before he shook her hand goodnight.

He wondered, more and more, just what could have made her act like that. He wasn't Sly Stallone, by any means—the mirror didn't lie—but then again he wasn't Quasimodo,

either. Something must have happened in Becky's past that
put her off men or sex, and the mystery was eating at him,
keeping him awake at night. At first he thought it might
have been a sour love affair while she was at college, but the
pieces didn't fit. It hurt when someone dumped you, but
Vickers had never seen a woman gasp and cringe the way
Becky had, not just from being jilted by some prick. It was
as if she had been hurt somehow, and not emotionally,
either, but he didn't have the nerve to ask.

Not yet.

In time, perhaps, when they had spent a bit more time
together, it would seem more natural for him to ask about
her past. He knew she was a local girl who went away to med
school in Los Angeles and wowed them with her smarts.
She'd done some time at one of those big hospitals, more
nurses on the staff than there were people in the whole of
Santa Rosa, but it hadn't lasted. Vickers wondered if there
might be some connection, linking Becky's job with her
uneasiness toward men. It didn't seem to make much sense,
but you could never tell.

If the vehicle had been passing through a couple hours
later, he might have overlooked it. There was more traffic
as the day wore on, but at the moment Vickers was all
alone... until the dark sedan turned out in front of him,
emerging from a narrow side street, and the driver swung
around in his direction. In a single glance, he made the
plates—from Mexico. The driver slowed a little as he came
abreast of Vickers's squad car, smiling at him like a hungry
weasel, nodding as though they ought to be the best of
friends from way back. Vickers gave the man the evil eye but
did not turn around to follow them or pull them over. They
were cruising well below the limit, and he did not want to
start his day by hassling nationals.

Grant Vickers did not know the driver or his passengers, but he could place the type. They came across the border on occasion, passing through, cold men in hot machines who rarely stopped in Santa Rosa, moving on toward other destinations in the north. Sometimes they passed the other way, toward Mexico, and he was never sad to see them go.

He did not know the strangers, but he had a fair idea of who they worked for, yes indeed. Thus far, their business interests had not clashed with his, and he would like to see things stay that way. He liked the hometown nice and peaceful, where the women and their kids were free to walk the streets. He wouldn't want it to become a shooting gallery, a modern Tombstone with himself in the unlikely role of Wyatt Earp.

Grant Vickers was a lawman who had come to terms with his limitations. He was not a hero, not an athlete, and he certainly would never pass for Sherlock Holmes. He had the common sense to recognize a lethal situation when he saw one, and whenever one confronted him, he had the brains to back away. If he could turn a dollar on the side, for doing what came naturally anyway, well, that was icing on the goddamned cake.

He curbed the cruiser, waited for the dark sedan to grow smaller in his rearview, but it turned instead of heading north. He frowned at that, and tried to put himself inside the driver's mind, discover what the bastard might be up to.

They were hunting, obviously. Here in Vickers's town. But who? And why? He would have known if there were any personal or business links to Santa Rosa, and he would have taken steps to sort it out, to warn the foolish locals off. But there was nothing. Zip. And that was what had Vickers worried as he put the cruiser back in motion and continued on his way.

The guns were out, and they were hunting. In his town. For someone Vickers didn't know. There was a wild card in the game, from out of frigging nowhere, and he didn't like the way that changed the odds. If they got lucky, if they made their tag in Santa Rosa, there would have to be an inquest, an investigation. He would have to act, and who the hell knew what might happen then?

His digital read 7:45. Old man Beamer would be open now. Grant Vickers cranked the squad car hard around and gunned it toward the diner, hoping that a cup of coffee might do something for his stomach. It was rolling now, as if he had consumed a couple bowls of Beamer's Texas chili, but without the pleasure that preceded heartburn. For a moment Vickers wondered if he might be working on a goddamned ulcer, finally deciding that it didn't matter either way. Some Rolaids ought to ease him through the afternoon, at least until he found out what—or whom—the Mexicans were looking for.

And once he knew...then what? Would he have nerve enough to throw their asses out of town? If they got lucky, dare he push the matter with indictments and arrests?

He had no answer at the moment, and he put the problem out of mind. He hoped the man they were searching for was a thousand miles away by now and running for his life. It wouldn't do him any good, of course, but once beyond the city limits he was someone else's problem. Someone else would have to scrape the victim up when the Mexicans were finished, and investigate the crime.

As long as it did not occur in Santa Rosa, Vickers would be satisfied. He was an easy man to please.

## 5

Darkness, and he was running toward the light of leaping flames, prepared to dodge each time a muzzle-flash cut through the night and angry hornets swarmed around his head. He answered fire when targets showed themselves, but they were few and far between. The hostile gunners had grown cagey, scoping out his battle plan and lying back to wait for him within the shelter of the shadows. If he wanted them, if he was going to complete his mission, he would have to seek them in the fire.

The heat was strong already, even at an estimated range of thirty yards. He raised one hand to shield his face, aware that he was framed in silhouette for any gunners who might choose to take advantage of the moment. Still, the fire was central to his strategy, his needs. And while he could not have explained his purpose at the moment, there was something in his gut that knew why he was here.

It was essential that he find Rivera, he remembered that much, but the man was laughing at him now, his low, reptilian chuckle emanating from the darkness. No. It was emerging from the flames, the very white-hot heart of what appeared to be a burning warehouse, miles across. A blazing structure that might stretch forever, from horizon to horizon, if he dared to look. He didn't, concentrating on the evil laughter, eyes like slits against the heat as he attempted to pick out his nemesis.

Just there: a movement in the fire. He hesitated, strained against the baking heat to make out shapes and sizes, finally deciding that the form was human, more or less. Too wide, perhaps, but otherwise complete with head and arms and legs, all wreathed in flame and moving jerkily, as if the puppeteer was having trouble with his strings. He waited, felt the figure drawing closer, though it scarcely seemed to close the distance for the longest time. At last, when he could tell the gap was narrowing, he braced himself, prepared for anything that might emerge out of the fire.

Rivera smiled at him through withered lips, his eyes like livid coals beneath a blistered brow. The fire had taken its toll, but he was recognizable, still on his feet. Incredibly he seemed to feel no pain. And he was laughing, softly, with a grim malevolence that chilled the watcher's soul.

Rivera held a squirming figure in his arms. Somewhere along the line, he had acquired a female hostage, and although she kept her face averted now, there was something terribly familiar in her stance, her general form. Unlike her captor, she had not been blistered by the flames, but while Rivera seemed immune to pain, the woman writhed and whimpered as the tongues of fire reached out to lap around her ankles, leaving not a mark upon pristine flesh.

The watcher realized that she was naked, while Rivera still wore scorched and tattered clothing. He kept one arm around the woman's slender waist, the fingers of his free hand tangled in her raven hair.

"You want her," he demanded, "come and get her."

The watcher tried to move, but he found that he was rooted in his tracks, as if he had been standing overlong in fresh concrete and it had been allowed to dry. He twisted frantically, endeavoring to put one foot before the other, his exertions only drawing further laughter from Rivera.

"Guess you're stuck, man," he exulted. "Guess this bitch belongs to me."

One blistered hand slipped upward from the lady's waist until the blackened fingers reached a breast. Rivera's laughter had a different quality about it now, almost maniacal. The watcher raised his weapon, set for autofire, and held the trigger down, intent on cutting off that evil laugh at any cost. Instead his bullets seemed to veer off course before they reached Rivera, vaporizing in the heat from leaping flames.

"You can't kill me," he jeered, secure within the fire. "I'm all you live for, gringo. Me. And *this*."

With one hand still caressing her breast, Rivera wrenched the woman's head back to expose her face. The watcher saw—

The ceiling.

Wide awake now, trembling as if with fever, Bolan knew that it had been a nightmare, nothing more. He tried to rise, but weakness and restraining hands prevented him. Above him, upside down, a woman's face intruded on his field of vision, giving Bolan something else beside the ceiling fan to focus on.

"You must lie still," she cautioned him.

"Who are you?"

"Dr. Kent. And who are you?"

The memories were flooding back to Bolan now, distinct from troubled dreams. He realized that he was lying on a padded operating table, with an IV drip plugged into his arm. His wounded side was numb.

"R. Kent, M.D.?"

"The *R* stands for Rebecca," she informed him. "We're in Santa Rosa, you've been shot, you broke into my clinic. Does any of this ring a bell?"

"How long have I been out?"

"You mean unconscious? I have no idea. It's been forty-five minutes since I found you on the floor. Of course, I wasn't here when you broke in."

"What time is it?"

She checked her wristwatch. "Eight o'clock. Expecting company?"

"I might be."

"Well, before they get here, I've got calls to make, and I'll need certain information. Like your name, for openers, together with an explanation of that gunshot wound."

He tried to rise once more, defeated by a giddy rush that might have been produced by chemicals or pure exhaustion. There was no pain in his wounded side now; in place of the incessant, burning ache, a pleasant numbness spread from hip to armpit. Dr. Kent was watching as he probed the bandaged wound with gentle fingers.

"Not to worry. It's a local anesthetic that I use with sutures. If you're smart, you won't disturb that IV hook-up. At the moment, you need all the blood that you can get."

"About those phone calls..."

"It's the law," she told him, "as I'm sure you're perfectly aware. All gunshot wounds must be reported by physicians in attendance."

"You're in danger here."

She stiffened, putting on a frown. "I don't respond to threats," she said. "I've put your guns away, and you're in no condition to go looking for them at the moment. If you can't behave, I'll have to offer you a sedative."

She was a gutsy lady. She was afraid, he felt it, but she hid her feelings well. And Bolan had no doubts that if it came to that, the sedative would be an "offer" he could not refuse.

"I wasn't threatening," he told her. "The men who shot me won't be satisfied until they're finished with the job. They might have traced me here already."

"All the more reason to call the authorities. They can protect you and sort this thing out."

The prospect of a small-town marshal guarding him against Rivera's army was so ludicrous that Bolan nearly laughed out loud. "The only thing they'll have to sort is bodies, if I'm found in Santa Rosa."

"Aren't we getting just the least bit overwrought?"

He glowered at her. "*We* are trying to prevent a massacre. If you prefer your killings wholesale, go ahead and make that call."

She hesitated, and the frown was deeper now. "Why should I buy all this? I still don't know your name."

He thought about it, finally figured *Hell, why not?* "The name's Mack Bolan. Ring a bell?"

From the expression on the woman's face, he knew that it was setting off a clamor of alarms. She almost took a backward step, but caught herself and stood her ground.

"The man they call the Executioner?"

"Some do."

"Assuming that it's true, what brings you into Santa Rosa?"

"Call it an unscheduled pit stop. If I hadn't stopped a bullet, I'd be somewhere else."

"My luck."

"You've got a chance to change your luck," he said. "That call you plan to make could get a lot of people killed."

"By you?"

The soldier spread his hands. "You've got my guns, remember?"

"Yes, and I intend to keep them safely under lock and key until the constable arrives."

As long as she was talking to him, she would not be on the phone, and Bolan knew he had to stall for time, attempt to win her over, or at least create a reasonable doubt within her analytic mind.

"The constable? What kind of force does he command?"

"You've seen the town," she answered. "It's a one-man show."

"I've got an army on my trail. Unless your constable's a kick-ass kind of guy, it might be better if you kept him in the dark. I wouldn't want to get him killed unnecessarily."

"All killing is unnecessary."

"There, we disagree."

"I've read a number of your clippings, Mr. Bolan. All about your so-called 'holy war.' I don't approve."

His smile was ice. "I haven't asked for your approval, Doctor. At the moment I have two priorities: survival and the prevention of a full-scale massacre in Santa Rosa. I would like to save your life, but if you won't cooperate—"

"*My* life? What have I got to do with this?"

"You're here," he told her simply. "We've had a chance to talk. My enemies will have to think I've told you something, and they can't afford to have you spreading it around."

There was a trace of panic in her eyes, immediately covered over.

"But you haven't told me anything. I mean, except your name and—"

"Cheap insurance," Bolan said. "No witnesses. How many people live in town?"

She frowned again, but clearly saw his point. "Around a hundred, if you count the local farmers and their families. Within the city limits, maybe thirty-five."

"I wouldn't want them on my conscience."

She was on the verge of a response but reconsidered, falling silent for a moment. When she spoke again, her voice was cautious, strained.

"I can't believe that these people—whoever they are—would murder everyone in town."

"You may be right. They'd only need to kill the ones who saw them, witnesses, but once they're on a roll..."

"And why should I believe your story?"

Bolan shrugged. "You've read my clippings, Doctor. You're aware of what I do, and who I do it to. You know the kind of people who have vested interests in my death."

"For all I know, that bullet might have come from a police revolver."

"If you think so, make your call. But be damned sure before you do. You'll have to live with the results."

She turned away, was almost through the doorway when she hesitated, turned to face him again. Beneath the fear and evident confusion, there was sadness in her eyes.

"I hate the kind of life you lead," she told him. "I despise the violence."

Bolan faced her squarely and responded, "So do I."

REBECCA KENT PICKED UP the telephone receiver, hesitated, listened to the dial tone for a moment, then replaced it gently in its cradle. If her patient had been truthful with her, if his story was not lies, half-truths and fantasy, she might touch off a bloodbath by alerting the authorities. If desperate criminals were hunting Bolan—if her patient even *was* Mack Bolan—his predictions followed a repulsive kind of logic. Violence fed upon itself, and men who made their living with the gun would not be shy about eliminating women, children, any witnesses.

She thought about Grant Vickers, wondering how he would cope with a full-blown shoot-out in the streets of Santa Rosa. He was big and strong enough, of course, but he was not a "kick-ass kind of guy." Despite a term of military service, he was no more of a match for armed professionals than she was. If she called him, if he recognized her patient, he would have to call the county sheriff, possibly the state police. Meantime, although he might be placed in custody, Mack Bolan would remain there, in her clinic, while his would-be killers searched the streets, eliminating his potential sanctuaries, one after another. If they knew that he was wounded . . .

She broke the train of thought before it reached its logical conclusion, looking at the problem from another angle. What if her persuasive patient was not Bolan? Or if he was the Executioner, suppose that he was running from police instead of criminals. What then? If she ignored her duty, she would automatically become the man's accomplice. She could lose her license, everything that she had worked for, suffered for, these past fifteen years. If she was so damned gullible that she believed the first lame story she was handed by a liar desperate for time, she might be sacrificing everything upon the altar of stupidity.

She reached for the telephone again, but hesitated. Something in the patient's eyes, his voice, had struck her as sincere. Rebecca Kent believed she was a decent judge of human nature—one appalling, hideous exception notwithstanding—and her instincts told her that the man had not been lying to her. There was danger close at hand, but having come that far, what could she ever hope to do about it?

If she could not hand off the problem to Grant without endangering his life, the lives of everyone in town, what *could* she do? She pictured Vickers in his uniform, the little half smile on his sunburned face, a pistol firmly planted on his hip. He tried so hard to be the classic Western lawman, but a town like Santa Rosa offered nothing in the way of challenges, no opportunities to deal with violence in a practical capacity. From dating Grant, she knew he was a gentle man, albeit rough around the edges. When he had tried to make a pass at her and she had shied away, he took the cold rebuff without a macho show of angry disappointment. There had been no bluster, no reminder of the money he had spent on dinner, nothing whatsoever in the way of force. She had respected him for that, and had been grateful at the time, but now she weighed the constable's potential as a rugged fighting man and found him wanting.

Rebecca Kent was not an expert, but she thought it must require a certain kind of man to kill professionally, in cold blood. Most men—most women, when it came to that— could take another life in self-defense, or in defense of those they loved. A smaller number found it in themselves to murder for revenge, an exorcism of their private demons. But the true professionals—assassins, mercenaries, and those of their ilk—were something else entirely. There was something in their makeup, or deleted from it, that permitted them to kill and kill again. For money, for the sport of it, or from commitment to a cause.

From her observation of the patient, Rebecca Kent believed he had that "something else" about him. She could not begin to understand his motivating cause, although, if she remembered rightly, stories in the press had mentioned something of a family tragedy behind his one-man war. In any case he did not strike her as the kind of mad-dog killer who preoccupied the media these days. Unless she had been absolutely taken in, he was a thoughtful man, concerned about the consequences of his chance intrusion in her life.

What was it he had said when she informed him that she hated his vocation, all the violence with which he surrounded himself?

*"So do I."*

And she believed him, foolish though she might have been. There had been no trace of deception in his voice, no cunning smirk behind his eyes. If he was Bolan—and she saw no reason, at the moment, why he should have lied— then he was certainly a killer. But Rebecca Kent would bet her life, her reputation, on the fact that he had never killed for pleasure, out of sport or spite. When he had killed, there must have been a reason that, at least to Bolan's mind, had been sufficiently persuasive to compel his actions.

She had pondered murder, briefly, years ago, before her thoughts of death had turned upon herself, and she had known that it was time to leave L.A. for good. She had been hiding out in Santa Rosa ever since, away from memories of all she had endured, all that she had contemplated, for revenge and out of self-disgust. She hardly ever thought of homicide in concrete terms these days, and on those rare occasions when she did, Rebecca Kent was filled with shame of such intensity that tears welled unbidden, in her eyes. A few more years, perhaps, and she might finally be able to forget.

But she could not forget her patient, lying in the other room, or the conflicting signals flashed by instinct and by common sense.

Instinctively she knew that Bolan had been truthful with her, that his secret presence in her clinic somehow posed a lesser threat than if his presence there was advertised. Meanwhile her common sense demanded that she carry out the letter of the law, inform Grant Vickers of her wounded patient, and divorce herself from any subsequent events.

Except that it would never be that easy. If she gave the wounded man to Vickers, she would be responsible for everything that followed, personally and directly linked to each and every act of violence that resulted from her phone call. By her silence she might save Grant's life, the lives of other neighbors.

And herself?

If Bolan was pursued, his enemies might well suspect that he was wounded. If they traced him there, to Santa Rosa, they would finally, inevitably, come to see her, asking questions, threatening, demanding. What could she accomplish if, as Bolan said, he had been followed by an army?

Nothing.

But the mere inevitability of failure did not release her from an obligation to try. Her Hippocratic oath had pledged Rebecca Kent to help the suffering, preserve all life wherever possible. To her, that meant not only Bolan's life, but any others that might be endangered by a revelation of his presence in her care. If she delivered him to Vickers, thereby saving herself but bringing a massacre upon the town, she would obtain no consolation from the knowledge that her actions had been legal. On the other hand, if she ignored the law and thereby saved an untold number of imperiled lives, had she in fact committed any crime?

Her head was spinning, and she fought to make her mind a perfect blank, erasing all the hypothetical for either side. The choice and risk were ultimately hers, but she had time.

How much?

Enough.

Enough to watch her patient, gauge his progress and decide if he was well enough to travel. Time enough to weigh his story carefully, compute the risks and hazards either way, before she rushed to a decision she might eternally regret.

If she decided that a call was necessary, it would simply be delayed. Grant would not argue with her judgment that a patient's treatment should take precedence above the legal niceties. If she decided not to call, then she would live or die with that decision in the long run.

Either way, the choice would be her own, and she would have to make it with her heart, as well as with her mind.

## 6

Hector Camacho scowled at the storefronts that slipped past his window. They all looked the same to him: dusty and lifeless, the signs of a town in the last throes of death. He had never enjoyed Santa Rosa, was never impressed by its stubborn resistance to change. Now, he thought, all it needed was one final shove toward oblivion. One little push. In his present mood, Hector would gladly oblige.

He had taken the flack for the raid on Rivera's *estancia*. Heat came with Hector's position—the second-in-command was always more responsible, somehow, than number one—but he had never been accused of negligence before, of sleeping on the job, and there was much to do before he could regain his pride. He must locate the gringo, first and foremost, bring him down before he had a chance to talk to anyone. Or, if he had shared his secret, if he even had an opportunity to speak, Camacho must eliminate his contacts on the spot. So easy, if only they could find the bastard.

Santa Rosa was their last real hope, Camacho realized. If their attacker had gone farther—if he had, for instance, thumbed a ride—then he would be beyond their reach. Rivera might put out a contract on him, through his contacts in the States, but it was virtually impossible to kill a man when you possessed no name or physical description of your victim. Stranger things had happened, true, but Hector did not put his faith in miracles.

All things considered, it seemed safe to say their enemy was still in Santa Rosa. He had lost his car a few miles south, and he had lost a lot of blood, as well, along the way. He might be dead already, sprawled beneath a cactus somewhere, waiting for the buzzards, but Camacho didn't think so. He had seen this one in action, and he had a rough idea of just how strong, how tough this hombre was. With his head start, there had been time to walk from the abandoned car to Santa Rosa, keeping well away from passing traffic on the highway. Once in town, the American would seek medical attention, but there was no hospital in Santa Rosa. Possibly a doctor's office. He would have to check it out.

The next priority was transportation. Once he was stitched and given medication for the pain, the gringo would be desperate to put some space between himself and Santa Rosa, running from the troops that would inevitably follow him. Except the troops were here already, and if the man had not stolen someone's car, it should be easy for Camacho's men to cover all the sources in a town this size.

The lone garage and service station was a possibility. Aside from that, there were no used-car lots, no dealerships, no nothing. People went to Tucson or Phoenix when they wanted to buy a car. They did not come to Santa Rosa for their major purchases. And, from appearances, Camacho would have said they seldom came for any reason.

He was satisfied their enemy was here, within his grasp, if only he could root the bastard out. A second car had been positioned on the highway north of town, its crew awaiting Rivera's order to seal the town. Before those orders could be issued, though, before Rivera risked a confrontation with the state police, the horrors of publicity, Camacho must convince him that their enemy was still in Santa Rosa.

Hector lit a cigarette and tried to put himself inside the gringo's mind. What sort of warrior were they dealing with? He was professional, no doubt about it, capable of taking on an army and inflicting heavy casualties before he slipped away. That ruled out the DEA, and Hector had already dropped the FBI from his considerations. They had no one like this man on their payroll, and the Bureau would not cross a border without filing forms in triplicate beforehand. CIA? It seemed unlikely. They were not concerned with drugs—unless they were involved in smuggling themselves—and they had once or twice relied upon Rivera as a source of contacts with the Contra movement to the south.

That left Rivera's various competitors, but once again Camacho had his doubts. If Esquilante or the others planned a move against Rivera's stronghold, singly or en masse, they would have sent an army to attack the rancho rather than a single man. And when their soldier fled, why would he run for the United States?

The more he thought about it, the more Camacho was convinced that they were dealing with an unknown quantity, a stranger—or a group of strangers—they had not encountered previously. Someone had decided that Luis Rivera should be driven out of business, and had taken steps to reach that goal. They had not been successful, even though they might have cost Rivera several million dollars in a single evening, but it was the very effort that disturbed Camacho, made him fearful for his own position. For his life.

He had come close, last night, with bullets snapping all around him in the fire-lit darkness, and he had not liked the feeling one damned bit. Camacho's idea of a shoot-out normally involved half a dozen guns—all his—against some solitary target who was taken by surprise, and preferably unarmed. This business of guerrilla warfare in the middle of the night was something else entirely, and it grated on Camacho's nerves. He might be dead already if another of Rivera's men had not been kind enough to step in front of Hector at a crucial moment in the action, stopping rounds that would most certainly have spoiled his day.

Camacho didn't like the sharp, metallic taste of fear. Since joining forces with Rivera, rising through the ranks to stand beside Luis, Camacho had become accustomed to inspiring fear, not suffering its chills and loss of face. He was a power to be reckoned with throughout Sonora, speaking for Rivera in his business deals and ordering elimination of the small-time dealers who attempted to encroach upon Rivera's territory. When Rivera fell, as he inevitably would, Camacho would be king.

Unless he blew it here, in Santa Rosa. If he let the gringo get away, he would be scum beneath Rivera's boots. The second-in-command could be replaced—could be eliminated—at any time. A word was all it took, and Hector knew that word was waiting on the tip of his employer's tongue right now. He had to prove himself, and soon, before Rivera started thinking that another man might do the job with more success.

His next step was immediately obvious. They had already searched the several streets and alleyways, without result. That meant the American was inside, somewhere, perhaps observing them right now. Hector knew what he must do to nail the town up tight, and he was ready to proceed. But first, he would require some inside help.

GRANT VICKERS FINISHED OFF his second cup of coffee, left a dollar on the counter and waved a hand to indicate he didn't want the change. Old Beamer's waitress was a sweet young thing named Rachel, and she flashed him such a smile that Vickers thought his heart would break. An angel face, a body like she had ... and Vickers would have bet his life that she was under seventeen. It was a crying shame.

He waved to old man Beamer, hitched his gun belt up and pushed through double doors to reach the sidewalk. It was heating up already, and it would be ninety in the shade by ten o'clock, assuming you could find a patch of shade, that is. The cruiser was not air-conditioned, thanks to misers on the town board, desperate to save a dime while everything around them went to hell. They couldn't tell the town was dying, but by God, they kept on top of "wasteful spending" by their constable.

He pulled up short before he reached the squad car, startled as he found Camacho lounging with his back against the driver's door. A little warning sounded in the back of Vickers's mind, and he recalled the crew he had encountered earlier that morning. Gunners passing through were one thing, damn it, but Camacho waiting for him out on Main Street in broad daylight was another game entirely.

"Hector, what brings you to Santa Rosa?"

"We have run into a little problem, Marshal."

"Constable."

Camacho shrugged and stared through Vickers as if he were made of glass. The lawman did not want to hear about his little problem, but he couldn't see a way around it now.

"Señor Rivera knows that, as a friend, you will be pleased to help him with his difficulty."

"I don't have jurisdiction in Sonora. You know that."

"Of course. The difficulty lies in Santa Rosa."

Vickers hooked both thumbs behind the buckle of his gun belt, frowning at Camacho. "Guess you'd better spell that out."

"Señor Rivera was attacked last night, at home. He is unharmed, but property was damaged, members of his household killed. The man responsible is here, in Santa Rosa.''

"What? One man? What kind of loco idiot would go against Rivera on his own?"

Camacho shrugged again. "This is a question *el jefe* wants to answer for himself. I have been sent to find the man and invite him back to share Señor Rivera's hospitality while they discuss these things."

It was a job to keep from laughing at Camacho, but the lawman had more sense than that. He also had no doubts about the form Rivera's "invitation" would be bound to take. And he was not excited by the prospect of a shooting war in Santa Rosa.

"So, what makes you think your man came here?"

"We found his vehicle abandoned on the highway south of town," Camacho answered. "Also, he is wounded and in need of medical attention. He could not go far."

He thought of Becky first, and wondered if the guy would try to get in touch with her for help. She would be bound by law to let him know about a bullet wound, but Vickers thought that maybe he should stop in at her office, just in case. If nothing else, it would provide him with a fine excuse to see her, pass the time of day.

The sound of Hector's voice snapped Vickers from his reverie. "How's that?"

Camacho's scowl was withering. "I asked if you have seen a stranger, anything unusual this morning."

Vickers shook his head in an emphatic negative. "I'll keep my eyes peeled, but the kind of man that you're describing won't be dropping by the diner here to catch himself a BLT. He'll go to ground somewhere, most likely. Try to flag himself an outbound ride."

"We have anticipated that," Camacho told him. "I am certain that Señor Rivera would appreciate your help. In case a stranger should present himself to you . . ."

"I've got your number," Vickers told him. "I know how to handle it."

"Of course. Good hunting."

"Listen, Hector, I don't want a lot of fireworks here in Santa Rosa, if you follow me."

"We do what must be done."

He didn't like the sound of that at all, but Vickers knew that it would do no good to argue with the gunman. Nodding solemnly, he waited until Hector stepped aside, then unlocked the car door and eased behind the squad car's wheel and fired her up. Before he had a chance to pull away, Camacho snapped his fingers and a dark sedan appeared from out of nowhere, nosing in to block the cruiser at the curb. Camacho took his place beside the driver, flashed a hungry smile at Vickers, and then the wheelman put his wagon through a sharp, illegal U-turn, headed north again, in the direction of the highway.

It was too much to expect that they were leaving town. He knew Camacho well enough to realize the gunner would not go home empty-handed. Hector and his sidekicks would be hanging in until they found their man, or until they satisfied themselves that he had slipped away.

Camacho had been right, of course. If he was wounded and on foot, their quarry could not have gone far. His hopes of flagging down a ride this time of day were slim and none, but even if he tried he would be forced to show himself along the highway, and the vultures would be waiting there to pick him off. If he had gone to ground somewhere in Santa Rosa, on the other hand, he would be hungry, thirsty, maybe dying from his wounds. The guy would have to try to get in touch with someone who could patch him up, at least enough for him to travel.

And his thoughts came back to Becky. As the only doctor in a radius of about thirty miles, she stood a decent chance of meeting Mr. X before he tried to hit the road. If he was armed and desperate, she might be in a dangerous predicament. Held hostage, maybe, in her own damned office by a raving lunatic.

It might be the solution to his problems, Vickers thought, if things worked out that way. He'd have a chance to rescue Becky, earning her eternal gratitude, while taking out Camacho's man without a lot of fireworks from the border rats. He would be forced to shoot the guy, of course; he couldn't have Rivera's people coming for him at the jail, and if Rivera didn't like it . . . well, he'd have to live with it.

Grant Vickers reined in his wild imagination before it had a chance to carry him away. He had no proof as yet that the stranger was in town, forget about the Dirty Harry number out at Becky's. Still, it wouldn't hurt to warn her, just in case. It was his duty as the law in Santa Rosa, and no one could ever say that he had left his duty unfulfilled.

Bud Stancell was surprised to hear the bell that signaled customers in need of gas this early in the morning. He continued to open at seven every morning, even though he seldom turned a dollar prior to noon, and lately there were days when only one or two loyal patrons—locals—stopped at all. Sometimes he thought he should have sold the business after Ellen died, and tried his luck in Phoenix or Las Vegas, but he could not bring himself to leave.

He had grown up in Santa Rosa, as his parents had before him, but the town was different in those days. There was more border traffic in the years before the interstate had placed a quarantine on smaller towns, conducting tourists in their air-conditioned Cadillacs to Tucson and points east without a necessary stop in Santa Rosa. Time had been when stores were flourishing on Main Street, dealing souvenirs and cactus candy, buckskin duds and beadwork from the Papagos, but that was old news now. A few more years, he thought, and Santa Rosa might dry up and blow away, another ghost town swallowed by the creeping desert, lost to living memory.

Bud Stancell would remain because it was his home, but he had other dreams for Rick, his son. Already taller than his father, Rick had been starting quarterback for Ajo's high school football team last fall, and if he kept his grades up, he was looking at a scholarship, no sweat. It made a father proud to realize his son was strong *and* smart, a combination noticeably lacking in a number of his teammates. Once he went away to college, Rick would have a new perspective on his life, a view of something outside Pima County, even outside Arizona. He would see there was a big, wide world out there, and no mistake.

Bud Stancell's time away from home had been accumulated in Korea, at the Chosin killing grounds, and he was grateful to return and find Santa Rosa more or less unaltered in his absence. All the changes had come later, after he had married, sunk his final dollars into the construction of a service station and garage. In those days, "service" meant precisely that; a patron didn't have to kiss your ass to get the windshield cleaned, and gasoline was nowhere near the price of liquid gold. Sometimes Bud wondered what had happened to America, allowing little piss-ant countries where they couldn't even grow a decent weed to treat the richest nation in the world like she was second-class.

Perhaps Korea was the straw that broke the camel's back. He heard a lot of people bitch and moan about the beating taken in Vietnam, but the States had settled for a draw at

Panmunjom some twenty years before the Nixon pullout from Saigon. Sometimes, especially when he'd had a beer or three too many, Stancell thought the creeping weakness might have started in Korea, taking years before it surfaced, like some kind of virus that lies dormant in your system, waiting for your natural resistance to break down. When the virus hit full-strength, it surely knocked the bottom out of Stancell's business, out of Santa Rosa as a whole.

He ambled toward the service island, hoping that it wasn't Charlie Maddox, not at this time of the morning. That old boy could talk your leg off, and he had a damned opinion about everything. You couldn't wish him Merry Christmas that he wouldn't let you have both barrels, running down commercialism or the heathen nature of the holiday. Bud wasn't up to Charlie's shit this morning, and if it was Maddox, if he started in on some wild hare or other, Bud would have to tell him so.

Except it wasn't Charlie. Hell, it wasn't even close.

Four Mexicans, all piling out of a late-model Chevrolet with plates that put them on the wrong side of the border. Stancell didn't mind, if they were paying cash, but there was something in their eyes that made him just the slightest bit uneasy. Something hard and hungry, like a pit bull's eyes before he took a piece out of your leg.

"G'mornin'. Need ta fill 'er up?"

The tallest of the men shook his head. "We're looking for a friend of ours. We were supposed to meet him, but his car broke down back there." A lazy thumb was cocked across one shoulder, indicating some point farther south. "Maybe you've seen him, eh?"

"Can't help you," Stancell said. "Nobody's been in here today, besides you-all."

"This hombre would be gringo," the interrogator said, as if Bud had not answered him already. "Tall. He might be looking for another car. You seen a man like that?"

"I told you, you're the first ones in today."

The tall man rattled something off in Spanish, shook his head again as if in weary disappointment. "It's important that we find this hombre," he explained. "We got some business with him."

Stancell didn't want to know about their business. He was smelling trouble now, the short hairs rising on his neck. He wished that he was in the station's office, where he kept the Smith & Wesson .38 tucked in a drawer underneath the cash register.

"I wish that I could help you," he responded, hoping that he sounded earnest. "If I see your friend, I'll tell him you were lookin' for him."

"Maybe you won't mind if we should take a look inside?"

"What for? I told you that there's no one here."

"A little peek, okay?"

They were advancing on him, slowly, closing in a pincer movement. Stancell dared not turn his back to run. Instead he started walking backward, toward the open door of the garage. If he could make it that far, he could duck into the office, get his gun and hold them off until he raised Grant Vickers on the phone. And if he couldn't make it to the office, there were wrenches, other tools, with which he could defend himself.

One of the Mexicans was about to cut him off, when Stancell bolted. Never mind the office, he was making for the tool rack, fingers outstretched for the pry bar when a flying tackle brought him down. He hit the concrete deck with someone riding his back, the impact emptying his lungs.

Before he could recover, they had jerked him to his feet. Two of the goons immobilized his arms and held him upright, almost at attention. While a third began to poke around his shop, the leader took a stance in front of Bud and kicked him squarely in the groin.

He would have fallen if the goons hadn't been supporting him. They couldn't stop his throwing up, a hearty breakfast splattering the leader's shoes before he stepped back out of range. Bud Stancell's lower body felt like broken glass.

"We need to find this hombre," he repeated patiently.

Bud gasped for breath. "The bugger hasn't *been* here!"

"Ah."

The man stepped closer and swung from the cellar with a fist encased in brass. One punch broke Stancell's cheekbone, and he felt his mouth fill with blood.

From that point on, Bud Stancell couldn't have responded to their questions even if he knew the answers, and they seemed to know it. Three of them were on him all at once, with fists and feet, and then the fourth was wading in from somewhere, getting in his licks while there was something left to kick around. They worked in silence, angry, driven by frustration, as they played a brutal game of soccer with his body.

Somewhere in the middle of it, after something like a minute, Bud got lucky and lost consciousness. Another seven minutes passed before his visitors got tired and ambled back in the direction of their Chevrolet.

## 7

After an hour or two, the Southern California desert begins to look the same. So many yucca palms and Joshua trees, so many tumbleweeds and cacti that they start to run together, merging in the driver's eye and mind. The land is not precisely flat, but there is none of the relief from boredom that is found in trying to negotiate the mountains farther north. In air-conditioned cars, the drivers set their minds on automatic pilot, try to find a station on the radio, and concentrate on staying off the shoulder of the road. In cars that have to use the four-and-sixty system—all four windows down while driving sixty miles an hour—the drivers bake and curse themselves for being stupid enough to make their crossing in the daylight hours.

Johnny Bolan knew the desert, understood it, but it held no abstract fascination for him at the moment. He was focused on his mission, on his brother's need, already calculating odds and angles from the meager information he possessed.

Somehow the move against Rivera had gone sour. That was bad enough, considering the days of planning Mack had put into the raid, but these things happened from time to time. A rotten break, a sentry with the flu backed up by more alert replacements . . . anything at all. His brother had been stuck in tighter spots, and he was still alive.

It was the wound that worried Johnny. Mack would not have referred to it if it was just a scratch. He knew that much and nothing more, the lack of information taunting him with mental pictures of his brother bleeding in an alley, running from the hunters while his life ran out through ragged wounds. No matter how he held the pedal down, he couldn't get there soon enough, and he could only offer first-aid treatment when he did arrive.

There ought to be a doctor in the town where Mack was hiding, but you never knew for sure. His atlas told him Santa Rosa had 157 residents in 1980, but surrounding towns were larger, and they might be forced to drive the twenty, thirty miles each time they broke a bone or came down with a virus. Many larger towns got by without a full-time doctor of their own, but John would keep his fingers crossed for Santa Rosa, hoping that it might be the exception to the rule.

Locating Mack could be a problem, even in a one-horse town with fewer than two hundred residents. Rivera's people would be after him, of course. Between his wound and hostile gunners trolling the neighborhood, he couldn't very well hang out on Main Street, waiting for a ride. Determination of his hiding place would have to wait on an examination of the town itself, but John was free to speculate while he drove. He would avoid the local sheriff, that was obvious. The doctor—if there was one—might provide a sanctuary, but there were assorted regulations bearing on reports of gunshot wounds. Mack would not want to hold the doctor hostage, if he should be fortunate enough to find one, but he might be forced to lock the old boy in a closet, say, or tie him to a chair, just long enough to buy some time, some combat stretch.

If it was up to him, a little town like Santa Rosa was the last place Mack would choose to make a stand. Endangering civilians ran against his grain, and if Rivera's army hit the town in force, the innocent were bound to suffer. Mack would try to minimize the damage, Johnny knew, by any means available. The damned guy might just sacrifice himself, if there were other lives at stake, and it was something of the sort that worried Johnny as he pushed the Jimmy up to eighty, held it there, his hands white-knuckled on the steering wheel.

He wondered how his brother might be armed. Mack would have carried ample hardware for the strike, but much of it would be expended, other items left behind when he was wounded, forced to ditch the car. It never paid to underestimate his brother; he had seen him work miracles from scratch, but even Mack could only do so much. Unfortunately courage didn't make a soldier bulletproof. Audacity could carry you against the odds, but it could only carry you so far. Once you had dazzled your opponents with the fancy footwork, you had to deal with them in concrete terms. With bullet, blade and strangling wire. A wounded man, with only side arms to rely on, simply had no business taking on an army.

But you couldn't tell that to the Executioner. Hell, no.

Mack didn't see himself as a superman; it wasn't anything like that. He simply had not learned to run away from trouble, let the bad guys have their fun and count your blessings if they left you out of it. He lived by an entirely different code, demanding action in the face of savagery, resistance when the cannibals were in control. If he was well enough to run and absolutely empty-handed, Johnny knew his brother would have done his damnedest to defend the residents of Santa Rosa from the plague that he, unwittingly, had brought upon their heads.

It was a sense of duty that might get him killed this time. But not if Johnny Bolan had a thing to say about it. Not if he could reach the tiny town in time to stand beside his brother. They might die together, if it came to that, but he would have tried. And if he came too late to help, well then God help Luis Rivera and his jackals.

Johnny knew their numbers and the names that counted, knew where he could find them. And if he came too late to help his brother, they would have another opportunity to curse the Bolan name. Another opportunity to feel the cleansing fire.

THE DAY WAS SHAPING UP to be another scorcher, but Rick Stancell didn't mind the heat. Hot days meant warmer nights, and that was fine. He called it drive-in weather, when the desert breeze was soft and warm, the sky so vast and dark that you could count a million stars if you had time. It was the kind of night just made for drive-in movies, with your best girl at your side, and given time and a little luck, you wouldn't even care about the movie on the big old weathered screen.

Rick didn't feel like working, but he had already promised, and he had his father's pickup truck to use tonight, together with some spending money, if he kept his word. He had invited Amy Schultz to see a double feature with him at the Ajo drive-in, and she had agreed. The films were nothing special—*D.C. Cab* and *Billy Jack Goes Hollywood*, definitely B grade—but Rick was not devoted to the cinema. He was devoted to Amy Schultz, and he was certain that with time and the necessary patience, he could make her come around.

She wasn't prudish, not exactly, but she seemed to be the kind of girl who saved the heavy stuff for marriage. Stancell didn't mind. He knew she would be worth the wait, but when his mind coughed up a thought like that, it made him hesitate and wonder what was going on inside himself. He was a senior—would be, come September—and a lot of kids got married right away, as soon as they could shuck the cap and gown. But Rick was bound for college, something better than a dead-end job in Pima County, sweating out his days behind a gas pump or a check-out counter at the hardware store. He knew that Amy liked him—maybe "loved" would be a better word—and most times, Stancell felt the same. But marriage was a fair piece down the road, five years at least, and in the meantime... Well, a guy gets itchy.

There were other girls at Ajo High who would have given Stancell what he wanted. It would have been so easy, but something held him back.

He didn't like to call it "love," with all the trappings of commitment that that term implied, but what else could it be? He had been dating Amy, going steady for the better part of six months, and while he often got the urge, he seldom had it anymore for other girls. It disturbed Rick a little, when he thought about the bridges that he might be burning, but it made him feel grown-up, as well. It made him feel...well, like a man.

The other guys at school were always talking about how much they got, and all of that, but when they asked about his dates with Amy, Stancell shined them on or shut them up with glaring looks. He did all right with Amy, to a point, but what they did or didn't do was not up for discussion on the Ajo High School grapevine. A week before the summer break, that asshole Tommy Pendergast had started wisecracking about "Rick's virgin queen," and Stancell had been forced to rearrange his bridgework for him. That had been the end of idle chatter—in his presence, anyway—and after Amy heard about it, she rewarded him with one of their more memorable dates. But they were both still virgins, and Rick had come to wonder if there was some way to correct that, short of trooping down the aisle at seventeen.

The thought of marriage didn't faze him. He wasn't frightened by the thought of Amy Schultz becoming Amy Stancell somewhere down the road. But not just yet. They needed time to grow, to see a little of the world. Time to learn about each other, and decide precisely what they wanted out of life. But none of that precluded having fun along the way.

He reached the service station, found it open and with his dad nowhere in sight. The empty service island came as no surprise; a customer this early would have been unusual, and Santa Rosa was not known for deviations from routine. If they were lucky, half a dozen locals might stop by to fill up this afternoon, but it had been a week or more since anyone had needed engine work. He had suggested that his dad cut back on hours, trim his overhead by opening at noon instead of seven in the morning, but he might as well have offered his opinions to the wall. Bud Stancell was enamored of tradition. He believed in change and progress, but for others, never for himself. Rick sometimes wondered how his father stuck it out, how he could love this dusty little town enough to struggle by on a subsistence income, pumping gas for people who were so appreciative that they took their heavy business into Ajo or surrounding towns. His father should have pulled up stakes when his wife died...but, then again, if they had moved, Rick never would have had a shot at Amy Schultz.

He passed the silent pumps, the empty office, entering the main garage. Still no sign of his father, though he got a strange, uncomfortable feeling in the shop. Tools were disarranged along the workbench, as if his dad had skipped the nightly cleanup yesterday.

He saw the retreads now. They had been neatly stacked last night, around a wooden spindle, but the pile was toppled, and two of them had rolled across the shop floor to rest against the opposite wall. A cabinet full of hoses, belts and other gear was standing open, as if someone had been interrupted in the midst of taking inventory.

"Dad?"

No answer. He was on his way to check the lot in back when something like a muffled groan, no louder than a whimper, reached his ears. He froze, turned back to face the empty room and waited for a repetition of the sound.

It came again, and Rick took all of half a second to pin it down. There was a row of cabinets underneath his father's workbench, stocked with odds and ends of the mechanic's trade, and he would swear the weak, inhuman sound was emanating from those cabinets, like a whisper from the tomb.

He crossed the floor in three long strides and ripped the cabinets open, startled into jumping backward as his father's body rolled out at his feet. No, not a body—he was still alive. Still breathing. But for God's sake what had happened to him in the hour since he'd left the house to open up his station?

If he hadn't known the man, Rick never would have recognized his face. The Roman nose was flattened, lying over his cheek, with one eye swollen shut, the other rimmed in drying blood. His lips were split and mangled, parted so that he could breath, revealing jagged vacancies where teeth had been in place an hour earlier. On impact with the floor, he curled into a fetal ball, knees up, both hands tucked in against his chest. Rick didn't need a medical degree to know those hands were broken; perhaps "smashed" would be a better word.

With sudden, crystal clarity, Rick realized that this had been no accident. He had been beaten, thoroughly and brutally, perhaps by several people working as a team. But why? A robbery? In Santa Rosa? Rick was tempted to duck back and check the cash register, but he could not desert his father. There might be internal injuries, and time was of the essence. What if he was dying?

Rick thought about his ruined date with Amy, and was instantly ashamed. What did it matter if he saw a movie, if he stayed a virgin, when his father had been attacked by strangers, beaten like an animal and left for dead?

But *were* they strangers? Was there someone here, in Santa Rosa, who might wish his father harm? He had not been aware of any enemies, but then again...

He broke the train of thought and let it slip away. The constable could worry over that, once Dr. Kent had finished working on his father. She was good, and she would know what to do.

"Come on, Dad, let's get up."

It took him several moments, but at last Bud Stancell made it to his feet, one arm around Rick's shoulders, grimacing at any accidental contact with his shattered hands. His steps were slow, his posture stooped, as though there might be broken ribs or other injuries, and Rick was weeping, seething, by the time they reached the pickup.

Someone had set out to maim his father, and if they had not succeeded, they had come damned close. Before the day was out, he meant to know their names and reasons for the cruel attack. If Vickers, with his badge and gun belt, could ensure swift justice, that was fine. If not...well, then, Rick Stancell just might have to take the law into his own hands. At that moment, as he slid in behind the pickup's steering wheel with angry tears still brimming in his eyes, the seventeen-year-old was looking forward to it.

PATIENCE WAS A VIRTUE that Luis Rivera had admired throughout his life, but always from a distance. He was not a patient man, had never been content to sit and wait when there was action to be taken, battles to be won. It chafed at him to sit beside the highway, smoking, while Camacho and the others scoured Santa Rosa for their prey, but he was not a fool. He knew that generals must rely on scouts and spies until their enemy had been discovered, his position and his strength reliably confirmed. That done, a field commander had the opportunity to plot his strategy and lead his troops to victory, instead of blundering around in unfamiliar territory, risking a fatal ambush.

He had joined his soldiers on the highway north of town, a small concession to impatience. Fully conscious of the risks involved, the greater distance to his native Mexico, he was determined not to miss the action if their quarry broke and ran. If anyone attempted to escape from Santa Rosa, he would be there, waiting with his men.

Another team still watched the highway to the south, and with Camacho's squad in Santa Rosa, that made a good-size army. It was enough to handle any threat that might arise, Rivera thought, and he was not without his friends inside the town itself. Strategic cash investments over the years had given him a lock on local law enforcement, scarcely worthy of the name, but if it came to violence, he was protected by the frail legitimacy of a tarnished badge.

Rivera checked his Rolex, scowling at the time. What could be keeping Hector and his crew? They had a radio; they should have been in touch by now, with some report of progress. Vickers should be helping them to search the tiny town, a task that might require an hour, two at the outside. Their prey was stranded, badly injured. How could he elude a team of able-bodied men?

Rivera lit a thin cheroot to calm himself and concentrated on the certainty of ultimate success. The time was not important; if it took an hour or an afternoon, it would be all the same to him. His honor would be salvaged, his supremacy assured. Competitors would have to reconsider their positions when they witnessed how he coped with grave adversity, the retribution he dealt out to his enemies at any cost.

Rivera hoped it would be possible to hunt down the American, retrieve him with a minimum of fuss and carry him back home for questioning. Ideally, no one in the tiny border town would know that he had passed among them, hunting for his prey. But he was ready for a siege. If necessary, he would level Santa Rosa, burn it to the ground and grind the ashes under foot. If Vickers could not help him by the authority of his position and his knowledge of the town, then he would cast the useless man aside and do it on his own.

Luis Rivera had not come up from the streets through countless brutal conflicts only to be beaten by a stranger he had never met. The gringo had some grudge against his operation, or against Rivera personally, but before the day was out he would know everything about his enemy. The man's own mother would not recognize him when Rivera finished drawing out the story of his life. And then, when he was finished, he would bring that story to an end.

Soon he would have his revenge. His reputation would be saved. No man would look upon Rivera as a weakling, someone to be trifled with, insulted by a member of the peasant class. He would again command the respect that was his due. He was the commander of a private army large enough and fierce enough to rule some modern nations, and if any of his rivals needed a refresher course in grim reality, he was prepared to tutor them in person.

Once again he checked his wristwatch. Seven minutes had elapsed, the seconds creeping past like hours as he waited for Camacho to report. Rivera arbitrarily picked out a deadline. Noon. If he heard nothing from his scouts by twelve o'clock, he would go looking for them, search the town himself if need be. One way or another he would see this matter finished, done.

He had more pressing business in Sonora, contacts to be made, incinerated merchandise to be replaced. His buyers in the States would not be sympathetic to an overlong delay; they might turn elsewhere for supplies if he could not fulfill their needs on time.

The present interlude was a distraction, though a necessary one. Soon Rivera could return to what he did best: generating wealth and enjoying the pleasures it could bring. It was his destiny.

But first, the American. First, the taste of sweet revenge. When he had had his fill, Rivera could relax and concentrate on business. When his thirst for vengeance had been slaked, his rage appeased.

Soon, now.

So very soon.

## 8

"What changed your mind about that call?"

Rebecca forced herself to meet her patient's eyes. "I haven't changed my mind. Not yet. It's just that...well, I'd like to try and understand you, why you do these things."

"Somebody has to do them."

"No." She shook her head emphatically. "I don't believe that. We have courts and laws to deal with criminals."

Mack Bolan smiled, without a trace of rancor. "Sure. And look how well they've done so far."

"We can't revert to vigilantism."

"I'm no vigilante. I'm in pest control."

"That's very glib, but we're discussing murder."

"Execution," he corrected her.

"The only legal executions are performed by order of the court, in manners prescribed by law."

"The law can't cope with syndicated crime," he said. "These savages have been evading laws and buying off the courts for something like a century, and that's just here, in the United States. In Sicily it dates back to the middle ages."

"Everyone has rights. The Constitution guarantees—"

"These so-called people threw their rights away," he interrupted her, "the minute that they started selling drugs to children, torching crowded tenements for the insurance, selling teenage runaways like cattle to the pimps in half a dozen countries. They convict themselves by every word they utter, every move they make. Their lives are one long guilty plea.''

''And you're the self-appointed judge.''

He shook his head. ''I'm not their judge, Doc. I'm their judgment.''

He was exasperating, so committed to his cause that everything she said was turned against her, twisted to become an argument on his behalf. And still she made no move to call Grant Vickers and report her wounded patient. She wondered if it might be something in herself that stayed her hand. Was she remembering the rage, the urge to kill that possessed her for a time, just after...

''This can't be much of a life,'' she said, determined to distract herself.

''It's not, but I get by.''

She was amazed by Bolan's tone of resignation. ''You've just been shot. You're stranded in a strange place, being hunted like an animal. I wouldn't call that getting by.''

''I'm still alive,'' he told her. ''What else is there?''

''Peace and quiet,'' she responded. ''Home and family. A life without the guns and killing.''

''Peace and quiet are expensive,'' Bolan said. ''Somebody has to pay the tab. Besides my family's all gone.''

''I'm sorry.''

''It's not your fault,'' he countered. ''The responsibility for that one's been assessed, the tab collected. It's old business.''

''So, you're fighting for your family? For revenge?''

''In the beginning,'' he admitted. ''But it didn't take me long to realize the savages were everywhere. My family's loss has been repeated every day, in every major city, since the mob got organized. If they're not bad enough, you've got the terrorists of various persuasions, racist groups and half-baked 'revolutionaries' killing for a cause that changes every hour, on the hour. Faces change, the propaganda varies, but they're all the same at heart. All savages.''

"You're taking on the world."

"Not quite. I still believe that the majority of people would prefer to lead their lives without the threat of being raped or robbed or murdered. Live and let live. But before we get to that point, certain people have to die.''

"And so you kill them, just like that?"

He thought about it, finally nodded. "Just like that.''

"Because they're evil?"

"No. Because they're predators, and while they live, they have to feed. Unfortunately you and I are on the menu."

She was startled by a sudden frantic rapping on the door, and realized that she hadn't opened up the clinic. So distracted was she by her wounded patient that she had ignored the time.

The pounding was repeated, a percussion beat of desperation. She was halfway to the door when something made her hesitate and glance at Bolan.

"My guns," he snapped. "Where are they?"

The doctor shook her head. "I won't have killing here.''

"You may not have a choice.''

"Lie still. I'll handle it.''

But she was trembling as she crossed the waiting room, caught up in Bolan's story, frightened by the thought of gunmen waiting on her porch. Would they have bothered to knock? Frozen with one hand upon the latch, she nudged the blinds aside and risked a peek, expecting burly ruffians with weapons drawn and poised to fire. Instead she saw Rick Stancell, slumped beneath his father's weight, supporting Bud with difficulty, smeared with blood that must have been the older man's. She hit the latch and threw the door back, stepping out to help Rick guide his father through the doorway.

"Rick, what happened?"

"Someone beat him up." The adolescent's voice was taut with grief and rage. "I found him like this, back at the garage."

"This way."

Without a second thought, she led her latest patient toward the tiny operating room. She thought of Bolan just before they crossed the threshold, almost steered the Stancells back to one of her examination rooms . . . and then she saw that Bolan had removed himself. The IV tube was clipped against its standing rack, where he had left it, and his bloody skinsuit lay folded on the counter, but the man himself was nowhere to be seen.

She and Rick helped Bud onto the table, then the boy backed off to let her do her work. A brief examination was enough to show Rebecca that she could not deal with Stancell's injuries in Santa Rosa. Both his hands were crushed, he almost certainly had broken ribs, and bleeding from the ears suggested damage to his skull. A neurosurgeon would be needed if her worst suspicions were confirmed, and there might be internal damage to Bud Stancell's lungs or other vital organs, suffered when his ribs were broken.

"I can clean him up and give him something for the pain," she told the young man, "but he needs treatment in a hospital as soon as possible. I'll make the call to the Grundys."

Amos Grundy was the chief of the volunteer fire department. His brother, Thane, had gone to paramedic's school in Tucson. They owned an ambulance, which they had purchased with the aid of county funds, and now monopolized the trade in patients being hustled off to hospital. They ran a decent service, Amos driving like a demon while his brother sat in back and tended to their passenger, and they had never lost a patient. Yet.

She snared the telephone receiver, raised it to her ear and waited for the dial tone. Nothing. She drummed the switch hook with impatient fingers, waiting, but to no avail. The line was dead.

FROM BOLAN'S HIDING PLACE inside a pantry room adjacent to the surgery, he could observe Rebecca Kent and eavesdrop on her conversation with the late arrivals. He was watching, listening, when she replaced the telephone receiver without dialing, turning with a frown to face the boy.

"The lines are crossed or something," she informed him. "Can you run on down to the Grundys? It would save us time."

"I'm gone," the boy replied, already suiting words to action as he raced out through the nearest exit, pounding out of sight beyond the windows.

Bolan stepped out of his hiding place, still woozy from the loss of blood and local anesthetic he had received. "You have that problem often?" he inquired.

The doctor almost jumped, then shook her head, returning to her battered patient on the operating table. "Once or twice," she said. "It's not unheard of."

"You assume it's a coincidence?"

"What else?"

He did not answer her directly, moving to stand beside the table. Dressed in Jockey shorts and bandages, he felt no chill. It was already hot outside, and Santa Rosa's clinic did not have the benefit of modern air-conditioning. An old swamp cooler labored on the roof, providing circulation for the rooms, but it would never be accused of freezing anyone to death.

"Who's this?" he asked.

"Bud Stancell, owner of the local service station." Dr. Kent glanced up at him, countless questions in her eyes. "Why do you ask?"

"Just curious. You get a lot of beatings here in Santa Rosa?"

She hesitated, even though she clearly did not have to think about her answer. "No."

"You've got a busy morning on your hands. A gunshot wound, a beating and your phone goes dead."

It hit her then, and she stood up to face the Executioner directly. "You believe there's some connection?"

"I'd give odds."

"Why would—whoever—want to hurt Bud Stancell? He has no connection with your private war."

"He didn't, till this morning. At a guess I'd say you're looking at the end results of an interrogation. Someone has been making sure I didn't get my car repaired, or find another one to take me out of town."

"And these same people cut my phone lines?"

"Maybe. It's more likely that they took the main lines down, outside of town. If anybody's interested, I'll bet you couldn't place a call on any phone in Santa Rosa."

"That's preposterous."

"So, prove it. Step next door and use a neighbor's phone. I'll keep your patient company."

She hesitated, finally shook her head. "I don't have time."

"None of us do."

Rebecca Kent ignored him. Stepping to the drug chest and unlocking it, she filled a hypodermic, locked the cabinet again and slipped the needle into her patient with the expertise of someone who has done it a thousand times before. A moment passed before the man relaxed, and then his moans receded, fading, until they had ceased entirely.

"He'll rest easy on the ride to Tucson."

"If he gets there."

"What? Oh, it's an easy drive. We have an ambulance in town."

"I wasn't thinking of the transportation."

"Oh? What, then?"

"Whoever put him through the ringer may have backup waiting on the highway."

"Mr. Bolan, I believe you're paranoid."

He smiled slightly. "Well, just because you're paranoid, Doc, doesn't mean that no one's out to get you."

"Mmm. You'll pardon me if I don't check for gangsters underneath my bed tonight? I can't believe these nameless heavies have the town surrounded."

"They have names," the Executioner assured her. "For the moment, you can call them Trouble."

"You look chilly, Mr. Bolan."

"I'm afraid I didn't bring my wardrobe with me, Doctor."

"Try the pantry. You should find some things inside the closet there. They won't be your style, but they'll cover the subject."

He backtracked, found the closet and opened it to find a couple of men's denim shirts, two lab coats, blue jeans folded on a hanger and a pair of slacks. He opted for a denim shirt and the jeans, surprised to find they fit him fairly well.

"Your husband's?"

"No, my father's." There was something wistful in her voice. "It's been a while. I never had the heart to throw them out."

He finished zipping up and left the shirttails hanging out to minimize the pressure on his wounded side. When he rejoined the doctor, she was swabbing down her patient's face with hydrogen peroxide, cleaning off the crusty blood and dabbing at his wounds, a pinched expression on her face betraying sympathetic pain.

"You care about this town," he said.

"Is it that obvious?"

"I wouldn't want to see you hurt. I wouldn't want to see this town destroyed."

"We'll make it."

Bolan didn't share her confidence. He did not want to think about the other innocents, across the years, who had been slaughtered when their paths had crossed his own. How many deaths of good people on his soul thus far? Too many.

He should leave at once, retrieve his weapons or depart without them. Either way, the simple act of getting out might spare her something, draw the heat away from Dr. Kent, her battered patient, and the town that was her home. If necessary, he could let Rivera's gunners see him, lead them out into the desert, let them take him there if it came down to killing. And it would, he knew that much. It always did.

On second thought, however, Bolan wondered if evacuation would achieve the ends he desired. If he was right, Rivera's gunners had already beaten one man, unaccountably allowing him to live. They were endangered by a witness now, the threat compounded by their victim's contact with his son and Dr. Kent. The ambulance attendants, if they came, would stand as two more leaks to plague Rivera, granting always that they were allowed to leave.

It would not matter, Bolan realized, if he exposed himself to the Rivera hit team now, or not. They had to finish mopping up behind them, and in the process, they were likely to encounter other witnesses in Santa Rosa. The stage was set for a chaotic bloodbath, and the Executioner could not escape a feeling of responsibility for having set the wheels in motion. If there had been something, anything, that might have been done otherwise . . .

He pushed the morbid train of thought aside. Regrets and self-recriminations would do nothing to prevent a massacre in Santa Rosa. On the other hand, there might be something that the Executioner *could* do.

"I'll need those weapons."

"No." The doctor's tone was resolute, as if she knew he would not resort to force. "Not yet."

He frowned. What was she waiting for? Could he trust *her* to decide when it was time, without delays that might prove fatal to them all?

He could have torn the place apart and found the guns himself, no doubt, but Bolan hesitated. It could wait, however briefly, while he calculated odds and angles. In a few more hours, it might make no difference either way.

RICK STANCELL HIT the sidewalk running, closing off his mind to the incessant heat and keeping up a driving pace around the back of Dr. Kent's clinic toward Main Street. Grundys' combination home and office was positioned on the southern edge of town, perhaps three hundred yards away. The pavement in front of Rick gave off waves of heat that made the storefronts shimmer like hallucinations.

He bolted across the sidewalk, onto Main Street in full stride, without a backward glance. He heard the screech of brakes, an angry horn and raised one open hand by way of an apology as he hot-footed toward the opposite curb. He spared a sidelong glance for the sedan that slithered past, a big dark Chevy, four men riding low behind the slightly tinted windows, plates from Mexico. It wasn't all that odd, and Rick had put them out of mind before he cleared another twenty yards, the Chevy disappearing down a side street, rolling lazylike, as if the driver were engaged in looking for an address that he couldn't find.

Rick Stancell didn't waste time wondering how anyone could lose their way in Santa Rosa. His thoughts were concentrated on his father and the hope that Amos Grundy wasn't sleeping off one of his famous drunks. If necessary, Rick would drive the goddamned ambulance himself, or take his father in the truck, if Dr. Kent would come along.

He trusted her implicitly and knew that she would never put his father into another doctor's hands if there was anything that she could do herself. He knew enough about internal injuries to understand you couldn't treat them in a doctor's office.

Dr. Kent would never let his father down, but now it was up to Rick—to secure the ambulance; to see him safely off to Tucson, following him in the truck as soon as he could close the station down; to wait beside his father's bed and find out what the surgeon had to say.

To find the animals who were responsible for his condition.

More than one man was involved; Rick knew that much instinctively. His father might be getting soft in middle age, but he could still defend himself, and he had not forgotten all those tricks he had learned in the Marine Corps, tricks that had been practiced time and time again on human beings in Korea. If he was afraid of anyone or anything, Bud Stancell never let it show, and Rick could not believe that he would take a beating passively.

Half a block now. Gaining. From the Grundys', he would race back to the clinic, wait until the ambulance arrived to pick up his father. The doctor's phone might be in service by that time; if not, then Rick would run to find the constable and tell him what had happened, set him searching for the bastards who had tried to kill his father.

First, though, he would have to check the station, find out if the cash drawer had been rifled. If it was a robbery—and what else could it be?—the constable and county sheriff could begin with roadblocks, searching cars for evidence and suspects. Even driving very fast, the bastards could not have escaped from Pima County yet.

They had a chance, and the odds would be improved once doctors had his father back in shape, once he could offer a description of the animals who had attacked him. In the meantime, though, there would be plenty for the constable to do. There might be fingerprints at the garage; he must remember not to handle anything except the doorknobs when he locked it up. He must try to anticipate the needs of lawmen working on the case.

But at the moment he was thinking only of his father, broken, cast aside like some discarded toy. Someone would have to pay for that, in court or otherwise. And at the moment, "otherwise" looked pretty good to Rick.

## 9

Grant Vickers parked his cruiser at the curb outside the Santa Rosa Clinic, frowning as he saw the Grundy brothers trundling their gurney from the ambulance along a narrow alley to the clinic's rear entrance. It was unusual enough to see them on a run at all, but when they worked, they usually made their pickups on surrounding farms or at the patient's home. The local population had begun to age, and there were heart attacks to deal with, broken hips and strokes from time to time. The farmhands, green cards for the most part, sometimes got a whiff of some insecticide or caught their hands in the machinery, but it was downright odd to find the Grundys at the clinic.

Instantly he wondered if the patient was Rivera's pigeon. Hector had been looking for a wounded man, and Becky was the only doctor in town. It added up, and Vickers saw a sudden gleam of hope. The Grundys might export his problem for him, if Camacho didn't tumble to the move in time. They could be on the road and running by the time Rivera's bloodhounds got the scent.

He locked the cruiser, hitching up his gun belt as he trailed the Grundys. They had their stretcher through the door when Vickers reached the porch, Rebecca waving them inside, and Vickers followed. She appeared surprised to see him, just a flicker in her eyes, but there was nothing of the usual smile this morning.

"Grant," she said at last, "I'm glad you're here. It's terrible."

"What happened?"

"Someone has attacked Bud Stancell. I'm afraid he has internal injuries."

Bud Stancell? Vickers frowned and moved around to stand beside the table, opposite the Grundys as they tried to lift the man to the gurney. Stancell looked like hell, no doubt about it. Someone—several someones, by the look of it—had done a nasty tap dance on his face and hands, with plentiful attention to the other areas as well. The constable had filed reports on road fatalities that didn't look as bad as Stancell did right now.

"Did he tell you anything?"

Rebecca stood to one side, arms crossed underneath her breasts. She shook her head. "He's been unconscious since Rick brought him in."

Vickers noticed the boy for the first time, standing in the corner, looking kind of pale and drawn, like someone suffering from heat stroke. Damned fine football player, Rick was. He had all the moves. Between his grades and speed, he could be Ivy League, no sweat. Some break, to get out of a piss-ant town like Santa Rosa, live a little, see the world. The only thing that Bud was going to see would be intensive care, and Vickers wouldn't have bet money on his hopes of coming out again.

"Did you see whoever did this, son?"

Rick shook his head. "No, sir. I found him in the cabinet when I got to his garage. They put him *in the cabinet*."

"Bastards." Vickers frowned. "It would have helped to have some kind of general description. As it is, I figure drifters passing through."

"You'll find them?"

"I'll do everything I can, boy, rest assured of that."

Grant thought he might have some idea of who the "drifters" were, but it was crazy, when you thought about it. Why would Hector and his hitters do a number on Bud Stancell, when they were supposedly involved with searching for some stranger? Hector wasn't anyone to trifle with, but Vickers hadn't thought that he was loco, either. Then again, Rivera's pigeon had supposedly been stranded when his car broke down outside of town. Camacho might have reasoned that the guy would look for a mechanic, might have dropped by Stancell's on the off chance, and the questions might've gotten out of hand. Too many "might haves," but it made a twisted kind of sense, if you considered Hector and his fondness for the rough stuff.

He studied Becky's worried face. Camacho knew their mark was wounded, just as he had known about the car. If he had tagged the town mechanic, it was only common sense that he would get around to looking for the doctor, and Vickers didn't want to think about Rebecca being handled by Rivera's animals. And yet, if he should try to warn her off...

The Grundys had Bud Stancell on their gurney now, and they were hauling him away. Rick followed, but Rebecca hung back in the doorway, staring after them.

"Are you all right?"

She turned toward Vickers with a curious expression on her face. "Of course. Why do you ask?"

"Just thinking that you looked a little peaked."

"Bud's a friend. I hate to see him suffering."

"Oh, sure. I just thought maybe there was something else."

"Such as?"

He tried a different tack. "Did you have another patient in this morning?"

"No. Why do you ask?"

"Oh, someone saw a stranger down on Main Street," Vickers lied. "They thought he looked like he'd been in some kind of accident."

"I haven't seen him. Sorry."

"If you do..."

"I'll let you know, of course."

"I'd appreciate it." Vickers hesitated, certain there was something else that he should say, unable to dredge up the words. He could not warn the doctor without baring guilty knowledge of a criminal assault, and worse. "I guess I'd better make some calls," he said at last. "See if I can find out who worked Bud over."

"Yes, I think you should."

She held the door for Vickers, saw him off, then closed it firmly. He spent a moment on the porch, then walked back to his cruiser, opened it up and slid behind the wheel. A dusty pickup had just pulled up outside the hardware store, a lanky farmer disembarking, but otherwise, Main Street was empty. No sign of Camacho's hunting party or the faceless stranger they were seeking. No damned way at all for Vickers to decide what action he should take.

It was too bad about Bud Stancell, and of course he had to go through all the motions, driving up and down the street, relaying a report to Sheriff Duffy up in Tucson. Even if by some bizarre coincidence the Stancell case was unrelated to Camacho's visit, there was little that the sheriff or the state police could do. Without descriptions of the men, their car, and so forth, they were pissing in the wind.

The constable was more concerned for Becky Kent. He couldn't watch the clinic obtrusively, but he could keep an eye peeled. And if Camacho tried to make a move against the doctor, then what? Did he have the hardware or the nerve to actively oppose Rivera's army? How long would he last, assuming that he tried? Could he face himself again if he stood back, did nothing, while they had their way with Becky, with his town?

Tough questions, and Grant Vickers wasn't ready with answers as he put his cruiser in motion, rolling slowly through the heart of town. When something happened, he would handle it. Beyond that, who could say?

He cursed the heat, Rivera and his hunting dogs, the desert that conspired to twist men's souls and drive them crazy. Some days, like today, Grant Vickers hated everything about his life. He hated breathing. Other days...well, living right on hell's back doorstep didn't seem so bad.

But for the moment he was trapped inside today, and he would have to give it everything he had, or he might never see tomorrow.

REBECCA KENT STEPPED BACK from the waiting-room windows, expelling a sigh of relief as the cruiser moved on, out of sight. She was trembling, unaccustomed to deception, certain that Grant Vickers must have seen through her. And yet, if he suspected she was lying, wouldn't he have asked more questions, badgered her until he had the truth? Their personal relationship, though ill-defined, might have prevented him from calling her a liar to her face, but he still had a job to do, and she was certain that she could not put him off indefinitely.

Sudden movement at the door, a hand upon the knob, and she was on the verge of crying out before she recognized Rick Stancell. Tears were in his eyes, but he was bearing up remarkably, all things considered.

"They just left with Dad," he told her. "I'll be driving up to Tucson in a little while to stay with him, but first I've got to do some things around the station, shut it down and all."

"That's quite a drive. Do you feel up to it?"

"I'm fine," he said. "No problem."

"Please be careful, Rick."

"I will."

And he was gone. The door had barely closed behind him when she was aware of movement on her flank. She turned to find the Executioner regarding her with cautious interest, looking almost folksy in her father's clothes. It was peculiar, but she never really thought of him as being gone, until some forcible reminder struck her square between the eyes.

"That's twice," the soldier said.

"I beg your pardon?"

"Twice you haven't turned me in. Why?"

"I really couldn't say."

And that, at least, was true. Rebecca could no more offer him a definition of her motives than she could take wing and fly. Above all else, she could not voice the dark suspicion that Grant Vickers had aroused. *"Someone saw a stranger down on Main Street."* Injured. Yet the constable had failed to offer a description, and his witness, if he existed, plainly had not marked the "stranger's" destination.

Why was she suspicious? She had lied to Grant, denied the presence of another patient in her clinic. Why should he have wasted time describing someone who, according to her own report, she had not seen? Was she becoming paranoid, infected by the mind-set that had kept Mack Bolan one short step ahead of execution squads throughout the years?

"You didn't trust him," Bolan said, and her reaction gave the lie to any answer her lips might form. It was as if the wounded man had looked inside her mind to read her private thoughts.

"I guess I'm getting jumpy, after everything that's happened."

"You've got reason," he replied. "I didn't trust him, either."

"Why?"

"There wasn't anybody on the street this morning. All the shops were closed. I didn't see a soul . . . except the people who are looking for me."

"No." Although her mind was edging toward the same conclusion, it was different, somehow, when he spoke the words aloud. She would not let herself believe that Grant could be allied with criminals of any kind. It was preposterous. Absurd. "I know what you're about to say. I don't believe it."

"How well do you know the constable?"

"We're friends." But Bolan's eyes elicited a more detailed response. "We've dated once or twice. It's nothing steady."

"But you like him."

"Yes, I guess so."

"And, for all of that, you thought that there was something strange about his questions, his behavior."

Bolan had her there. She tried to meet his eyes and failed, eventually focusing upon the IV rack.

"Are you feeling stronger?"

"I'm all right."

It wasn't true, of course. He must be weakened by the loss of blood, by shock, the trauma of his wound and all that happened afterward. He should have been in bed, and preferably in a hospital, but she did not waste breath on the impossible suggestion.

"You should rest."

"No time. The opposition won't be taking any coffee breaks."

"And if you leave? Where will you go?" He had no answer for her, and she forged ahead. "You said yourself, they may be watching all the roads. Suppose you took my car, or someone else's. How far would you get before they ran you down?''

Again, no answer from the Executioner.

"And when they see your bandages, the sutures, they'll be certain that you've seen a doctor. When they trace the car, whoever you decide to steal one from, that makes another witness to eliminate.'' She paused for breath, and felt him watching her. "One man has been severely injured as it is. How many others will it take?''

The soldier frowned. "You aren't exactly safe right now, with me around.''

"I fooled the constable. I'll manage.''

Bolan shook his head. "I'm not so sure you sold your friend on anything, but that's beside the point. You had a look at the mechanic, Doc. For all the good it did, he never laid eyes on me in his life. Imagine what they'll do to someone who has all the answers.''

"So, I'll have to be convincing.''

"These men aren't renowned for graceful losing, Doctor. They don't take no for an answer when it *is* the answer.''

"So, help me. Tell me who 'they' are.''

The soldier hesitated, staring hard, as if he meant to read her soul. And then he said, "All right.''

LUIS RIVERA STUBBED OUT his cheroot and shifted in his seat, uncomfortable after two long hours of waiting. Hector should have been in touch by now; regardless of the motive, his continued silence was not comforting. Rivera had been stewing in the desert heat too long, without reports of progress from his men in Santa Rosa, and his mind was turning slowly, inexorably, toward revenge against his own subordinates. If Hector did not call in, say, within another twenty minutes—

*"Mira!"*

Instantly alert, Rivera saw the ambulance from half a mile, its multicolored lights revolving, flashing, their display diminished by the glaring sun. He stepped out of the car, his gunners following. Other doors were slamming behind him, his men taking up their stations on the baking pavement. Someone drove one of the backup cars diagonally across the road, blocking both lanes.

The driver of the ambulance applied his brakes fifty yards from the roadblock. He had his window down, red-faced and growling as the van decelerated, coasting to a stop no more than twenty feet from where Rivera stood, his men already closing in to surround the new arrivals.

"What the hell you think you're doin', boy?" the driver shouted, glancing left and right, his anger losing steam as hardware was displayed. "I'm on official business. An emergency."

"I also have a small emergency," Rivera told him, smiling in anticipation of the kill. "We need to see your passenger."

"The hell you do! This man's en route to Tucson. He's hurt bad."

"I have the cure for his distress." Rivera nodded, and the nearest of his gunners put a bullet through the driver's forehead, silencing his arguments forever. Others had the rear doors open; an automatic weapon stuttered briefly as the paramedic riding with the patient was eliminated. Anxiously, Rivera circled to the rear and thrust his men aside to face his enemy, now helpless on a gurney in the ambulance, his arms strapped down.

Except that this was not the man. He was too short, too heavy, almost certainly too old. His injuries, while numerous, did not include a bullet wound.

Rivera drew his pistol, leaned inside the ambulance, and cured that omission on the spot. He felt the others watching him, prepared to carry out his orders, but the dealer found himself dumbstruck, immediately at a loss for words. He had been certain that the ambulance was carrying his enemy away from Santa Rosa, bound for some emergency facility and treatment that would save his life. It would have been the perfect wrap-up to a miserable morning, but, instead, he was confronted with an aging stranger, almost certainly the victim of a savage beating, unrelated to the man he sought.

Rivera thought at once of Hector and the others, reasonably certain that he recognized their handiwork. They had encountered a suspected witness, he surmised, proceeding to interrogate the man, and they had foolishly allowed him to survive. Hector and his men were still hunting, with information gathered from their victim or without it, using precious time.

"The radio," he snapped, his pistol holstered now, one empty hand outstretched and waiting. Someone handed him the walkie-talkie and he keyed the button for transmission, speaking with his lips almost against the mouthpiece. "Hector, do you hear me?"

Several seconds passed before the small receiver crackled in response.

"Yes."

"Come to me."

"Immediately."

He returned the radio to waiting hands and barked an order to his *pistoleros*. One of them reached through a window of the ambulance to shove the lifeless driver from his seat, then climbed behind the wheel. It took a moment, but he finally killed the flashing lights and got the van in gear, proceeding to park it behind the caravan of waiting cars.

Luis Rivera had run out of patience. When Camacho and his men arrived, it would be time to visit Santa Rosa as a group, and find some answers to the questions that were plaguing him.

Where was his enemy?

*Who* was he?

Was the gringo still alive, or had his wounds proved fatal?

Either way, Rivera's visit would be most unfortunate for Santa Rosa. Tired of the delays, enraged by the interminable waiting, he was in a killing mood. The murder of a battered stranger in the ambulance had merely offered him a taste of things to come. There might be nothing left when he was finished with the tiny border town, and, then again, he might decide to leave a grim reminder for his enemies.

A warning sounded in his mind, alerting him to danger. There was no threat from the constable in Santa Rosa, but the people of the Arizona desert were a rugged species, used to dealing with their problems privately, by force. Some of them might resist him, take up arms against him when his mission was revealed. He could not hope to strip them of their weapons absolutely; searching house-to-house would spread his force too thin, and even so they might miss something. But he could eliminate the source, make sure that no one had a ready call on extra guns or ammunition when he made his move.

"Jorge. Esteban." When the gunners stood before him, he explained their mission, forced them to repeat it, making certain that they understood. He could as easily have raised Camacho on the walkie-talkie, but he was afraid that Hector might get side-tracked, waste more precious time.

When this matter was finished, he would have to take another long, hard look at Hector, and decide if he was truly leadership material. So far this day, Rivera had not been impressed with his performance. It was possible that soon he would have need of someone to replace his second-in-command. This afternoon would tell the tale.

He watched Esteban choose a third man to accompany them, all piling into a sedan equipped with radio and automatic weapons. They would pass Camacho on the highway into Santa Rosa, but Rivera's number two already had his orders, and he would not think of turning back to follow. He had better not.

Within the hour, Santa Rosa would be ready for him, still unconscious of the blow about to fall. He cherished the advantage of surprise, aware that it could make the crucial difference in a situation where his men would be outnumbered five or six to one. Discounting women, children and the elderly, the odds might still be even, but the populace of Santa Rosa numbered no proficient killers in its midst.

Well, there just might be one.

The man Rivera hunted, whom he would destroy before he slept again. The bastard who had cost him millions, slaughtered members of his household, brought him here to save his reputation while some tatters of it still remained.

Before Rivera finished with him, he would know the gringo's name, the names of his employers, everything there was to know about the man who had attempted to destroy him. Death would not come easily or swiftly for Rivera's nemesis. The bastard would be praying for oblivion before he was allowed to rest in peace.

Luis Rivera smiled in sweet anticipation. The day might not be wasted after all. There might be entertainment still in store, a treat before the sun went down in violet shadows to the west.

A feast of blood Santa Rosa would not soon forget.

## 10

"Your change from twenty comes to seven ninety-five. You-all come back now."

"Sure, Gib, sure."

Gib Schultz stood back and watched his only customer of the morning disappear through the swing doors. Old Arnie Washburn was a character, and no mistake. He had a fresh supply of ethnic jokes on hand each time he stopped into the hardware store . . . although that wasn't near as often as it used to be. Three weeks—or was it four?—had passed since Arnie had been in the last time, and his purchase today would not put Gib in another tax bracket with the IRS. You had to see the bright side, though; at least he was a customer with money in his pockets. That species had been rather few and far between of late, as witnessed by this morning's trade. One customer, a lousy thirteen-dollar sale, since eight o'clock. Gib figured he was well below the minimum wage now, and smiled sourly to himself. If he still had employees, Schultz would have been forced to lay them off.

It had not always been hard times in Santa Rosa. Years ago, when he and Vi were newlyweds still bursting with their dreams, there had been decent business for a hardware dealer. Farmers needed this and that, a little bit of everything, and other local merchants had relied on Gib and Vi for all their hardware needs. The businessmen of Santa Rosa had been good that way, as far as hanging tight and throwing trade to one another, but the few remaining locals couldn't keep a decent hardware store alive, not when their income had been cut by eighty-five percent within ten years.

Schultz blamed the highway, which had bypassed Santa Rosa with a faster route to Tucson, but he knew that was at best a partial answer to the general malaise that had gripped the town. Where farms and businesses had once prospered, you found For Sale signs and empty acreage, abandoned by the victims of inflation, rising interest rates, declining income. Schultz had hung on more from stubbornness than anything else. He had been born in Pima County, married there, and reared three children, more or less removed from the malignant perils of the city. Robert, their first-born, was a successful tax attorney in Phoenix. Cynthia was teaching high school in Los Angeles, but she was up for an assistant principal's position in the fall. The baby of the family, Amy Lynn, would be a senior in September, and with grades like she brought home, she wouldn't have a bit of trouble getting into the college of her choice.

Provided Gib and Vi could raise the tuition. That was a problem, when the mortgage value on the store that you had worked for thirty years was lower than the 1950s purchase price. He had no doubt that Amy could secure a scholarship, but there was pride involved. It hurt a man to tell the state that he could not provide an education for his children.

They would get by. Somehow, they always did. When Robert had his motorcycle accident in '81, the smart-ass doctors said that he might never walk again, but he had fooled them all. The boy had finished law school leaning on a cane, but he could do without it now, and you would only catch him limping if you made a special point of looking for it. People would survive, no matter what. It was a lesson the bureaucrats in Washington had never seemed to grasp. No matter how you beat a man and pushed his face in the dirt, he would return and get his own back from you one fine day. Unless you killed him.

Gib Schultz had seen his share of killing in Korea, up around the Chosin Reservoir, in early 1951. He and Bud Stancell had called it Frozen Chosin, with the temperature so far below the freezing point you had to dig a hole for your thermometer to catch the falling mercury. Guns froze, trucks froze, and you could lose a hand by touching anything at all without your heavy mittens on. It was a wonder to him that the Chinese soldiers had been able to attack with such ferocity through gusting sheets of ice and snow. It was a wonder to him that he had survived.

He started dusting counters, though the shop was clean enough already, and as always, he began in Sporting Goods. It was an ostentatious label for one tiny corner of his store, but it had always been Gib's favorite. There had not been much call, of late, for fishing gear or hunting knives, but he kept both in stock for old times' sake. The long guns were his first love. Shotguns, rifles, no more than a dozen of them now, and half of those had been on hand for better than a year. But while he had a store, Gib would continue stocking guns and ammunition. In the old days it had been a decent money-maker; recently, he saw the oiled and polished weapons almost as a symbol of resistance to the changing times, one man's refusal to be pushed aside.

He smiled, imagining what Vi would say if he began to spout philosophy and wax poetical around the house. He was a simple man, but that did not diminish his perception of established values, his belief in the traditions of America. Gib didn't buy the argument about a Soviet invasion, all that crap about the farmers and the gun buffs forming a militia to repulse the Reds. You couldn't drop an ICBM with a 12-gauge, but it wasn't foreign enemies that worried

Schultz so much these days. He watched the news and read his daily paper out of Tucson, saw enough of life in general to know that something had gone fundamentally, perhaps irrevocably, wrong in modern-day society. Convicted criminals were wandering around in perfect freedom, while their victims lived in cages, bars on windows, triple locks on doors. You couldn't turn on the television or pick up a paper without encountering some judge or politician who was on his way to jail. One federal "jurist" from Nevada had been drawing $75,000 a year from his prison cell, and would have kept on drawing it for life, except that someone in Congress got around to calling for impeachment. Even then, the bum had nerve enough to go on television, blaming prosecutors and the FBI for having nerve enough to double-check his tax returns.

Venality in politics was nothing new, but recently the stain had seemed to filter downward, through society, affecting damn near everyone. You had more raving psychos on the street today than you could shake a stick at, crazy bastards who would kill a man for the fun of it and then drive on and do the same to someone else a few miles down the road. You heard about young kids in grade school taking dope and sacrificing animals to Lucifer, like something from a cheap horror movie on the late show. Runaways, child prostitutes, sadistic crimes where one kid turns upon his playmates with a knife or Daddy's .38. Sometimes Gib wondered how his own three kids had turned out normal. God knows he and Vi had beaten all the odds.

And he was thankful. You'd have to be an egotist, an atheist, or just plain stupid to believe that you could pull it off alone. The kids spent too much time away from home as they were growing up for Mom and Dad to take the credit for themselves. You did your best, instilled a sense of values where you could, but then you had to turn them loose and put your faith in something greater than yourself. Sometimes it even worked. Sometimes.

It hadn't worked for Jack Washburn. He had raised the sweetest boy you'd ever want to meet, provided for him, watched him grow to young adulthood with his mind and body both in decent working order. He had staked his future, all his dreams, on his boy, unmindful of the trouble that was brewing half a world away in Vietnam. When Tommy Washburn went to war, his father had been proud, convinced that nothing could go wrong. When Tommy came home in a box two weeks later, old Jack's dreams had frozen in their tracks, and they had never budged again.

Sometimes you just got lucky, damn it . . . and sometimes your luck went sour, all at once, without a hint of explanation. It was like the shifting wind, one minute at your back, propelling you along, the next directly in your face, with sand and grit to sting your eyes. You couldn't trust the desert wind, no more than you could trust in luck. But faith . . . that was something else again.

He caught the blinding glint of sun on metal, glancing up in time to see three Mexicans unloading from a dark sedan. He didn't recognize them, but their presence came as no surprise. These days, the traffic passing through was mainly headed north, and if they stopped to spend a dollar, Schultz was not inclined to ask about their green cards. Strangers didn't stop into a tiny, rural hardware store unless they needed something, and he only hoped that he would have whatever it might be on hand. Gib Schultz was smiling as the first one entered, jingling the little bell he had mounted on the left-hand door. It sounded just like money, and the sound was music to his ears.

SANTA ROSA'S MAIN STREET was deserted, baking in the heat, as Esteban Rodriguez parked outside the hardware store. He took a moment to adjust his shades and double-check the .45 he wore beneath one arm. He was aware of Julio and Ismael breaking out their weapons, checking loads and safeties. Opening the driver's door, he grimaced at the furnace blast that greeted him. It would be hotter in Sonora, but there he would have been indoors, attending to Luis Rivera's personal security in air-conditioned comfort. Soon, with any luck, they would be home again, and he might be in line for a reward.

Hector Camacho had incurred Rivera's anger, wasting time in Santa Rosa when he should have had the gringo safely under wraps. He might still talk his way out of a demotion, but if Esteban impressed his boss with his own performance here, it might just tip the balance, move him up into a job with more responsibility, increased prestige. A bodyguard's life was reasonably safe—until last night, at any rate—but it was also tedious. Esteban relished the idea of moving up and out in the Rivera empire, managing a territory of his own one day. With everything that he had learned, he was already on his way.

But first he had to show what he was made of here, in Santa Rosa. It had been a good idea, this raid to search for weapons and effectively disarm the town. A tour of Main Street had revealed the hardware store to be their only target; they had found no gunsmith's shop, no sporting goods emporium with rifles in the window. If the town had any guns on sale at all, they would be here, and Esteban would have the shop secured in a few more moments.

He was not concerned about resistance from the local peasants. Granted, they were superior in numbers, and many of them would undoubtedly have arms at home. Rodriguez scanned the weathered, faded storefronts, and he sensed that they would offer no resistance as a group. Confronted with a team of tough, professional assassins, armed with automatic weapons, Santa Rosa's citizens would slink off to hide until the danger passed. Except, Rodriguez thought, this time Rivera might not let them hide.

The hardware store was cooler than the street, but only by a few degrees. An ancient cooler labored on the roof, but it was in a losing battle with the Arizona sun. Rodriguez waited for the door to close behind him, feeling Julio and Ismael like two shadows at his back, and scanned the store for any sign of weapons on display. He found them easily, before he even saw the store's proprietor emerging from a nearby aisle, a feather duster in his hand. Four shotguns, half a dozen rifles, neatly racked and well tended, with ammunition boxes shelved on either side. To Esteban, it was the mother lode.

"Can I help you gents?"

"We're interested in guns," he told the owner, noticing a flicker of concern behind the man's washed-out eyes.

"Yes sir, I've got 'em," he replied, with just a trace of hesitancy in his voice. "What were you looking for, exac'ly?"

Esteban brushed past him, moved to stand before the rack of long guns, studying the polished barrels, hand-rubbed wooden stocks. Three 12-gauge shotguns and a 20-gauge, three .22s, a lever-action .33, and two sporting rifles, probably ought-sixes, both with telescopic sights. It wasn't much to stock an army, but he would feel better knowing that these weapons were in friendly hands.

"We'll take them all," he said.

The merchant could not find his voice at first. He glanced from Esteban to his companions, back again, attempting to decide if the man was playing with him, joking. "That's a decent piece of cash," he said at last.

Esteban shrugged. He saw no point in mentioning that he did not intend to pay for anything. "We'll also take your ammunition."

"All of it?" Schultz squinted at Rodriguez, as if by screwing up his face he might somehow improve his hearing.

"Yes."

"Some of it doesn't fit these guns. I got some .38s in there, .223s, .410s, a few more odds 'n' ends."

"We'll take it all," Rodriguez repeated patiently, putting on a plastic smile.

"Well, shoot, I reckon you know what you need." He led them back in the direction of the register. "If you'd be kind enough to show me some I.D., I'll ring that up for you right now and we can see you on your way."

"I.D., *señor*?"

"A driver's license oughta do it," he replied. "You know how Uncle Sam can't get along without his paperwork."

"Of course." Esteban slid a hand inside his nylon jacket, hauled the Colt Commander out and aimed it at the man's face. He thumbed the hammer back and smiled across the open sights. "Will this be good enough?" he asked.

Schultz stared at Esteban, his pistol, the other gunmen. He slowly raised his hands to shoulder-height, then made a sudden lunge for something on a shelf beneath the register. Esteban could have killed him easily, but it would have been noisy and unnecessary. Lashing out, he whipped the automatic's muzzle across the man's skull with enough force to open his scalp. The thin man staggered, slumped against a shelf supporting cans of motor oil, which tipped and broke away beneath his weight.

Rodriguez placed one hand upon the counter, vaulted it with ease and landed in a crouch beside his victim. The man was stunned but conscious, cursing breathlessly and struggling to rise, his progress hampered by the cans of oil that rolled beneath him every time he made a move. Rodriguez kicked him in the ribs to slow him down, and then again, because it felt good. Finishing the job, he slashed his .45 across the balding, unprotected skull once more and stepped back satisfied. Before rejoining Julio and Ismael, he retrieved a .38 revolver from the shelf beneath the register and tucked it in the waistband of his slacks.

Rivera would be pleased with their achievement. They had not disarmed the town by any stretch of the imagination, but in one bold stroke they had eliminated a cache of weapons that the citizens could have drawn upon in their hour of need. A few more moments were required to stow the arms and ammunition in their trunk, and then they could rejoin the column waiting north of Santa Rosa.

Smiling to himself, Rodriguez missed the woman's entry through an open doorway on his left. When she saw her fallen husband, she screamed. Rodriguez was already rushing toward her, gaining, when Ismael drew his nickel-plated .32 and put a bullet through the open oval of her lips. The little gun's report was understated, probably inaudible outside, but the projectile's impact was dramatic and completely final. Lifted off her feet, the woman struck a bank of shelves, rebounded like a rag doll, bonelessly crumpled to the floor.

Rodriguez did not waste a glance on the gunman, knowing he would have to punish Ismael if he saw his grinning face. The woman's life meant nothing—less than nothing—to Esteban, but a *pistolero* was supposed to follow orders. When they started killing on their own initiative, control was jeopardized, a precedent for independent thought established. He would have to nip it in the bud.

Already stalking toward the Main Street exit, Esteban tossed orders back across his shoulder. "Kill the other gringo, quietly, and get the weapons loaded. I will tell Luis what has happened.''

In his heart, he knew Rivera would not mind the deaths of two more Anglos. They were nothing to him, and he would be pleased to hear about the guns. So far, the siege of Santa Rosa had been carried off without a hitch.

AMY SCHULTZ WAS LATE, but she was certain that her parents would not mind. They made her work for spending money through the summer, but they never treated her like an employee, never nagged her if she was a little late, or left a little early, for a date with Rick. In fact, he was the reason for her tardiness; she had been trying to call him all morning, but there was no answer at home, no answer at the service station. That was strange: Bud Stancell never closed on weekdays, and he never had so many customers that neither he nor Rick would not hear the telephone.

If they had lived in Tucson or in Phoenix Amy might have worried, but in Santa Rosa, "trouble" meant a blow-out on the way to work, or something equally mundane. It was unusual that no one at the station would pick up the phone, but it was not mysterious. Most likely they were in back somewhere, or Rick had gone for lunch and Bud was tied up with a customer. No big deal.

She was looking forward to their date that night, their time alone together at the Ajo drive-in. Thinking of Rick's kiss, his strong, insistent hands, made Amy tingle with excitement, but she knew that she could not give in. Not yet. But soon, perhaps.

This time next summer they would both be packing up for college, and the thought of being separated from the only boy whom she had ever really loved made Amy nervous, cold inside. They had discussed applying to a list of colleges together, going with a school that would accept them both, but in reality, she knew that Rick would have to take the best deal he could get on an athletic scholarship. That shaved their chances of togetherness, and while her grades were good enough to win acceptance anywhere, she feared that something might prevent them from enrolling on the same campus.

Something like her father, for instance. He was fond enough of Rick, had nothing but the highest praise for Amy's choice, but she could tell that he was skeptical about their long-run chances of success. They were too young, he said, to really know their minds where romance and the future were concerned. Another year, another five years, and they might not feel the same about each other. In the meantime, it was vital that they not become too close and gamble everything they had upon a moment's pleasure.

She reached the hardware store at last and let herself in through the back. She heard her parents rearranging stock out front and called to them, a cheery greeting with a suitable apology for being late.

No answer.

Could they be that angry with her? Or were they preoccupied with taking inventory? Maybe her father was with a customer. She hoped so; they could use the money. Amy took her bright red smock off the hook and slipped it on. She left the storeroom to join her parents and was surprised to find a short man, Mexican by his appearance, standing at the rifle rack, two guns tucked underneath each arm. A callused hand was clamped across her mouth, a strong arm circling her waist and pinning both arms tight against her sides.

She struggled, kicking backward at her captor's shins until he gave her head a vicious twist and colored lights exploded on the inside of her eyelids. Amy felt as if she were about to faint, but she was clearheaded enough to see the short man lay his weapons down and approach her with sudden hunger in his eyes. She knew the look, although when Rick had looked at her that way there was a gentleness in his eyes instead of cruelty. She knew precisely what the stranger wanted, and she tried to kick at him, humiliated when her legs would not respond to orders from her brain.

The man's hands were on her now, inside her smock, and Amy heard him shred her blouse. His laughter was a mocking sound, indecent, and she cursed herself for weakness as the angry, helpless tears welled up beneath her eyelids. Desperately she made another bid to break the grip that held her fast, expecting yet another twist to strain her aching neck. Instead the faceless stranger let her go. Before she had a chance to see if she would stand or fall, the short man stepped in close, still grinning, cocked his fist and struck her squarely in the face.

The drab linoleum that she had mopped a hundred times rushed up to meet her, but the impact failed to put her under. Amy Schultz was conscious when the rough hands turned her over, pinned her to the floor, and started ripping at her clothes. She thought of Rick, for just the barest fraction of an instant, and then, hopelessly, began to scream.

## 11

Johnny Bolan picked the trooper up a few miles east of Yuma, clocking close to eighty-five on Interstate Highway 8. He had been careful in the towns, obeying posted limits and avoiding notice, but the interstate had been his chance to make up time, unwind the Jimmy's power plant and let his mind free-float toward possible solutions for his problem. Thus preoccupied with private thoughts, he missed the tiny winking lights at first, receiving no warning from his radar detector. The cruiser had been parked along a side road, screened by billboards and accumulated tumbleweeds. Its driver had been on the verge of dozing when the Jimmy hammered past him, giving him a final chance to make his quota for the day.

The patrolman had closed his distance to a hundred yards when Johnny caught it, and the younger Bolan spent a heartbeat weighing possible reactions. He could always stop and take the ticket, but there might be other problems if he did. The radar-sensitive ''fuzz buster'' mounted on his dashboard was illegal in several states, and if the cop took umbrage to it now, there might be an arrest, a comprehensive search that would uncover weapons and explosives, sundry other gear. Above all else, an interruption of his journey put more heat on Mack, and that was Johnny's prime consideration as he floored the 4 x 4's accelerator.

He would have to lose the tail, and while that would involve a detour, some wasted time, it had to be a damn sight faster than submitting to a search and possible arrest. Whatever, he was in it now, the Jimmy pulling slowly but inexorably out in front, the squad car dwindling in his rearview mirror as he held the pedal to the floor.

The patrolman would not be shaken off easily. Engaging the Police Pak in his cruiser, he was after Johnny like a shot, his siren whooping in syncopated rhythm with the flashing colored lights. A straight shot into Pima County on the interstate would gain him nothing but a caravan of cruisers, Johnny knew, and long before he got that far, there would be roadblocks waiting for him on the highway. He would have to lose his tail, and soon, then settle down somewhere to wait it out while troopers scurried up and down the highway, searching for their prey. They would grow tired of it eventually, but it was a nuisance, and he didn't like to think what might be happening in Santa Rosa while he dawdled in the desert, wasting time.

Above all else, he did not want to think about what might already have transpired in Santa Rosa. Knowing that he might be too late, that the aborted phone call might have been the last that he would ever hear from Mack, he could not let it go. While there was any hope at all, he would continue, and when hope was gone, he would begin the task of dishing out revenge.

But at the moment he was searching for a side road, anything to get him off the interstate and offer him some room to run. A half mile farther he caught one, cranked the Jimmy through a hard left turn, fishtailing as his tires bit into dirt and gravel, spewing shrapnel in his wake. The trooper nearly overshot his turnoff, but he made it with a scream of tortured rubber, jouncing after Johnny on the one-lane track. The younger Bolan was already generating clouds of choking dust, and while it would not put the trooper off his track, it had to slow the opposition down a little.

Johnny took advantage of his lead, accelerating, conscious of the fact that if he blew a tire or fouled his engine with accumulated dirt and sand, he would be finished. No more speeding ticket, now; he would be on the hook for reckless driving, resisting arrest and any other charges the trooper could dream up before they reached the local jail. A search of his belongings would be mandatory, and from there, the list of charges would begin to snowball, adding felonies to misdemeanors, piling time on top of time.

And time was something the younger Bolan did not have.

Another dirt road branched off the first, and Johnny took it on an impulse, following the rutted tracks that other off-road drivers had prepared for him. The cruiser on his tail was built for highway driving, flat-out speed, but it was not a rover. Lacking the Jimmy's four-wheel drive, stronger springs and armored undercarriage, it should not be able to compete long-distance over rugged, rocky ground.

John lost him at the next branch in the road. It came upon him suddenly, without a hint of warning, and he took the south fork, curving back in the direction of the interstate by slow degrees. A quick glance through the driver's window showed him that the narrow track lay close beside a deep ravine, all choked at the bottom with tumbleweeds and cactus, the remains of some forgotten, prehistoric stream. Behind him, choking on his dust and blinded for the moment, his pursuer overshot the track, his squad car losing traction, nosing into empty space and tilting crazily before it made the twelve-foot drop. The highway patrolman might scramble free with only minor whiplash to serve as a reminder of the episode, but it would take a wrecker to extract his cruiser from the steep ravine.

They would be hunting for him on the highway, soon, from Yuma eastward, all eyes searching for a Jimmy bearing California plates. It had to figure that the trooper had his number, that it had been broadcast well before the cruiser had been taken out. It was a problem he could live with, given time to make some superficial changes to the 4 x 4, and while he was reluctant to invest the time, he was not willing to accept the grim alternative.

He drove another seven miles on dirt and gravel, running roughly parallel to Highway 8. He found a row of dunes to screen him off from prying eyes along the road and pulled between them, shutting down the Jimmy's engine and climbing out to stretch his legs. He opened up the back and rummaged underneath the spare for tools and backup plates, selecting Arizona's from the several sets he kept on hand against emergencies. Five minute's work, and they were mounted, California tags sequestered with the other spares beneath the Jimmy's carpeting. He couldn't change the paint job, but there had to be a thousand similar vehicles on the road in Arizona, and the troopers would be looking for specific plates. Before he reached the highway, the new tags would be as dusty as the car itself, and no one would be able to detect the switch without a thorough search.

When he was finished, Johnny returned to the highway, drove another twenty miles to Wellton and found a drive-in restaurant. He killed an hour with a burger, fries and milk shake, watching squad cars rocket past, westbound for Yuma. When Bolan was halfway through his meal, a motorcycle officer pulled in behind him, eyed him hard for several seconds, then revved up his Harley and continued on his way.

The younger Bolan felt as if he might have aged a decade in that hour, waiting for a fraction of the heat to dissipate.

He would be forced to watch his speed from here on, avoiding further contact with the state patrol. He had already used his quota of luck for one day, borrowing against tomorrow, and he didn't need another run-in with the law to make that point. He still had miles to go before he reached the killing ground in Santa Rosa, and he had already wasted too much time.

GRANT VICKERS RETURNED the microphone to its hook, frowning as he leaned back in his swivel chair and cocked his boots up on a corner of his desk. The sheriff's deputy had been properly solicitous, reminding Vickers that there wasn't much for them to do without at least a general description of the suspects or their vehicle. It was a not-so-subtle way of telling Vickers he was wasting everybody's time, and they would doubtless share a laugh at his expense in Tucson, but he had been left with no alternatives. Emergency receiving would report Bud Stancell's injuries, and it would be peculiar if the local law did nothing in a matter of felonious assault. His contact with the sheriff was routine, and he would let the matter rest right there unless somebody on the home front started asking questions. If it came to that, he knew that he could always stall them, falling back on lack of evidence, descriptions, and the like to camouflage his own deliberate inaction on the case.

He had gone looking for Camacho after leaving Becky at the clinic, and had been relieved to find the bastard gone. There was no sign of Hector, his companions, or the souped-up Chevy they had driven into Santa Rosa. Maybe they had gotten lucky, Vickers told himself; they might have found their pigeon, wrapped him up and hauled him back across the border to Rivera. Maybe.

But he didn't think so.

It would take a sheer, remarkable coincidence to put the stranger in their hands. Bud Stancell hadn't seen him, Vickers would have bet his life on that. Camacho had been angry and frustrated when he turned the jackals loose on Stancell; if their quarry had been hiding out at the garage, they would have simply murdered Bud, to silence him, before they stuck their excess baggage in the Chevy's trunk. The beating, Bud's survival, were a testament to Hector's failure in the hunt, and while he might have been recalled, Camacho's absence did not mean his boss was giving up, by any means. There would be other hunters, other crews, and that meant Becky Kent was still in jeopardy.

The lawman sat up straight and eased his gun from its swivel holster. Neither he nor the weapon had seen combat, but he knew the gun would do its job, provided that he had the nerve to use it. Opening the cylinder, he checked the load. He kept an empty chamber underneath the hammer, force of habit, even though he knew it wasn't really necessary. Now, considering the fact that he might actually have to fire the weapon, Vickers dug a box of ammunition from his top desk drawer and slipped another hollowpoint into the vacancy. That made it six potential deaths instead of five. Vickers thought it should have added more weight to the pistol, but he felt no change.

Six dead men in his hand. But would he have the guts to stand against Rivera? He had been on the bastard's payroll longer than he cared to think about, and there was every chance that he would be committing suicide by opposing Rivera's army. But if it came down to killing, and if he could get in close enough...

It all hinged on Rebecca Kent. If push came to shove, Vickers didn't give a damn about the town; a year or two at this rate, Santa Rosa would dry up and blow away. But Vickers held the woman in high regard. It would have been too much, perhaps, to say he loved her, but it could have come to that, in time. Unfortunately, time was something he did not have a surplus of just now.

It would be easier for all concerned if he could simply find the man Rivera's goons were looking for. He could arrest the stranger on some trumped-up charge, pretend that he was driving Mr. X to Tucson for safe keeping, and deliver him to Hector or whomever on the highway outside town. Unfortunately, Vickers had no more idea of where the stranger might be hiding than he had of where Camacho and his troops had gone. The bastard might be anywhere, assuming that he ever got to Santa Rosa in the first place.

Wounded, walking in from somewhere to the south, it would have been so easy for the pigeon to collapse and die before he reached the city limits. Hector might be wasting everybody's time and raising hell for no good reason, but the lawman knew Camacho and his boss would never understand that point of view. It would require a vast expenditure of time to search the desert thoroughly, and in the meantime, if the hunch was wrong, their quarry might be miles away and singing to the state police.

If only Vickers had some rough idea of who Rivera's men were looking for. A "gringo," sure, but what the hell did that mean in the States? It ruled out Mexicans and Indians, for openers, but Vickers knew that even blacks might be considered gringos, based upon the attitude of those applying labels at the moment. As a positive description, it was worse than useless, fitting four-fifths of the country's populace. He could go out in search of tramps, pick one at random, shoot him before he turned him over to the drug lord. But if Rivera had some means of identifying the man he wanted, it would be a wasted effort. And he knew that an effort to deceive Rivera, if discovered, just might get him killed.

There would be time enough for that, and if he had to risk his life, Grant Vickers did not plan to waste it on a goddamned tramp. He checked his watch, saw it was time to make another driveby on the clinic, just to satisfy himself that none of Hector's goons had doubled back to play the answer game with Becky. If they touched her, tried to harm her...well, he would be forced to make a choice when that occurred. But in the meantime, there was time to kill, and he would kill it on the road.

Before he reached the sidewalk, Vickers turned and went back to his office. He opened the top drawer of his desk, withdrew the box of hollowpoints, another box of shotgun shells that lay half-hidden under rumpled correspondence. He would not be needing them, of course, but it was better to be cautious when tomorrow started looking shaky and you couldn't count on waking up to see the sun. The constable was not declaring war, by any means, but if war came, he meant to have an edge.

All things considered, Vickers thought it was the only way to fly.

"WHY DO YOU DO IT?"

Bolan did not have to ask what "it" was. They had danced around the subject of his occupation once before, and he had watched the lady chewing on it in the meantime, getting nowhere with her own attempts to put herself inside his mental process. Frowning thoughtfully, he cocked a thumb toward Main Street, baking in the noonday heat, and answered with a question of his own. "Why do you stay?"

She came back at him quickly, without hesitation. "People need me here. This is my home, I grew up just a quarter-mile away and went to school here, through eighth grade. Of course, there were more children then." She seemed to lose her thread of concentration for an instant, but she snapped back quickly. "I fulfill a necessary function."

Bolan spread his hands and offered her a weary smile. "My story in a nutshell."

Dr. Kent appeared incredulous. "You can't be serious. I help the sick, the injured. You kill people for a living. Any effort to compare the two activities is, well, ridiculous, that's all."

"Not really. Every time you clean a wound with antiseptic, you're killing germs. When you remove a limb that can't be saved, or cut a tumor out, you're acting in the interests of your patient . . . but you're also taking life."

"There's no comparison. To kill a human being—"

"May be absolutely necessary," Bolan finished for her, weary of the old debate and anxious for a change of subject. "All men have the right to kill in self-defense, or to protect their loved ones. I believe we have a duty to use force, if it will help prevent atrocities." He saw the skepticism in her eyes and gave it one last try. "If you could travel back in time and murder Hitler, thereby saving countless people from destruction, would you do it?"

"Certainly."

"If you observed a rape in progress, would you pull a trigger to protect the victim?"

Something like a shadow fell across her face, and there was a surprising gruffness to her voice as she responded. "I believe so, yes."

"And if you knew, beyond the shadow of a doubt, that John Q. Public has committed murder, that police can never touch him, and that he will escape, scot-free, to kill again unless you take him out yourself? What then?"

Uneasy, she turned away from him. "It's hypothetical. I couldn't answer that."

"I can. There's nothing hypothetical about the syndicate, the terrorists, the animals that prey on people after dark in every major city, coast to coast. You read the papers, Doctor. It's a jungle out there."

"So, we all pitch in and act like animals?"

The soldier shook his head. "Not even close. We use our human senses, our intelligence, our strength, and stop the animals before they eat us alive."

"You've obviously given this a lot of thought," she said. "I happen to believe there's too much violence in the world already."

"Granted. But you don't eliminate the problem by ignoring it or forming a discussion group. You'd know that if you'd ever tried to talk a rapist or a killer into reconsidering his crime beforehand."

The shadow had returned to haunt her eyes, and now Rebecca Kent was looking at him strangely, looking *through* him, with her thoughts a thousand miles away. When she regained her voice, it was as distant as her gaze. "I don't presume to judge you, Mr. Bolan, but I can't believe you'll save the world by killing everyone who disagrees with you."

"If that was the plan of action, Doctor, you'd be dead already. We're not talking philosophical agreement here. It's raw survival, plain and simple."

She got up, restless, tried the telephone again, then sat back down. "Still dead," she said by way of explanation.

Bolan was not startled by the news. He would have bet that all the lines in town were dead, and they would stay that way until somebody on the outside had their fill of listening to busy signals and reported something wrong in Santa Rosa. Depending on the timing of that call, it might be hours more before a lineman started checking out the wires and found the point where they had been brought down by insulated cutters or a well-placed charge of buckshot. Hours more, perhaps, to fix the break, and only then would anyone begin to think about what might be happening in town.

Rivera would be finished with his work by then. Whatever he might have in mind for Santa Rosa, he would have time to spare before the outside world had an inkling of what was happening. The soldier wondered what would happen when the drug lord showed himself, how citizens of Santa Rosa would react. The constable would be outgunned, but he might rouse the townspeople, given half a chance, and offer some resistance to the occupying army. Individuals might take up arms against Rivera, in defense of homes and families. The dealer's mercenaries would have modern, paramilitary weapons and an old familiarity with murder on their side. In combat situations, Bolan knew, the numbers only mattered if the quality of troops on either side was roughly equal. Half a dozen seasoned veterans could stop an untrained army in its tracks, defeat them with a small assist from Fate.

Unless the inexperienced militia should get lucky.

In his youth, the Executioner had seen the plot spun out a hundred times on movie screens and television. Farmers, simple people, laying down their plows and taking up their guns against the bandits who were threatening their homes. It didn't matter if the heavies rode on horseback or on motorcycles, in a Model T or in the turret of a Panzer tank: the story was the same. In films, the good guys won because it made a better story, and you needed heroes if you meant to keep on selling popcorn at the matinees. In life, however, it was something else again.

In Vietnam and afterward, the Executioner had learned that there was never any guarantee of happy endings. In a real-life close encounter with the Reaper, you were satisfied if you could walk away, and never mind the hypotheticals about what had been gained or lost. The winners were the living, and the losers got a toe tag for their trouble. A few days in the ground, and they would all look pretty much the same.

But it still mattered, damn it. Any way you stood the rule book on its ear, a few hard basics always read the same. Like good and evil, right and wrong. The fact that certain crimes against humanity could simply not be left unpunished, if humanity itself was to retain its meaning. Certain enemies were simply *wrong*, and you opposed them not because of politics or artificial border lines, but rather out of a concern for all mankind, a recognition that their evil, left unchecked, would constitute a danger to the species. Hitler had been such an enemy, but he was not alone, by any means. You did not have to look in chancellories or throne rooms for an enemy these days. Some of them rode in limousines, but others took the bus and bore a strange resemblance to the boy next door. You took them where you found them, and *when* you found them, you were ready for them, or they served you up for dinner like a sacrificial lamb.

The sound of wailing sirens cut the noonday heat like razors ripping parchment, drawing closer. Bolan fought a minor wave of dizziness before he regained his balance, then followed Dr. Kent along a narrow corridor to the waiting room.

"Grant got the county sheriff," she suggested, trying to sound hopeful as they peered through separate windows.

"Maybe."

"What else could it be?"

The soldier didn't answer, waiting for the sounds to take on substance, for the source to show itself. It might have been the county sheriff, but there was an alternative that came to mind.

It might be Doomsday.

For the Executioner.

For Santa Rosa.

## 12

Esteban and his companions rendezvoused with Rivera bearing their collection of assorted small arms from the hardware store. Rivera heard them out, dismissed the deaths of two more gringos as inconsequential. Something else had happened on the brief foray to town—he read it in the eyes of Jorge and Ismael—but he did not press them for details. In a few more hours, nothing they had done would matter in the least. It would be over, finished, and Rivera could relax.

Rivera's trademark was a mixture of audacity and caution. Always careful when it paid off, the dealer knew precisely when to gamble on the long odds, risk his life, if need be, in pursuit of wealth and power. He had risen through the ranks on nerve alone, and made his fortune in a business where strength alone was not enough to guarantee survival. Early on, he learned that cunning was essential in his chosen trade. While other dealers hid behind their walls and barbed-wire fences, trusting in their private armies, he had infiltrated their territories, sniffing out ambitious underlings, recruiting them as spies in hostile camps. The major dealers had ignored him, for the most part, totally preoccupied with their omnipotence until, one at a time, he had eliminated them. In five years time, Rivera had arisen from the gutter to command the largest private army in Sonora, dealing marijuana, heroin and cocaine to syndicates throughout the States. His reputation as a winner was established, but he knew that it could all be taken from him, just as he had taken it from others.

There had been other challenges before, but none as serious as that which he was facing now. On previous occasions he had seen the trouble coming, recognized its source, and moved to neutralize the danger in advance. Two dozen small competitors, and half as many larger ones, had come to grief because they thought that they could prey upon Rivera's empire, emulating his old tactics, using them against the king himself. But they were gambling on his own forgetfulness, the apathy that sometimes comes with power, and they had been fatally mistaken in their estimation of his cunning.

For Rivera had forgotten nothing, and he took no chances with his own subordinates. His payroll was extravagant, perhaps, but he was buying loyalty from the soldiers in his ranks, the lawyers and accountants who were necessary evils in a business such as his. He paid them more than they were worth, and let them know precisely what they stood to lose by crossing him, betraying him to his competitors. Whole families had disappeared upon the rare occasions when a traitor was exposed, and Rivera's personal ferocity, his thirst for disloyal blood, was legendary with his gunmen. Some of them had witnessed the punishments he had inflicted, and they spread the word, embellishing the stories until he emerged as something of a demon cast in human form. Rivera did not mind; the legends served a useful purpose, and his richly padded payroll was a form of cheap insurance, well worth the investment.

As his convoy reached the outskirts of Santa Rosa, he felt another legend in the making. Members of his entourage would talk about this day for years to come. Authorities might question him, and some of them, at least, would whisper his involvement as established fact, but there would be no evidence on which to base a legal charge. Rivera might inform a chosen few—his favorite bought-and-paid-for *federales*, for example—but the story would spread through the grapevine, and his potential enemies would stand in awe.

He had originally hoped for a more peaceful solution, but time was running short, and Rivera felt a sense of urgency. He had already stayed too long in the United States, and every hour added to the visit magnified his risk. Despite connections with the Mafia and Latin syndicates, despite the small-town marshals on his payroll, an arrest in the United States could ruin everything. Rivera did not have the pull with federal agents and the courts that he possessed in Mexico; he could not bring the heat to bear on politicians with their hands out, deep in debt to him for campaign contributions, "favors" of all kinds. A bust in the United States—especially on a charge as serious as murder, or the paramilitary seizure of a town—could land him in a cell for life, without parole. Without a diplomat's protection, nationality meant nothing to the Arizona State Police or FBI, and some of them, he knew, would shoot him down with relish, given half a chance.

It was essential that his business be concluded soon, before the silent cordon he had thrown around the tiny crossroads village could be cut. In spite of his precautions, there was still a chance that someone might escape from town, or see the roadblocks and find a way to call for outside help. There were many possibilities for error, and Rivera recognized that natural audacity was lapsing over into desperation. It would take a master's hand to keep the two apart, but he was equal to the task.

Rivera had expected something of a crowd, but now he saw that he had overestimated Santa Rosa. No more than a dozen people had emerged from shops and homes to investigate the sirens, while several others peeked timidly between drawn blinds. The rest, he thought, must be at work on nearby farms or in surrounding towns.

For his purposes, it was enough. The word would spread throughout the tiny crossroads town, and if the population was diminished from his own first estimate, that left him fewer witnesses to deal with, fewer people to interrogate.

He gestured absently with one hand, and Camacho killed the squad car's siren. Seconds later, someone hit a switch inside the wailing ambulance, and silence fell across the heart of Santa Rosa like a shroud. Rivera swung his legs out of the cruiser, straightened slowly to his full height, letting each of them examine him. It made no difference if they saw his face, since none of them were going to survive his visit.

He lit a cheroot, then reached inside the cruiser for the microphone that Hector offered to him. Jiggling the switch, he tested it, made certain that the squad car's PA system was engaged. Rivera held the microphone against his lips and spoke with slow precision, measuring his words.

"Citizens of Santa Rosa! Your attention, if you please!"

REBECCA KENT STOOD SILENTLY behind venetian blinds and watched the dark man with the microphone as he addressed the town. Her heart caught in her throat at the sight of Amos Grundy's ambulance, the last vehicle in the line, its colored lights still winking silently even though the siren was shut down. She could not see the man behind the wheel, but knew instinctively that she would not have recognized his face. She did not want to think about Bud Stancell or the Grundys, and she forced herself to concentrate upon the stranger and his entourage.

The leader stood beside a pale green squad car bearing the insignia of the Border Patrol. No uniforms were in evidence, and Dr. Kent felt certain that its presence here was not indicative of an official visit. Like the ambulance, it had been commandeered, its legitimate passengers disposed of. She closed her mind to thought of where they might be now, what might have happened to them, listening to the stranger's voice.

"Citizens of Santa Rosa! Your attention, if you please!"

His voice was cultured, in an artificial sort of way, and redolent with strength. She felt as if his eyes, invisible behind dark glasses, might pierce her if he turned in her direction.

"I am speaking to you on a matter of supreme importance," he continued. "There is hiding in your town a fugitive from justice, wanted for the crimes of murder, arson and assault.

"This individual presents a danger to your town, your families," the stranger said, his voice a deep, metallic echo in the street. "As long as he remains at large, no person in this town is safe."

He waited, letting that sink in, and scanned the sidewalks from behind his shades. Rebecca saw a handful of her neighbors watching, waiting for the stranger to continue. All of them looked curious, confused, suspicious. None of them knew who or what the man was looking for, and the secret settled on Rebecca's shoulders like a heavy yoke. Whatever happened next would be her fault, as much as Bolan's, but she never once considered giving up her patient to the gunman on the street.

The leader spoke again. "I am requesting your assistance in the capture of this fugitive," he said. "The man is wounded, and in need of medical attention. Also, he does not possess a car, but may attempt to buy or steal one."

Silence, when he finished speaking. On the sidewalk, several of the locals whispered to one another, clearly sizing up the stranger and his entourage, concluding from the lack of uniforms, the presence of the Grundys' ambulance, that he had no official sanction, no authority beyond the weapons visible inside a couple of his backup cars. The mood was apprehensive, not yet hostile, but Rebecca knew her neighbors, and she realized they might not knuckle under passively. If they were pushed too far...

She stiffened as old Enoch Snyder took a long stride forward, his companions hanging back. Dressed in faded overalls, a straw hat cocked to one side, hands in pockets, Enoch was the quintessential prospector, prepared to stand up for his claim. With every eye upon him, Snyder cleared his throat, spit brown tobacco juice into the gutter and began to speak.

"I don't believe I caught your name," he said.

The stranger frowned. "My name is unimportant. I am looking for a fugitive—"

"I heard all that the first time," Enoch interrupted him. "Fact is, we've got a constable in town to handle any violations of the law, an' I'm not clear about your jurisdiction here in Santa Rosa. That's a federal car you're ridin' in, but you ain't federal, 'less I miss my guess. You sure ain't from the county, and I know damn well you ain't connected with the state police."

"We are from Mexico," the stranger told him.

"Maybe you should check your road map. You-all are parked in the United States right now, which means your badges ain't worth squat...assumin' that you got 'em."

"I am trying to protect your town."

"We done all right without you, up till now."

"You have not faced this individual before. He is extremely dangerous."

"That why you brought the ambulance along?"

"In case of injuries—"

"You people down there do a lot of business with the Grundys?"

For a moment there was utter silence in the street, and then the stranger turned, barked something to the men still seated in the cars behind him. In another moment they were scrambling clear to form a skirmish line, all bristling with submachine guns, shotguns, pistols. Rebecca caught her breath and took a step back from the window, fearing that they were about to open fire. She nearly stumbled into Bolan, stifling an outcry.

Old Enoch had immediately fallen silent, but he held his ground, unmoving. Other citizens up and down the sidewalk were edging towards doorways or looking for cover. If the gunmen opened fire, Rebecca thought, none of them had a chance. She was about to watch a massacre, and there was nothing she could do to head it off, prevent the slaughter that was coming. If Snyder said another word, the stranger might unleash his wrath upon her neighbors. And after he was finished there, then what?

The old man took his time, examining the guns, the hard-eyed man who held them leveled toward the citizens of Santa Rosa. Slowly, with a fine contempt, he spit another murky stream into the street and took a long stride back to lounge against the grocery's brick facade. Rebecca Kent felt the tension gradually unwind her, sensing that catastrophe had been averted for the moment. But she knew that it was only a postponement, rather than a true reprieve. Her mind made up, she turned to Bolan in defeat.

"Your guns are in the first examination room," she said. "A cabinet underneath the sink."

GRANT VICKERS WATCHED the sideshow through binoculars from his position at the southern end of Main Street. The approaching sirens had alerted him, but Vickers knew

Rivera's reputation and had not been overanxious to respond before he checked out the situation. A glimpse of the Grundys' ambulance, the Chevrolet Camacho had been driving, told him everything he had to know about the noisy caravan. The presence of a squad car was distinctly ominous, but Vickers was concerned with number one right now. The border boys could damned well take care of themselves.

Old Snyder was a spitfire, but he backed down quick enough when guns were drawn. Rivera was the first one who had ever shut the old bird up, and Vickers gave him points for that, but he was worried now about the confrontation shaping up in Santa Rosa. If Rivera lost his cool, or if some local boy got itchy, made a careless move, they could be ankle-deep in blood before the sun went down. Grant Vickers didn't want that on his conscience, but he didn't want his own blood on the pavement, either. Somewhere, in between the two extremes of martyrdom and crass desertion, he would have to find a not-so-happy medium and try to make it work. Somehow he had to try to save the town.

There was no question of a face-off. Vickers had lost count of the armed men down there, and there might be others hiding in the ambulance. It was an army, and he was just one reasonably frightened lawman with a job to do. It didn't help that he had never faced a hostile gun before, and his involvement with Rivera through the past few years was icing on the cake. When a person accepted money from a man like that, his soul was pawned without a ticket. Vickers hoped there was a way to pull it out before the whole thing blew up in his face. With any luck at all . . .

He listened as Rivera stated his demand: delivery of the stranger in an hour's time or there would be unspecified reprisals. Vickers had no doubt that blood would spill. Rivera wasn't on the list of gracious losers, and he would not leave until he had his quarry, or until his anger had been spent upon the town. If no one gave the stranger up...

But what if no one had him? What if no one in the tiny, godforsaken town had seen him. If Rivera was mistaken, or if the elusive hit man had already found himself a place to hide, unknown to any resident of Santa Rosa, they were up the creek. There were abandoned mobile homes and houses on the outskirts of the town, a scattering of shops downtown that had been closed for eighteen months or more. A couple of the houses had been broken into by tramps or bikers, and there would be nothing to prevent a fugitive from holing up in one of them to lick his wounds and watch the hunt go by. If Vickers could persuade Rivera to begin a search of the outlying empties, he was betting they could bag the guy in question and avert a massacre, but touching base with his employer would not be as easy as it seemed. He lived in Santa Rosa, after all, and there were still proprieties to be observed.

Downrange, Rivera wrapped up his ultimatum with the announcement of a lesson for the populace of Santa Rosa. At a gesture, one of his gorillas revved the ambulance and put it through a backward U-turn, parking in the middle of the street with rear doors angled toward the small crowd on the opposite sidewalk. Rivera snapped his fingers, and a couple of his henchmen opened the doors, began unloading something heavy on the pavement.

Vickers took another look through his binoculars, then closed his eyes and groaned. There would be no more time to waste, he realized. It might already be too late to head off the bloodbath; there might already be too many witnesses.

Rivera and his men were pulling out the stops, going for broke, and they had left no doubts concerning their intentions. If he still had any hope at all of heading off disaster, Vickers had to act before somebody in the town panicked and took it on themselves to even up the score. If there was time. If there was any hope at all.

RICK STANCELL HAD BEEN DRAWN from the garage by ululating sirens, startled at the sight of the Grundys' ambulance bringing up the rear of a motley parade. There had not been sufficient time for them to get to Tucson, let alone return, and that meant someone must have stopped them on the highway. Rick observed the squad car at the head of the procession, realized its driver and his passengers were not in proper uniform, and knew that something had gone desperately wrong in Santa Rosa. He thought of Dr. Kent's phone, and his own back at the service station. Dead. And suddenly his father's beating seemed a part of something larger and more sinister, a threat not only to the Stancell family, but to the town at large.

Rick listened from the sidelines as the tall Hispanic stranger made his statement, sparred with Enoch Snyder, finally calling up the guns. It was apparent that the town was under siege, perhaps cut off from any contact with the outside world, but Rick's predominant concern was for his father. Dr. Kent had made it clear that he was desperately in need of treatment that the local clinic could not offer, and prolonged delays while strangers played their macho games in Santa Rosa might prove fatal. Rick was tempted to approach the leader of the raiding party, make a personal appeal, but something told him that he might as well be talking to the wall.

The dark man finished threatening his audience and smiled. In stilted, formal tones, he offered them "a lesson," something to consider if they were tempted to defy him. At a gesture, one of his companions backed the ambulance around until it stood directly in the middle of the street, its double rear doors pointed toward the combination grocery store and post office. At a finger snap, two gunners trotted to the van, swung back the doors and reached inside. Rick froze in shock as work boots wriggled into view, pursued by khaki legs, the swollen paunch of Amos Grundy. The gunmen dumped his body on the pavement as though it were a sack of grain, reaching back inside to haul his brother out and place them side by side. The flaccid postures, ragged wounds and crusty, drying blood left no doubt that both men were dead.

Rick held his breath, already sick with horror as a third limp body was wrestled from the inside of the ambulance. He did not have to see the battered face, now vented with a bullet wound above one eye, to recognize his father. The remains of breakfast came up and Rick was doubled over, retching, by the time Bud Stancell's body hit the pavement in the middle of the street.

He could hear a woman sobbing somewhere behind him, two men cursing softly beneath their breath. The world was spinning, tilting crazily beneath his feet, and for a moment Rick was frightened that he might collapse, lose consciousness, before he had a chance to break away. The blinding rush of panic-rage was fading, and while he longed to lock his hands around the stranger's neck, move on when he was finished there to throttle each of his companions in their turn, Rick knew that he could never hope to reach his target in his present state. A rush from where he stood, barehanded, would be tantamount to suicide, and he was suddenly committed to survival. Long enough, at least, to pay back something of the debt he owed to nameless men whom he had never seen before this afternoon.

He straightened slowly and with difficulty, and turned his back upon the hollow shell that once had been his father. There was nothing he could do to spare his father from the pain and the indignity he had suffered in his final hours, but there might be something Rick could do to even up the score. His father kept a .38 at the garage, in case of robberies, and while there had been no occasion for its use, he had kept the weapon oiled and loaded. Rick had failed to check to see if it was still in place this morning, but if it had not been taken by the men who had attacked his father...

There was still a chance that he could have some measure of revenge, and while he knew that it would never be the same again, it might just be enough to keep his mind within the borderlines of sanity. But first...he thought of Amy Schultz with sudden longing, totally divorced from sex, and knew that he should see her, just once more, before he took a last, irrevocable step against his enemies. Avoiding glances from the other citizens of Santa Rosa, stepping wide around the hands that sought to stroke him in condolence, Rick struck off in the direction of the hardware store.

**13**

He had promised them an hour, and Luis Rivera was a man who kept his word from time to time. No more than forty minutes left, but he would wait and see if any of the gringos had a shred of common sense. If one of them had seen the soldier, even sheltered him at home, it would be so easy to step forward, save himself, his family, by offering the information Rivera sought. Of course, it would save no one in the long run; all of them would have to die, now that Rivera had been bold and brash enough to show his face, but no one in the tiny town of Santa Rosa knew that. Yet.

Rivera honored promises as long as they were useful to him. In a business deal, if he agreed to pay a large supplier on delivery of merchandise, he kept his word, thereby ensuring future shipments. If he made the promise to an independent runner, trying to retire in sunny Florida on income from a one-off deal, he simply took the merchandise by force, retired the would-be dealer to a sandy grave, and went about his business. Compared to some of his competitors, Rivera was a paragon of virtue. You could trust him just as far as you could see him, on a foggy day.

With Hector, Esteban, and half a dozen of his gunners, he had moved inside the air-conditioned diner, seeking refuge from the sun. His other troops were left on guard around the vehicles and out back, preventing any two-bit local from attempting to become a hero overnight. The bodies from the ambulance still lay on Main Street, lined up on the center stripe, and they would soon begin to smell. Rivera didn't mind, especially—he was accustomed to the stench of death from long experience—and the aroma just might serve as an incentive to the people of the town.

Or one of them, at any rate.

The stranger's presence was not general knowledge. He had searched the faces of his sidewalk audience for hints of recognition as he spun his fabricated story, seeking a response and finding none. No hint of shock or guilt, no trace of lingering anxiety. Rivera now considered two alternatives: the people he had spoken with, thus far, knew nothing of the gringo's presence in their town; or else one of them was a great deal stronger than he looked.

Or she. A woman might be tempted by a wounded warrior, taking him to heart and standing firm against a threat to his well-being. Despite Rivera's heritage, his personal commitment to machismo, he did not regard the female as a weaker sex. They suffered much in life, not least in childbirth, and their lust for vengeance could be awesome. If a woman had the stranger in her clutches, and especially if she was unmarried, then Rivera's task would be that much more difficult. She would not give the gringo up as readily as, say, a man with a wife and children to protect.

But he would let them have their hour, keep his fingers crossed and hope that someone, anyone, would point at his neighbor, whisper in Rivera's ear. A fearful man will sell his neighbor, and his neighbor's children, to survive. With three dead men—their friends—already lying in the street, the townspeople knew that he was serious, that it was not a game. They would think twice before they tried to call his bluff.

His chief lieutenants sat in silence, sipping coffee, killing time, and waiting for their orders. Esteban had done a decent job of rounding up assorted weapons from the hardware shop, reducing chances for a vigilante ambush on the street, and he had briefed Rivera on the incident involving Jorge and Ismael with the merchant's daughter. The gunners would be dealt with later, when Rivera had the time to teach them discipline, but at the moment he was thinking of the girl. Allowing her to live had been a judgment call, with which Rivera did not totally agree, but he could understand Esteban's reasoning. The girl would certainly be found. Her injuries, the liquidation of her parents, would spread further terror among the locals, prompting them to take whatever steps might be required to save themselves. Potential problems lay within their choice of methods for survival. While the rational recourse would be delivery of the wounded stranger to Rivera, some among them might decide to fight. It was a risky game, this playing with men's minds, and he would have to wait to see the outcome first, assessing methods with the benefit of hindsight prior to making any judgment on Rodriguez.

As for Hector, he had been chastised, in private, for his failure to maintain communications with the column while he made his own reconnaissance of Santa Rosa. There had been no need for public confrontation, with Camacho losing face in front of his subordinates, but if he failed a second time, Rivera would be forced to reinvestigate his options. And, if Hector failed him once again in Santa Rosa, he would not be going home alive.

Rivera called for coffee, studying the slender waitress as she served him, noting how she trembled in his presence. She was young, no more than twenty, probably eighteen, and she excited him, but he resisted the temptation to reach out and slip a hand beneath her skirt. She would not resist him—he could see that fear had sapped her will to fight—but he did not have time for games. Rivera's mind was focused on the task at hand, and a distraction was the last thing he needed. Maybe, when his work was done in Santa Rosa, he would take the waitress with him, keep her for a day or two to celebrate and pass the time. When he was finished with her, she could join the others in oblivion.

The dealer lit another of his cheroots and checked his watch against a large clock on the wall above the door. The townspeople had already wasted half of their allotted time, but he could wait. No one would interrupt them here. His men were on the highway, north and south, and the telephone lines had been cut down on either end of town. There was no local operator, no telegrapher, and as for CB radios, he would have to take his chances. If anyone got on the air, if anyone was listening...

He pushed the thought aside. Less than thirty minutes remained, and he would be long finished with his business in the little town before assistance could arrive. The sheriff's office was in Tucson—more than sixty miles away—and any solitary deputies who might respond, meanwhile, would be destroyed by his rear guard before they reached the town limits. Santa Rosa, for the moment, was entirely his, and he would use its people as he chose, in order to get answers, revenge.

The answers were important—who and why—but after so much wasted time, Rivera knew that he would settle for the gringo's head, a trophy that would prove once more that he was no one to be trifled with. There might be other ways to learn which of his many competitors had tried to put him out of business in a single stroke, and if he never learned the name at all, it might be enough to let the jackals know that they had failed, that their efforts were in vain.

Rivera could survive without the answers, but he could not go home without the stranger's head. Defeat would inevitably lead to other challenges, eventual defeat by someone stronger, quicker, and more cunning than himself. There was no point in leaving Santa Rosa if the stranger was alive, and so Rivera made his mind up that he would not leave, his gunners would not leave, until their job was done. No matter if the county sheriff came, the state police or the National Guard. Better for them all to die in combat than to tuck their tails and run like yellow dogs. Far better for them to find the gringo soon, mop up the witnesses and head for home.

His coffee had gone cold, and he called for more, eyes fastened on the waitress as she moved to serve him. The border crossing might yet have its rewards, he thought, and smiled.

KEEPING TO THE ALLEYS, crossing two blocks down from where his father and the Grundys stretched out side-by-side on Main Street, Rick spent thirteen minutes on his trek to reach the hardware store. Granted he had stopped to vomit twice along the way, but now the rolling of his empty stomach had subsided into steady, throbbing pain, and he was confident that he would not be forced to stop again. The image of his father hung before him like a grim mirage.

From the hardware store, he would be forced to cross the street again, but it would be all right, if he did not delay too long. The bastard with the microphone had promised them an hour, of which twenty-seven minutes remained. The gunners, standing watch beside the caravan, had not molested anyone so far, but Rick had felt compelled to reach the hardware store by a circuitous, deceptive route. He would not draw attention to the Schultzes, would not let himself be seen with them, not with the actions that he had in mind for later. If he failed—an almost certain bet, considering the odds and arms against him—Rick would not bring further wrath upon their heads. If he was not seen entering the store, or leaving it, the bastards might not take it out on Amy, on her parents.

Even as the thought took shape, Rick knew that he was being childishly naive. His father and the Grundys had been murdered in cold blood by men who did not take the time to hide their faces. Clearly they were not expecting any witnesses to walk away and spread the word of what had happened here today. The stage was being set for wholesale slaughter, but the leader of the wolf pack had delayed his final stroke while waiting for some stranger to be found in Santa Rosa. Once he was discovered and in the bag, there would be nothing to restrain the gunners, nothing to protect his neighbors, Amy, any of them.

But he still had time. While the invaders waited for their break, he had an opportunity to move against them, strike a blow for those they had already murdered. It was foolish to believe that he could kill them all before they cut him down, but if he took out a couple, if he did any good at all, it might encourage others to defend themselves. By his example, he might move the others to respond in kind, and if they pulled together, there was still a chance that they might win. A chance, at least, that some of them would walk away.

Rick Stancell did not think in terms of martyrdom or sacrifice. He had not come to terms with the idea that he was, suddenly, an orphan. There was no place in his mind for an examination of some hypothetical tomorrow: where he might wind up; who might be left among the dwindling stock of relatives to take him in; what would become of his ambitions, college, all the rest of it that added up to some uncertain concept called "the future." There could be no future now. If he disgraced himself and tried to run away, the animals would hunt him down and kill him. If he tried to move against them, they would surely drop him in his tracks, but he could salvage something of his pride, his self-respect, along the way.

No point in thinking of his father. His deep, abiding rage was there to keep him warm, and it would never go away, but Rick was focused on Amy. Her softness and her warmth, one final touch, perhaps a kiss goodbye before he set about his final business with the jackals on the street. Just like the movies. "We, who are about to die, salute you," and the credits roll across an image of a fallen warrior as the world goes up in flames.

He was surprised to find the back door of the hardware store half-open, silence warning him away and simultaneously urging him to enter, have a look inside. The open door was nothing, really. In the present circumstances, it was less than nothing, trivia beneath consideration by the conscious mind. But Amy's parents *never* left the back door open. Never.

Pushing through as quietly as possible, he closed the door behind him, heard the latch engage. The storeroom was as silent as a church when all the members of the congregation have departed for their homes, a hush that somehow was not reassuring in the least. He listened briefly at the open doorway to the store itself, stepped through...and froze.

He spotted Amy's mother first, a crumpled rag-doll figure to his right, her face averted, wispy hair in back all clotted with blood and something that resembled suet. Stancell felt his stomach lurch again, but fought it down, eyes traveling around the store until they came to rest on Amy's father, sprawled behind the register. The whole top of his head was gone, and there was no need for a check on vital signs.

A moaning, whisper-soft, distracted Rick and brought his heart into his throat. It came from the direction of the rifle rack, which Amy's father kept well-stocked, empty now, together with the shelves that usually supported ammunition boxes. In a flash, it registered that someone had cleaned out the weapons, obviously trying to disarm the town, and then his thoughts were back with Amy, focused on that feeble moan.

He stepped around the counter and the first glance told him everything. Naked, she huddled against the wall, her knees drawn up and encircled by her arms. Her face was hidden, muffling the hollow sound of weeping, but she flinched and screamed out loud as Rick knelt down beside her and rested one hand on her shoulder. It took several moments for the girl to recognize him—one eye was swollen nearly shut from the explosive impact of a fist or boot heel. Blood had dried in abstract patterns on her face, but Rick ignored it, busy helping her to stand, supporting her while she tested her legs to see if she could walk with his assistance. Holding her against him, standing between Amy and the lifeless bodies of her parents, he eventually steered her toward the storage room and found a long smock hanging behind the door. He helped her into it, but Amy folded as he fumbled with the topmost button. He caught her halfway to the floor.

He held her in his arms, and she was feather-light, as if the substance of her soul had already flown. He checked her pulse with trembling fingers, pressed his ear against her lips and held his breath until he felt hers, faint and tickling on his skin. She moaned when he lifted her again, and Rick was thankful for the smallest sign that she was still alive.

The Santa Rosa Clinic was a hundred yards from where he stood, but Rick knew he would make it, as he had succeeded with his father earlier that morning. This time, with a little luck, his trek might not end up in death for someone he loved. This time there might still be a chance.

He carried Amy, and the rage within him had a different thrust, a different focus now. He knew precisely what had happened in the hardware store, what she had suffered—granting that a man *can* understand the pain, the stark humiliation. He hurt for Amy, for his father and the Grundys, and his burning anger made itself apparent in the tears that streaked his face, the wordless curses that emerged in primal snarls as Rick pushed through the doorway, out into the alley and the noonday heat.

One final stop to make before he doubled back and got his father's pistol at the station. One more stop before he set about exacting his revenge. It might be brief, but it would still be sweet, for all of that. When he was finished—when they finished him—the bastards would be conscious of the fact that someone had opposed them, someone had resisted to the death. It wasn't much, but at the moment it was all Rick Stancell had. And it would have to do.

ENOCH SNYDER HAD BEEN OLD as long as anyone in Santa Rosa could remember. He had been Old Enoch, since the fifties, maybe earlier. He had been old at twenty-two, when he came home from Tarawa with steel enough inside him to make magnets go berserk, and scars like some demented road map covering his slender frame. At twenty-three, his hair had been snow white, and he had been Old Enoch ever since. A man could only see so much and cling to youth, a solemn fact Enoch viewed with philosophical acceptance, leaving the regrets to others who were cursed with worse misfortunes than himself. He did not really mind the way his body ached all over just before a rain; the rains were few and far between in Santa Rosa, as it was, and he had not seen snow in more than thirty years. At sixty-six, the wiry former Leatherneck admitted that *was* old now, but he was far from finished.

Those madmen in the street had startled him—with all their guns, and bodies being hauled out of the ambulance that way—but he was not afraid. He knew that he would miss Bud Stancell and their conversations over coffee in the afternoon. Ex-Leathernecks were hard to find these days, and Stancell knew—had known—what it was like to lose your youth inside a foxhole, waiting for the enemy to hit you one last time before the break of dawn. Korea wasn't Tarawa, but hell was hell, no matter where you found it. And if you came out of the flames at all, you were a different man. You came out old before your time, with something hard and cold inside that never really went away. The memory of wholesale killing followed you around forever, waiting on the fringe of your unconscious for a chance to haunt your dreams, but you survived and went about your life as if that frozen part of you inside was still alive and well.

For Enoch Snyder, fear had been erased at Tarawa, blown out of him along with spleen, appendix and eighteen inches of intestine. Having seen the worst that life could offer, having dragged himself away from it and lived to walk again, he knew that fear was nothing more than dread of the unknown. He did not pass his hand through fire or pick up rattlesnakes, because he knew precisely what would happen, but he did not fear tomorrow, either. Having seen and done the worst that man could see or do, he had no time for fear. He would survive, or he would die, depending on his timing, whether it turned out to be his turn, and in the end, it would not make a bit of difference either way.

But in the meantime he could make the dirty sons of bitches dance a little, yes, indeed.

The M-1 rifle was a classic carbon copy of the one that he had used on Tarawa. He had not fired the piece in over seven years, but it was oiled and polished, sighted in and ready. Once a week or so, he took the weapon out and cleaned it, for the practice, for the memories it held. They did not give him nightmares anymore; they were the stuff of Snyder's life, and he had learned to live with them, as he had learned to live with stiffness in one hip, the aches and pains of growing old with bits of shrapnel in your flesh.

His eyes were clear, his vision twenty-twenty, uncorrected, and his hands were steady as he raised the rifle to his shoulder, looped his index finger through the trigger guard and sighted on a mental image of the dark man's face. On Tarawa, he had been taught to kill up close and personal, before the world exploded in his face and he was hauled away for makeshift reconstruction on the mercy ship offshore. How many had he killed before they nearly killed him back? No way to tell, at this late date. In the confusion, with steel and smoky thunder in the air, you killed with the finesse of a demented butcher run amok, and some of those you killed got up a moment later, slashing at your back, your friends, with bayonets and sabers. It's hard to keep a tally when the dead don't die, and all a man can think about is whether he has ammo left to kill again, again, again.

Old Enoch had sufficient ammunition for the job at hand, and no mistake. A thousand rounds of ought-six, eight rounds to a clip, all ready for the big Garand to feed. In Snyder's mind, he could already feel the recoil kicking at his shoulder, rapid-fire reports like thunder in his ears. He had a GI bayonet to fit the rifle, but he would not need it; there would be no place, no time, for any action hand-to-hand. If they got close, if he was still in any shape to notice, he would fall back on his .45 for mopping up. If that was not enough to do the job, or if he moved too slowly, they would kill him, sure, and that would be the end of it.

But not before he made the sons of bitches dance.

He owed Bud Stancell that, at least, and while he never had much dealings with the Grundys, it was wrong for some slick shit to take them out that way. A lesson was required, and Enoch Snyder was the very man to teach it, while he lasted. Enoch loaded the Garand and set its safety, smiling to himself.

A little while, and school would be in session for the grown-ups. He was betting that the class would be a damned sight smaller when the last bell rang, but no one would be bored. Hell, no.

Old Enoch was about to make a cameo appearance in the hottest show around.

## 14

Rebecca Kent was startled by a sudden rapping on the back door of the clinic. There was something less than fifteen minutes left before the expiration of the stranger's cryptic deadline, and his men were still on Main Street, so it must be someone else. Without a word Bolan faded into an examination room and closed the door behind him. She could almost see him, standing in the darkness of the little cubicle with gun in hand, prepared to kill a total stranger if he was discovered. Strangely, though, his presence gave her comfort, as if he were a living talisman that warded off evil.

More like a lightning rod, she thought, proceeding through her surgery to reach the door, where someone had begun to knock insistently. On second thought, it sounded more like they were kicking at the door. She peeped through the venetian blinds and was immediately stricken by a sense of déjà vu.

Rick Stancell stood outside, a woman cradled in his arms, all swaddled in some kind of pink material. Rebecca threw the door back, motioned him inside and saw at once that it was Amy Schultz. Her face was bruised and swollen, there were other bruises on her legs, and she was obviously naked underneath what seemed to be a smock of some sort, draped around her body like a cape.

"In here," she said, and realized at once that Rick would know the way. It had been—what? three hours—since his father had come through that door in need of help, and now Bud Stancell was a corpse, stretched out on Main Street with the Grundy brothers. In a flash, before she concentrated fully on her patient, Kent had time to wonder what must now be going through the young man's mind.

"Where did you find her, Rick?"

"The hardware store," he grunted, lifting Amy up onto the table, stepping back, as if afraid to touch her now. "Her mom and dad are dead."

Another jolt, but she was getting used to sudden death. "What happened?"

"They hit the store for guns and ammunition," he replied, and there was no need to explain who "they" might be.

"She's fortunate to be alive." And even as she spoke the words, she thought, *or is she?* Having glimpsed the smear of drying blood on Amy's thighs, she knew the teenage girl had suffered more than just a beating. Sometimes, Dr. Kent suspected—or had once believed, at any rate—survival was the worst of it.

"I need some time alone with Amy, Rick."

"Oh, sure. I've got some business at the station, anyway." His voice was strange, remote and lifeless. Glancing at him now, concerned, Rebecca scarcely recognized the boy whose life she once had saved.

"Rick?"

"Mmm?"

"You won't do anything . . . well, foolish, will you?"

"No."

"You promise?"

"Sure."

"I'm sure the state police will be here soon."

"Okay."

She was not getting through to him, but Rick was level-headed, sober, and her more immediate concern was Amy Schultz. The girl was drifting in and out of consciousness, and Dr. Kent was worried that she might have suffered a concussion. Rick was gone before she could come up with any other platitudes to pacify him, and he left a residue of rage behind him, like another living presence in the room.

With trembling hands, she peeled away the smock that Amy wore, examining her briefly for external injuries or any sign of broken ribs. She had been beaten, but her wounds were not on par with those sustained by Bud Stancell. Sated by the act of rape, her tormentors had done a sloppy job of finishing the girl. In retrospect, considering the grim experience she had undergone, the murder of her parents, Dr. Kent could only wonder if the girl would count herself lucky, or cursed.

The memories came back upon her in a sudden, dizzy rush, and for an instant she could almost feel the grasping hands, smell alcoholic breath as she was trapped, surrounded, pinned. She nearly slapped at those imaginary hands before she caught herself, face flushed and short of breath, remembering that it was all behind her now. She had survived—as Amy would survive, God willing—and if she had not exactly prospered, neither had she thrown her life away.

In retrospect, survival was the best that you could hope for in some situations. You survived, by nerve and force of will, and when survival was assured, the danger past, you could start to build your shattered life from scratch. God willing. If you had the strength, the courage to hold on.

Rebecca knew—had known—the Schultzes, as she knew most everyone in town, but Amy was a virtual stranger, never sick enough these past few years to need a doctor's services. Her luck had run out with a vengeance, but Dr.

Kent could call upon her own experience to help the girl, at least to some extent. As much as anyone could ever help another person cope with pain that went beyond the physical to scar the soul.

She felt a sudden rush of anger, first at men in general, finally focused on the girl's attackers and upon Grant Vickers, for his failure to control the situation and protect the townspeople. On one level she was conscious of the fact that he was hopelessly outnumbered, powerless to break the siege, yet it was his duty to the people of Santa Rosa and the badge he wore. There should be *something* he could do, despite the overwhelming odds.

She went to work on Amy Schultz with hydrogen peroxide and merthiolate, attending to the superficial cuts and bruises first, allowing Amy time before she undertook the pelvic work. A few more moments, either way, would scarcely matter now, and it was critical that Amy should not lapse into hysteria, or slip into a catatonic state. The mind was more important than the body at the moment, and Rebecca knew that it could still go either way, depending on the treatment the girl received.

She spoke to Amy, softly and continuously, telling her that it would be all right, the worst was over, she was not alone. Of course, the words were only partly true; in every way that mattered, Amy Schultz would always be alone with her experience, compelled to deal with it in private dreams and waking nightmares. Even with another victim, there were thoughts and fears that never could be truly shared.

But for the moment, having someone close at hand might be enough. At any rate, it was the best that Rebecca Kent could do.

GRANT VICKERS PULLED his cruiser in beside Rebecca's car as young Rick Stancell left the clinic, double-timing back along the alley toward his dad's garage. Poor kid. He never spared a glance for Vickers, and the constable could scarcely blame him. Vickers felt about as useful as tits on a bull, and there was no point in reminding himself that he was helpless, outnumbered, outgunned. He had the two-way radio in his squad car, the base station in his office for emergencies, and he had not used either in an effort to obtain assistance. Later, when it came to playing Twenty Questions, he would claim that he was cornered by Rivera's men, ordered to maintain radio silence under threat of death, convinced that outside intervention would precipitate a bloodbath in the streets. It just might work . . . if there was anybody left to listen.

Gravely worried by the murders of Bud Stancell and the Grundy brothers, Vickers had begun to wonder if it might be too late already. Normally discreet, Rivera did not seem to mind the threat of witnesses this time, as if he had a practical solution already in mind. It didn't take a genius to surmise what that solution might entail: the witnesses from Main Street were as good as dead, but once Rivera started killing, would he dare—or care—to stop? If he was forced to massacre a dozen people, why not raze the whole damned town? And if he leveled Santa Rosa, why would he need the constable alive?

The train of thought was ominous, and Vickers let it go. If it began to look like doomsday, he could always meet with Rivera, let the bastard think he was easy pickings, and then treat him to a magnum-load surprise. It would be suicidal, but desperate cases called for desperate measures, and if it came down to that, his hours would be numbered anyway.

He locked the cruiser then checked it, afraid that someone might attempt to tamper with the radio or lift his shotgun from the dashboard rack. He would be needing both if he decided to defy Rivera, and at this point, even with their past relationship in mind, the constable did not delude himself that he was trusted by the dealer. He was a hired hand, one of hundreds on Rivera's payroll, and he would become expendable the moment that he ceased to meet Rivera's needs. Indeed, he might already be a liability as one more witness to a triple murder, one more target for Rivera's henchmen when they started mopping up. Except that he did not intend to be mopped up. At any rate, he would not go without a fight.

He climbed the concrete steps, knocked once and waited for Rebecca. When she answered, he was startled by her pallor, the expression on her face. If anyone had asked, he would have guessed that she had opened up the gates of hell and peeked inside.

"What is it, Grant?"

The frost beneath her tone made Vickers lose his sense of purpose for an instant. "I stopped by to see how you were holding up," he said at last.

"Come in."

She stepped aside and held the door, then closed it after him. Without another word, she led him toward the surgery with long, determined strides. Before they reached the doorway, he could see a figure swathed in blankets stretched out on the padded table, blond hair haloing a battered face. He recognized the Schultz girl, Amy, a second before Becky spoke.

"She's been beaten and raped. Her parents have been murdered. You can find their bodies at the hardware store."

"Sweet Jesus."

She was looking at him with a vague expression of contempt. "You sound surprised," she said. "Does it surprise you, Grant?"

"What happened?"

"How should I know, Grant? I'm not the constable."

He made an effort to ignore her bitter tone. "You seem to know a lot," he said. "You been down to the hardware store yourself?"

The doctor shook her head. "Rick Stancell found her. Gib and Vi had both been shot. The guns were taken from their store."

A warning prickle started at Vickers's nape and worked its way across his scalp like frigid fingertips. Rivera had anticipated trouble from the citizens of Santa Rosa, taking steps to nullify resistance in advance. He had disarmed the town.

"You have to stop this, Grant."

"And how would you suggest I do that, Becky?"

"Call the state police, the sheriff...anyone. There must be someone who can help."

"I've tried," he told her, lying through his teeth and wondering if she could tell. "The lines are down."

"You have a radio," she countered. "You could try."

"Too far," he answered, praying that she would not recognize the lie. "The mobile unit won't reach Tucson, and I can't raise anybody closer. I've been having trouble with the CB in my office for a coupla weeks."

She seemed to look directly through him, but if she suspected he was feeding her a line, she kept it to herself. Instead of challenging the lie, she said, "You *will* keep trying."

"Sure I will, but in the meantime we can get along without damn fool heroics in a losing cause."

"You're giving up?"

"I'm trying to avoid a bloodbath, Becky."

"I'd say you're a little late."

"You want me to go out and play *High Noon*? A little gunplay out on Main Street? Think that might help cheer you up?"

"There must be *something* you could do."

"You've seen that crew. They've got an army out there, automatic weapons, you name it. How am I supposed to put the cuffs on twenty men?"

No answer, but her eyes were ice. Again he wondered if she might have realized his role in what was happening, perhaps through intuition. Vickers put no stock in ESP or like phenomena, but there was no denying that some people had a knack for picking out deception, spotting liars from a mile away. Rebecca might have such a talent, or she might just be distraught at what was happening around her, knowing that it would get worse before it had a chance in hell of getting better. Either way, he sensed a barrier between them, recognizing that it would require decisive action on his part to bridge the gap. He wondered, then, if he was equal to the task.

Whichever way it went, he stood to lose. He had already lost his town, for all intents and purposes, and he could kiss his job goodbye if anybody ever learned about his tie-in with Rivera. Assuming that there was any job to lose, once the dealer and his goon squad finished with Santa Rosa. Nonexistent towns had precious little need for constables, and it was looking more and more like Santa Rosa was about to self-destruct. Five dead already, that he knew of, and a single spark would put the frosting on it, set the town on fire.

A single spark, and Vickers realized with sudden crystal clarity that he was sitting on the powder keg.

BOLAN GAVE THE CONSTABLE a chance to clear the premises before he left the small examination room. He wore the sleek Beretta 93-R in its shoulder rigging, carrying Big Thunder in his left hand, with the web belt wrapped around its leather sheath. Rebecca Kent was working on her latest patient, and she did not look up as he passed before the open doorway to the surgery. Her anger toward the lawman had been obvious, his own reactions more subdued than Bolan would have privately anticipated. The man had almost sounded guilty, whether in the face of anger from a woman he respected, cared for, or for some reason that was more obscure, the soldier could not tell. In any case, the constable had not been able to repel Rivera's raiders, and he showed no inclination toward a showdown with the dealer's private army. His reaction was entirely logical, and yet...

"She's resting now."

He turned to find the doctor watching him, her features drawn and pale. The young girl's injuries had touched her in a way that earlier events—including revelation of a triple murder—had not managed. Bolan wondered if it was exaggerated empathy, or something else entirely.

"Want to talk about it?"

"No." She shifted warily away from Bolan's gaze and poured herself a cup of coffee, sipping at it slowly. Glancing at the clock, she said, "We're almost out of time. Do you believe he'll carry out his threat? Against the town, I mean?"

"He has to. They're already in too deep to let it go. Too many witnesses."

"He's bound to kill us, then, regardless..."

"Whether he finds me or not," the soldier finished for her. "Yes."

"Is there anything we can do?"

"We can fight," Bolan answered. "We can kill Rivera if we get the chance, or make it so expensive for him that he has to cut and run."

"How can you discuss another person's death so casually?"

"It's never casual," he answered, "but I won't lose any sleep over Rivera."

Dr. Kent shifted subjects, uneasy with the conversation's trend. "I just feel terrible for Amy. She's so young."

And suddenly he knew. The truth was written on her face. "How old were you?" he asked.

The lady dropped her eyes. "It shows? I guess I'm not as good at covering as I thought."

"You do all right."

She hesitated for a moment, then continued. "I was finishing my residency in Los Angeles. There was a doctor on the ER night shift I'd been seeing off and on. Nothing serious. One evening we were on our way to catch a movie, and he said he had to stop by his apartment for a minute. I went up with him; I didn't see the harm." There was a catch in her voice now, and angry tears were welling in her eyes. "They call it date rape these days. I was so ashamed, I never got around to calling the police."

"But you survived."

"After a fashion. I went through all the phases: guilt, denial, anger, thoughts of suicide and murder. Finally I ran back home to hide."

"I'd say you're needed here."

"I used to think so," she replied. "But Santa Rosa's dying on its feet. This afternoon should finish it, one way or another."

"Maybe not. Towns live, like people. Sometimes they get stronger at the broken places."

"You surprise me, Mr. Bolan. I've never met a battlefield philosopher."

Bolan smiled. "You still haven't. I'm just a sucker for lost causes."

"I don't think so. And I don't think you're the bogeyman I've read about in all the papers."

Bolan shrugged. "It won't matter, either way, unless we stop Rivera."

"What can I do?"

"Stay frosty," he suggested. "How much do you know about the constable?"

"I told you, we've been out a few times. He's a local boy who never found the nerve to leave. We all hide, one way or another."

"Does he live above his means?"

"I don't . . . What are you asking me?"

"He didn't seem too hot for facing down Rivera."

"Can you blame him?"

"It's his job."

"All right, so he's afraid. We can't all be commandos."

"Did you buy that line about the broken radio?"

She thought about it for a moment, finally answered, "Sure, why not?" But he could read the hesitation in her voice, her eyes, already giving way to doubt. "I can't believe that he's connected with the others."

"Still, you haven't told him anything about my being here."

"I didn't want to get you into trouble."

It was so outrageous that they both were forced to laugh, and he could feel the ice dissolving slowly. When the moment passed, they stood and faced each other silently. The spell was broken by a whimper from the other room.

"I'd better check," the doctor said, and Bolan watched her go, aware of all the pain and fear that she was carrying inside. But she was a survivor; Bolan read it in her eyes, had glimpsed the fire within. She might have run to Santa Rosa as a form of sanctuary, but she was not merely hiding there. The lady led a useful life, was of service to her fellow man. Above all else, she cared. That much was obvious.

She would survive the coming storm. His visit to the sleepy desert town had cost too many lives already, and the soldier knew it wasn't over yet. There would be hell to pay before the storm blew over and Bolan knew that none of them might make it to the other side intact. But they could try, damned right. They could give it everything they had, and make the cannibals pay dearly for their gains, and there was still a chance.

A slim one.

But there was still a chance.

RICK STANCELL STOOD in the garage and scanned the gray perimeters of his collapsing world. His father's life had been confined within these walls, but Rick had always wanted more. He could forget about that now—the football, college, Amy at his side. It was a washout, all of it. Rick knew that it would be a total fluke if he survived the afternoon, and if he did, there would be welfare workers and counselors prepared to deal with orphans like himself and Amy Schultz. They would be separated, torn apart, and shipped to foster homes like so much excess baggage.

No. Correction. Amy might be going to a foster home, assuming that she lived, but Rick would not be going anywhere, for he had no intention of surviving. He was moving on a hard collision course with death, and he had no intention of attempting to avoid his fate. His world, his life, had been effectively destroyed within a span of hours. There was nothing left except revenge, and he was well aware of what revenge would cost him.

Rick checked his wristwatch, found they were already out of time. He chose the largest lug wrench from the rack in front of him and weighed it in his palm, deciding that it would suffice. Retreating to the office, where his father kept the .38, Rick checked the register to verify that nothing had been stolen. Not that it would matter. The least of all his worries now was money.

He was opening the drawer, about to rummage underneath accumulated papers for the pistol, when a scuffling
sound surprised him, brought his head around. A slick
Hispanic with a phony smile was standing in the office
doorway, watching him with interest. The gunman wore a
pastel leisure suit, the jacket open to reveal a nickel-plated
automatic pistol tucked inside the waistband of his slacks.

"I see you on the street before," the gunner said.

"Could be."

"You run this station, one so young?"

"My father."

"Ah." If it meant anything to him, the gunner did not let
it show. "You know we're looking for a gringo stranger."

"Haven't seen him."

"That's too bad. You better come with me, I think."

"I can't. I've got to watch the station."

"It's not going anywhere."

Rick shrugged, scooped up an undernourished pile of tens
and twenties from the register, and was about to stuff them
in a pocket when the hoodlum took his bait.

"You won't be needing the money," he explained, all
smiles. "You let me hold it for you, *sí*?"

"Well, if you say so." Offering the money with his left
hand, Rick allowed his right to slither backward, close
around the lug wrench jutting from his pocket. He would
have to time it perfectly, deliver everything he had in one
swift stroke. Instinctively he knew that there would be no
second chance.

The gunner stepped in closer, caution fading in the face
of greed, and Stancell took a short stride forward to meet
him, putting all his weight and strength behind a vicious,
hacking swing. The wrench impacted dead on target—in the
middle of the gunman's forehead—with a force that burned
along Rick's arm. A sickly *crunch* announced steel's raw

superiority to bone, and then the gunner folded, sprawling on the worn linoleum.

Rick stood above him, panting, knowing that his adversary might be dead, immediately certain that he must make sure. He focused on a picture of his father, lying dead on Main Street, then replaced it with a memory of Amy, huddled like a wounded animal in pain, and finally he found the strength he needed. Three more times he brought the lug wrench down, and when he finished, there was no more need for guesswork on the gunner's state of health.

He stooped, retrieved the automatic from his fallen adversary's belt, and saw it was a custom .45. He tucked it in his waistband beneath his shirttail at his back, and slipped his father's .38 beneath his belt in front. Thus armed, he grasped the man by his wrists and dragged him through the office doorway, halfway across the garage, until he reached the grease pit. Stooping, straining, he maneuvered the deadweight to the edge of the pit, rolled it over the brink, watched it fall. Retrieving a tarp from the storeroom, he fanned it like a cape and let it fall across the body, covering the evidence. The others might have little difficulty finding him, particularly if he had been detailed to the station under orders, but at least Rick felt that he had bought himself a little time, while doubling his stock of weapons.

He was ready for them now, at least as ready as he ever would be. He had taken one step on the road to vengeance, but he was not finished by any means.

One down, more than a dozen to go. How many could he kill before they cut him down? Did he have any hope at all?

It didn't matter. Simply trying was enough. He had already accomplished more than he had expected. Given half a chance, he would destroy them all.

## 15

Grant Vickers parked his cruiser in the alley and approached the diner from the rear. No witnesses so far, except the pair of lookouts posted by the exit, but the lawman knew that he could not expect his luck to hold. There would be locals in the diner, trapped at their respective jobs when the invaders commandeered their place of business as a field command post. They might start putting two and two together, but Grant thought that he could bluff it out. Provided any of them lived to talk about it afterward.

He would fall back upon his badge, if questioned, and remind his critics that it was a lawman's duty to maintain the peace. How better than by meeting with the enemy commander, trying to convince him that his game was up and he should leave before an ugly incident degenerated into total, screaming chaos? It was thin, but he could sell it if he really tried, persuading his constituents that he was trying to reduce the risk of further bloodshed, minimize the damage after damage had been done. They knew he wasn't frigging Gary Cooper, but if there was any doubt on that score, he intended to erase it, pronto.

They were waiting for him, automatic weapons leveled at his navel, and he kept it cool, approaching with his empty hands raised up to shoulder level. Edging closer, one of them relieved him of the Python, slipping it inside the waistband of his slacks. They shook him down for hidden hardware, came up empty; he had never been *that* stupid. Finally the taller of them ducked inside to huddle with Rivera, and returned a moment later with a cautious come-ahead.

Half of the diner's dozen tables were now occupied by members of Rivera's team. It was the biggest rush the place had seen in years, but none of them were paying, and the owner, Eddie Beamer, would doubtless have preferred a safe and sluggish afternoon. The waitress caught his eye with something like a hopeful smile, but curiosity replaced it as he veered away and headed for Rivera's table. Sipping on a bottle of Dos Equis, the dealer muttered something and the guards on either side of him evaporated.

"Constable, sit down."

He faced Rivera from across the narrow table, leaning forward on his elbows, lowering his voice to a conspiratorial whisper. He could feel Rachel watching him, frowning, and he could half imagine Eddie Beamer out back, behind the grill, all eyes. Well, damn it, let them wonder. He was fighting for their town, their lives.

"This thing has gone too far," he said.

"I quite agree. Your people have defied me long enough."

"They're not defying you, Rivera. They don't have your man, *comprende*? My guess is, he bought it in the desert, south of town. And if he is here, then he's found himself a place to hide, and no one's seen him."

"Someone must have seen him, Grant."

It was the first time that Rivera had ever addressed him by name, and it made the lawman's skin crawl, like a kiss of death. Already knowing that his efforts would be wasted, Vickers forged ahead.

"You've been here too damned long already," he informed Rivera. "Hell, the state police or Pima County deputies might cruise through here at any time."

Rivera smiled. "They would not pass my men unless they come in force, prepared for battle. But you have no reason for concern, unless outsiders have been warned, somehow..."

His eyes burned into Vickers's and the lawman went all cold and dead inside. "They haven't heard a thing from me," he said, "but there are other ways. Some cowboy with a CB rig could blow it for you."

"I will take that chance." Rivera checked his watch and frowned. "Your people have five minutes left before I must begin to search myself. I have allowed myself to hope that it would not be necessary, but I see now that I have been foolish, treating peasants as if they were equals."

"People in this town won't take a roust like that without a fight."

"Then they will die."

It was his last word on the subject, and the lawman knew that there would be no point in reasoning or pleading with Rivera. There were too damned many witnesses already; all of them would have to die before Rivera's army headed home. There would be questions, either way, but with survivors there were likely to be *answers*, and the dealer could not take that chance. Investigation of a massacre in the United States might force the government of Mexico to take another, harder look at the Sonoran empire that Rivera had constructed for himself. With diplomatic protests flying, routine payoffs would not do the job. There would be too much blood to cover with *mordida*. But sometimes blood washed blood away, and if you spilled enough of it, you covered up your tracks.

Rivera would be capable of wiping out the town, Grant Vickers realized. The dealer would not lose a moment's sleep about a few more lives—or deaths. How many people had he killed already in the name of "business"? Hundreds? Thousands?

Grant Vickers had an obligation to the town of Santa Rosa, to its people. He had abused their trust, but until this afternoon, the payoffs, lies and secret dealings with Rivera had done nothing to diminish his performance as protector of the tiny town. He had performed with honor, and if certain shipments of narcotics passed through town, northbound, without a second glance from Vickers, it was nothing to the people whom he served. The drugs would not be dealt in Santa Rosa, and it was not Vickers's job to second-guess the DEA boys by obstructing traffic at the border. If the Feds could not prevent Rivera from importing dope, how could a small-town lawman hope to stem the tide?

Rivera smiled across the table, and his grin reminded Vickers of a hungry shark. "Relax, amigo. We are partners, *sí*?"

Grant forced himself to smile and nod as though he were buying it, when all the time he knew it was a crock of shit. Rivera had him measured for a box already, with the rest of Santa Rosa's citizens, and Vickers knew that he could never hope to save the town unless he saved himself as well. No matter that he didn't feel worth saving. It was simple: dead men couldn't fight, and they were way beyond negotiations with Rivera now.

He rose to leave and felt the dealer's weasel eyes like gun sights boring in between his shoulder blades. He reached the exit, waited with a hand out for his Python, while the sentry glanced back at Rivera for instructions. At a nod, the gunner shrugged and gave the Colt to Vickers, stepping back to let him pass. Outside, the noonday heat struck Vickers like a fist above the heart.

It was as hot as hell already, but he knew that it would be a damned sight hotter in the coming hours. When it was done, he might just have a chance to sample hell and make a real comparison. Unless he found some luck he didn't know about. Unless he found the nerve, the guts, to stand against Rivera's men and make it stick.

It was as good as suicide, but Vickers knew he had no choice. He owed the town that much, at least. He owed that much to Becky Kent.

LUIS RIVERA LIT ANOTHER of his cheroots and blew a cloud of acrid smoke in the direction of the diner's ceiling. Vickers would bear watching; he could feel the man about to break, and when it happened, Vickers might surprise him. Weak men sometimes found an inner well of courage, strength that they, themselves, had not been conscious of until a crisis brought it forth. Such men were dangerous, but only if you let them take you by surprise.

It would have been so easy to eliminate the constable just now. A simple gesture to his men and Vickers would have been cut down before he cleared the exit. Simple. But the dealer had more pressing matters on his mind, and Vickers was not going anywhere. His life was here, in Santa Rosa, and he clung to foolish hopes that something might be salvaged from the town. If nothing else, he cherished hopes of personal survival, counting on his past association with Rivera to secure his life. The gringo might not realize that their connection marked him as a liability; while Vickers lived, the secret of this day would not be safe. Rivera had not reached his present age and station by allowing loose ends in his business dealings. Careless errors were often fatal, and the dealer planned to reach a ripe, old age.

The peasants had refused to give up his quarry, but he was not persuaded by the lawman's arguments about the gringo

dying in the desert, unobserved. Rivera felt his prey in Santa
Rosa, knew that they were close, and if the people of the
town would not cooperate, he would be forced to search the
hamlet door-to-door until he found the soldier, trussed him
like an animal, and took him home for the amusement of his
troops. If he could not find out who had employed the man,
Rivera thought that he might try another tack. It might be
fun to issue invitations, bring his chief competitors together for a demonstration of his vengeance on the gringo
warrior. One of them, at least, would get the message; all of
them would realize that he was no one to be trifled with.

But first Rivera had to find the man.

He checked his watch again and saw that it was time. The
townspeople had ignored his offer, spurned his generosity,
and now the time had come for them to pay. It was a lesson
Rivera knew he would enjoy.

He summoned Hector from his table near the diner's entrance, issued orders for the sweep to be initiated, starting
from the north. Half of the gunners were to stay with him,
securing the diner, while the others worked the street,
checking every shop and home in turn. Before they finished, he would have his man in the bag, and then he would
be free to finish with the peasants who had dared defy him.

Beckoning the waitress to his table, he requested beer and
smiled at her, excited by the fear he saw behind her eyes.
Again, Rivera thought that it might be amusing if she came
with him to Sonora for a while. She would resist, but he
would offer her an option: life or death. Reduced to basic
terms, the most unpalatable notions grew persuasive, and if
she resisted him in bed, so much the better. He enjoyed resistance, to a point; it made the ultimate surrender that
much sweeter.

He waited for her to return and then ordered food. Rivera was not hungry, but he liked to watch her work, and he

would have to keep his strength up for the test to come. They might be challenged yet, by one or another of the locals, and he wanted to be ready for the challenge, if and when it came. He might enjoy a contest, come to think of it . . . provided that the outcome could be guaranteed. It would not do for him to be embarrassed by the residents of Santa Rosa, not when so much was at stake.

He turned to face the diner's broad front window, watching Hector as he issued orders to the troops. The wholesale killing would not start until they had their man, but in the meantime, any obvious resistance would be dealt with harshly and irrevocably. If the townspeople wanted war, he would provide them with the opportunity for martyrdom. It was the very least that he could do, and it would be a pleasure.

And while he waited, there was still the waitress, curiously childlike and appealing in her linen uniform. Rivera teased himself with mental images of her, at home in his *estancia*. She might be good for more than momentary dalliance. She might . . .

But he was being foolish now. She was nothing, no more than a trifle in the scheme of things. Rivera might find time to play with her a little, but he dared not make more of her than she was. If he attached undue importance to the woman, he would have to think of her as human, and it would be that much harder to dispose of her when it was time. He could not let himself become attached to anyone or anything that he might later have to throw away.

Outside, his men were dispersing, moving out to start the sweep that could have only one result: the capture of his enemy and destruction of the tiny town that had inadvertently sheltered him. He felt no pity for the town; it had been dying over time, by slow degrees, and now Rivera had arrived to end its misery. He was performing something of a

public service, eliminating what had come to be a laugh-
ingstock, an eyesore on the highway. In death the crossroads hamlet would achieve a fleeting place in history before
it faded, out of sight and out of mind. Its fate would rank
along with other legends of the desert: Superstition Moun-
tain, the Lost Dutchman mine, the Seven Cities of Gold.
For a time, men would speak the name of Santa Rosa with
a kind of wonder, speculating on the perpetrators of a massacre that would make history. And gradually, when no answers were forthcoming, it would be forgotten like the
desert's other unsolved mysteries.

In time.

Rivera was concerned about the present. If he could not
unearth his quarry, it would matter little what became of
Santa Rosa. With the gringo bastard still at large, his operation would remain in constant jeopardy from unknown
enemies. If they could penetrate his best defenses once, they
would be capable of doing it a second time, keeping on until they finished with him, left him empty, ruined, like the
peasant he had been in childhood. Scowling, Rivera took a
silent oath that he would not allow himself to be defeated by
the faceless enemy. He would prevail and force the opposition to acknowledge his supremacy before he snuffed them
out like cockroaches beneath his feet.

Rivera thought that it would be a pleasure. And, in any
case, he owed it to himself.

TWO HOURS OUT OF SANTA ROSA, Johnny Bolan had to stop
for gas. The station was a weathered, two-pump pit stop on
the edge of nowhere, manned by a proprietor who seemed
to have absorbed the brutal sun for years on end, his skin
becoming taut and as brown as leather. Johnny left the guy
to fill his tank and wipe the dead insects off the windshield,
making for a phone booth tucked around the side. There

was no trace of a directory, but Johnny punched up Information, receiving the area code for Santa Rosa, along with the numbers for the constable, a clinic and the only service station in the town. With quarters stacked in front of him, he tried them all...and each time heard a busy signal droning in his ear.

He gave it up and called the operator to get assistance with the call. He let her have the clinic's number, waited while she patched it through and grimaced as a recorded voice came on the line. "We're sorry," it informed him, "but your call cannot be completed as dialed. Please hang up, then check your number and try again. If you still cannot complete your call—"

"I'm sorry, sir," the operator broke in, interrupting the recording. "All our circuits into Santa Rosa show up busy at the present time."

"Is that unusual?"

"I really couldn't say."

He fought the urge to curse and shout at her, aware that it would gain him nothing. "Let's assume it *is* unusual," he said. "And let's assume that everybody didn't use their phones at once, okay? Is there another reason why the lines might show a busy reading?"

"Hypothetically, if there was damage to the lines, they might report as busy, sir."

"In that case, I would like to file a damage report and request immediate repair service."

"Are you in Santa Rosa, sir?"

"Of course not. How could I be calling Santa Rosa if I *was* in Santa Rosa."

"I'm sorry, sir, but you must be in Santa Rosa to request repairs on lines in Santa Rosa."

"How can I request repairs from Santa Rosa if the lines are down?"

"I'm sorry, sir—"

"Can you at least break in and see if anybody's on the lines from Santa Rosa?"

"We are not permitted to intrude on private conversations, sir, except in cases of emergency."

"All right. I'm Dr. Joseph Gray, and I have urgent business with the Santa Rosa Clinic. I take full authority for any inconvenience you might cause by breaking in—"

"I'll have to get permission from my supervisor, sir."

"How long will that take?"

"If you'll just hold on a moment, sir..."

The Jimmy had been gassed, its windshield cleaned and it was ready for the road. He slammed down the telephone receiver, aware that he could be in Santa Rosa by the time he got in touch with someone who had both authority and guts enough to break in on the busy lines from Santa Rosa. And if back-checks from a distance proved the lines were down, then what? The process would have wasted precious time, and gained him nothing. While he waited on the phone to speak with faceless supervisors, Mack was trapped in Santa Rosa, maybe fighting for his life.

He passed a wad of rumpled bills to the attendant, slid behind the Jimmy's wheel without his change, and put the vehicle in motion, headed east. Two hours, give or take, and there would still be daylight left when Johnny reached the killing ground. Still time to find his brother...or, at least, determine what had happened to him, the direction his killers might have taken. Not that there was any doubt about Rivera; he would run for home when he was finished, and the younger Bolan would eventually find him there. It might take time, but he had time to spare. It might take everything he had, in worldly terms, and it would still be cheap at half the price.

But helping Mack was the priority. If John could reach him while he lived, before it was too late, then he would find a way to pull his brother out of Santa Rosa, more or less intact. If battle had been joined before he reached the tiny crossroads, he would wade into the middle of it, strike whatever blows he could against Rivera's team. He might find unexpected allies in the populace, and then again...

It didn't matter, Johnny knew, if anybody stood with them or not. Together, he and Mack could choose their ground and make a stand their enemies would not forget. Together, they could take apart a strike force many times their size.

Together...

Johnny pictured Mack, stretched out and lifeless on some dusty sidewalk, while the locals gawked and fought for scraps of clothing from the famous dead. A three-ring circus, with Rivera in the role of ringmaster, calling the tune as his brother's corpse lay in state beneath the broiling sun.

Except that it would never be like that. The citizens of Santa Rosa would not have an opportunity to join the hunt, assuming that they had the urge. If they were cognizant of what was happening and free to talk about it, someone in the outside world would certainly have gotten word by now. The hamlet's several lines would not be engaged all day long if everyone in town was busy hunting Bolan in the streets. That left one possibility, and Johnny knew it was the truth before he ever set foot in the little town. He knew that Santa Rosa was besieged.

Rivera would be taking every possible precaution to ensure success and ward off interruptions. Taking down the phone lines would be basic, child's play, and it would prevent the citizens of Santa Rosa from communicating with the outside world when things got tight. Roadblocks were a possibility, although they might be subtle, letting unofficial traffic in and no one out. The heavy hardware would be closer in, downtown, prepared to move on contact with the Executioner. If John was cautious, if he kept his wits about him, there was still a decent chance that he could get inside the first perimeter, make contact with the enemy's main force before they knew that he was coming.

And if they tried to stop him on the highway, he would find a way inside, in any case. He would not let them turn him back when he had come this far, endured this much, to reach his brother's side. He was prepared to charge the gates of hell, if necessary—and, the warrior knew, it just might come to that. But hell was only frightening to those who feared the flames, and Johnny Bolan had been burned before. He recognized the heat, accepted it, and it held no more terrors for him.

He was ready for anything Rivera might have waiting on the streets of Santa Rosa. And if death was waiting for him there, as well, so be it. Every man had an appointed hour of destiny, but few were privileged to choose the ground, the cause in which they fell. It came as a relief to know that he would not be swept away by circumstance, the victim of some random accident or careless Sunday driver. Death was too important to be left to chance.

If it was time, the younger Bolan meant to make his final hours count for something. And Rivera would remember him, whichever way it went in Santa Rosa. He would rue the day when he had taken on the Bolan brothers, even with an army at his back.

The fire was waiting. John could feel its heat already, drawing closer, and he craved it now, to keep him warm.

**16**

Sitting in his cruiser on the northern edge of town, Grant Vickers knew that there was nowhere left to run. His effort to negotiate a cease-fire with Rivera had been doomed from the beginning. There was nothing he could do to save his town from ruin, nothing he could do to save himself. But he could still resist, make things a little tougher for Rivera on the road to final victory. With any kind of luck at all, he might get one clean shot off at the man himself.

With luck.

The lawman's luck had been all bad, so far, and he did not anticipate a change, but it did no harm to be ready, just in case. With leaden fingers, Vickers freed the 12-gauge pump gun from its dashboard rack and retrieved the box of surplus shells from the cruiser's glove compartment. He worked the Remington's slide, chambering a live round, then withdrew another magnum cartridge from the box and fed the shotgun's tubular magazine. It gave him seven rounds, for starters, and if he could not hit someone with a shotgun, at the range he had in mind, he might as well give up.

He set the riot weapon's safety, laid it to the side, and set the open box of cartridges beside him on the seat. There would be no question of reloading if he stumbled into any kind of ambush situation, but it never hurt to be prepared. And if he played his cards right, he might lay an ambush of

his own. Rivera might get careless and drop his guard
enough for Vickers to attempt a kill. It was a long shot,
granted, but it might be their salvation if he came up empty
on more practical ideas. And in the meantime, there was
Becky Kent, her teenage patient, and the clinic to be
watched, protected.

Scanning with binoculars, the lawman watched Rivera's
gunners scatter from their tight perimeter around the diner,
fanning out across the street. It was beginning, and he didn't
care if there was a stranger hiding out in Santa Rosa. It was
*his* town, not Rivera's, and *he* carried the law, in his badge
and in the swivel holster on his hip. It didn't matter that he
had spent years ignoring portions of his duty; he was ready
*now* to take a stand, and if he was too late to win, at least he
knew that it was not too late to try.

They were beginning at the southern end of Main Street,
going door-to-door from all appearances, and at their present rate they might not reach the clinic for an hour. Then
again, Rivera had had ample time to scan the local telephone directory or question hostages inside the diner. He
might know about the clinic, give it top priority, in case the
wounded stranger had succeeded in his search for medical
assistance.

If there *was* a stranger.

If he had ever been in Santa Rosa in the first place.

Vickers put the riddle out of mind. It did not matter in the
long run if Rivera was correct or not. The bastard had already killed five people, maybe more that Vickers didn't
even know about, and he was bent on wiping out the town
to keep his bloody secret safe. The question of the stranger
had become superfluous, irrelevant to everything that was
about to happen. If he found the guy right now, this instant, and delivered him into Rivera's hands, the dealer
would no doubt proceed with his annihilation of the town.

It was a no-win situation, but surrender only made Rivera's job that much easier, and Grant was in no mood to make things pleasant for his enemy. He was about to light a fire beneath Rivera, and he hoped the dealer would go up in flames. If not, at least his pride might get singed around the edges, and he would remember Santa Rosa as a town where one man found his guts and made a stand.

One man.

It had a solitary ring about it, chilling Vickers to the bone. And there was no one he could turn to for assistance. Maybe, if Gib Schultz or Bud Stancell had still been alive... But they weren't, and there was no damned use at all in crying over spilled blood. The other able-bodied men in town were working on surrounding farms, some of them traveling as far away as Tucson for the daily grind, and by the time the first of them returned from work that evening, it would all be over. That left Vickers with a pool of children, housewives and a few old men to staff his army, and he knew it wasn't worth the time or effort to begin recruiting now. Whatever he accomplished, he would have to do alone, and that was fine. The lawman thought that he deserved no better, and the thought did nothing to improve his mood.

He put the cruiser in reverse and backed into the alley, cranking hard around until its nose was pointed toward the clinic. There might still be time to see that Becky Kent was safely under cover while Rivera's goons were busy canvassing the street for prey. He might succeed in persuading her to leave town, seek shelter...

They would have to take the girl, of course. He knew Rebecca would not leave a patient to the wolves; it was against her nature. Vickers didn't mind transporting Amy—they were in so deep already that it couldn't get much worse—but what if Becky's patient was not fit for travel? Could they somehow fortify the clinic, drive Rivera's raiders back before they got inside?

It was a fantasy. One man, a woman and a wounded girl could never hope to stand off an army. He might take down the scouts, but once Rivera's reinforcements arrived, the outcome would be swift and certain. Still, the prospect of a valiant sacrifice possessed a certain morbid charm. It would be bitter irony if he became a hero, after selling out the town for so damned long, but stranger things had happened.

Too bad, Grant thought, that he had lost his faith in miracles. He could have used one now. Hellfire, he could have used a dozen.

AS HE PASSED THE PHARMACY, Rick Stancell hesitated on a hunch and tried the back door, found it open. Locking doors had never been a top priority in Santa Rosa, where security came first from knowing everyone in town, and people found their solace in the thought that neighbors wouldn't steal. Such thinking wasn't always accurate, but there had been no ugly incidents within Rick's memory. Until today.

Today had ruined everything, thrown trust into the trash, along with justice, honor, decency. Rick knew that he would never trust another stranger, but it scarcely mattered, since his life was measured out in moments now. Men with automatic weapons were already moving door-to-door on Main Street, in search of someone Rick had never seen. Unless he missed his guess, they would be killing as they came, eliminating witnesses in what would surely be a full-scale massacre before they finished.

Standing on the threshold of the pharmacy with two guns tucked inside his belt, Rick felt like an invader, as if he had somehow joined the enemy. It did no good to tell himself that he was fighting for the town where he was born and raised. In truth, he knew that he was seeking plain old, everyday revenge. For Amy. For his father. There was something painful in the knowledge, something *guilty*, but he pushed the thought away and concentrated on his mission, on his enemies.

They would be close at hand. They had begun at this end of the street, and he was standing in the third shop on a north-south axis formed by Main Street. A feed store and a tiny Laundromat, both out of business, were the only structures to the south, and it would not take long to scour their interiors. He would be stunned if either building hid the Mexican's stranger, but Rick knew it would not matter either way. The gunmen had to make a clean sweep and they were coming, even if they found their prey the first time out.

As if on cue, the front door opened to admit a pair of grim-looking thugs, and Rick stepped back behind a stack of cartons, scrutinizing them. One had a shotgun propped casually across a shoulder, his partner had an automatic pistol tucked behind the buckle of his belt, easily accessible. As they sauntered toward the register, Rick knew instinctively that he would have to neutralize the shotgun first. The handgunner would require some time, however brief, to draw and fire, but his companion only had to drop the weapon from his shoulder, point and squeeze the trigger.

Though a novice when it came to firearms, Rick was conscious of the captured automatic pistol's greater rate of fire and stopping power in relation to his father's .38. He had already checked over the pistol, satisfied himself that it was loaded, with the safety off, and now he drew it from his belt, the hammer locking under pressure from his thumb, one eye closed as he sighted down the slide. He aimed directly at the shotgunner's chest, following his target as the goon stopped short before the counter, lowering his weapon, grinning at the pharmacist, the man he was prepared to kill.

"You know why we are here, *señor*?"

Before the druggist had an opportunity to answer, Rick squeezed off two rounds in rapid fire. He was astonished by the recoil, thankful that the gun was braced in both hands, with his elbows locked. His first round drilled a hole in the gunner's chest and knocked him off his feet; the second missed completely, detonating bottles of cologne that were arranged behind him on a shelf. The empty cartridge cases struck the wall to Stancell's right, rebounded, clattering around his feet.

The second gunner was already digging for his weapon, scanning for the source of danger, when Rick put a bullet through his gut. The human target staggered, reeling, but he somehow kept his balance, hauling on the pistol that protruded from his belt. He had it now, and bloody hands were tracking onto target acquisition when a lucky second round sheared through his throat and slammed him backward into a display case, which collapsed beneath his weight.

Aware that time was counting down, Rick stood above his kills and scanned the battleground. The shotgunner was still alive, but fading fast, and Stancell did not waste a mercy round on what was soon to be a corpse. He pried the 12-gauge pump from flaccid fingers, moving on to claim the second gunner's pistol. He turned toward the counter and slapped the automatic down in front of Arnie Jefferson, the druggist.

"Use it if they come again," he said, and put the place behind him without waiting for an answer. There was too much left to do and he had only made a start. There was no time to waste in idle conversation, trying to convince a frightened man that it was preferable to stand and die than take it on your knees. If Jefferson could find the strength to fight, so be it. If he chose to die without a whimper, then the choice was his, and it would not affect Rick's future in the least.

Uncertain of his enemy's reaction to the burst of gunfire, Rick was conscious of a need to keep himself in motion and prevent the hostile guns from fixing his position. He had taken out three so far, which left God knew how many still on their feet and up for battle, anxious for a chance to bag themselves a gringo. Stancell had no doubt that one of them would nail him soon, perhaps the next time that he showed himself, but fear played no part in his thinking. He was numb, burned out, experiencing nothing in the way of terror at his prospects or elation at his recent victories. If they picked him off before he had a chance to do more damage, then at least he would have tried to even up the score. Three lives for one, and for the damage that the animals had done to Amy.

Rick was cursing as he put the pharmacy behind him. He wanted all of them, goddamn it, stretched out lifeless at his feet. If there had been time, he would have paused to mount their heads on poles, for all the town to see, but Stancell knew that he would have to be content with simply killing them, their deaths the only monument that he could hope to leave behind.

He was surprised to note that killing did not seem to faze him. He experienced no nausea, no dizziness, no nagging pangs of guilt so often emphasized in movies and on television. There was nothing, other than the cautious satisfaction of a job well done, a job Stancell knew was not complete.

The others would be waiting for him when he showed himself. They would not know his name, might not be conscious of his physical existence at the moment, but it would not take them long to realize that someone was resisting, fighting back in Santa Rosa. They would be on guard, prepared for trouble, as the milk run turned into a contest for survival. Three of them would not be going home alive, and that would have to give the others pause. If they were frightened, if they hesitated on the firing line or wasted rounds on shadows, Stancell would be points ahead. He could not hope for victory, but there was still a chance to shave the odds before he cashed it in.

And every gunner that he dropped was one more victory. Another strike against the animals who had destroyed his world. It was the least that he could do, all things considered, and the former high school football star was gratified to learn that he could do it fairly well. He wasn't equal to the pros, but he wasn't doing badly, either. Three of the exalted pros were dead already, and he was not finished yet, by any means.

In fact, Rick had the feeling he had only just begun.

REBECCA KENT WAS STARTLED by the muffled sound of gunfire that came somewhere to the south on Main Street. Turning to the Executioner, she swallowed hard and said, "It's started."

Bolan did not answer her directly. He was buckling on his web belt, with the giant silver handgun in its leather holster dangling on his hip. She watched him, silent, as he drew the weapon, checked its load, returned it to its sheath. "They're starting to the south," he said. "That gives us half an hour, max."

"For what?"

"To make this place defensible. Do you have any weapons on the premises?"

The doctor thought about it briefly, finally shook her head. "No, nothing."

"Tools or instruments?" he prodded. "Anything at all?"

"I have a set of scalpels," she responded hesitantly. "There should be a hammer and some other tools back in the pantry."

"Anything at all," he said. "And while you're at it, think about your drug stock, any sort of lethal chemicals or heavy sedatives. If you could mix a killer cocktail and have it ready in syringes—"

"No!" The vehemence of her reaction startled Dr. Kent, and that, in turn, was mortifying. He was asking her to kill with medicine, and for the barest fraction of a heartbeat she had actually considered it. "I can't do that."

"Fine." He did not seem inclined to argue with her. "You won't mind if I look through your stock, for something that could save our lives?"

The doctor blushed bright crimson, bit her tongue and handed him the key to her drug locker. Bolan turned his back on her, opening the whitewashed cabinet and scanning the contents of its shelves, selecting half a dozen bottles and arranging them along the countertop. She saw that one of them was hydrochloric acid, and she closed her eyes, refusing to participate by indirection in the grim perversion of her healing tools.

"You'll need to move the girl," he told her after several moments. "She's exposed right now. Pick out an inside room and get her moved while there's still time." Almost as an afterthought, he added, "She'll be safer on the floor."

"How so?"

The warrior frowned, reached out and rapped his knuckles on the nearest wall. "Too thin," he said. "A burst of automatic fire will cut through this like it was paper. On the floor, she'll have the added cover of your cabinets, baseboards, furniture. It isn't much, but it's the best we've got."

"I see."

"We haven't got a lot of time to waste."

"I'm going!"

She had finished moving Amy, settling her in a corner of the third examination room, when she was conscious of a rapping on the clinic door that fronted Main Street. Moving cautiously toward the reception room, she heard the Executioner fall in behind her. From the side of the waiting room, she saw two men outside the door and knew that they were members of the raiding party that was laying siege to Santa Rosa.

She half turned toward Mack Bolan. He had drawn the pistol from his shoulder holster, and he held it with its muzzle toward the ceiling, one hand cupped around the other, in an attitude of readiness. "What should I do?"

"Go on and let them in," he said, "then hit the deck as if your life depended on it."

She had no doubts whatsoever that her life depended on following his orders precisely, and she nodded dumbly, conscious of the fact that he was using her to kill these men whom she had never seen before today. She salved her conscience with the knowledge that these men were no doubt murderers themselves, that they would kill her, and her patient in the other room, if they were not prevented by brute force. She recognized the grim necessity of what the soldier was about to do . . . and still it was no easier.

Her hand was trembling as she gripped the doorknob, turned it, swung the door wide open to admit her uninvited visitors. They shouldered past her, brandishing their weapons in her face, the taller of them reaching out to slam the door behind. His companion was examining Rebecca with disturbing frankness, grinning like a hungry jackal. *"Muy bonita,"* he informed his sidekick, reaching out to cup her breast through the material of her blouse and lab coat.

Sudden panic gripped her, and she batted at his hand, her nails raking at his face. He caught her by the jacket, but she brought her heel down on his instep, grinding with all the pressure she could manage, and he gasped in pain, released her with a violent shove that sent her sprawling to the floor.

It was the shove, she later realized, that saved her life. Behind her, Bolan had emerged from hiding, leveling his pistol at the human targets, and she would have been directly in his line of fire if she had not been thrust aside so violently. The Hispanic gunmen saw Death coming, tried to beat the Reaper's time, but they were still off balance from the scuffle on the threshold, tracking with their weapons while the soldier was already squeezing off. It was no contest, and Rebecca watched them die.

The first round drilled her attacker through the forehead, exiting in a crimson mist that etched a grisly pattern on her wall. The dead man tumbled backward, jarring his companion's aim and giving Bolan time to place another round on target, this one drilling through the taller gunman's chest and slamming against the doorframe, pinning him in place while Bolan put another slug between his eyes.

Rebecca felt her stomach heaving, casting up its meager contents, choking off a startled scream as number two collapsed across her legs and briefly pinned her to the floor. She kicked out, desperately, and freed herself before Mack Bolan had a chance to reach her. He was bending down to offer her his hand when they were mutually startled by the back door's sudden and explosive opening. It slammed against the wall, the doorknob buried deep in plaster, and a crouching figure sprang across the threshold, sweeping left and right with what appeared to be a submachine gun.

Bolan was already pivoting to face the unexpected enemy, releasing Becky's hand, his weapon rising into target acquisition much too late, when thunder seemed to rip the corridor apart. Their adversary was immediately airborne, hurtling toward Bolan, spinning into rough collision with a wall and toppling to the carpet. Smears of blood stained the plaster where his shoulders had made contact with the wall.

They waited, frozen—Bolan in his combat crouch, Dr. Kent still on her knees beside him. He was poised to fire as yet another silhouette blocked out the doorway's light…and then he recognized the lawman's uniform.

It was Grant Vickers, with a shotgun cradled in his arms.

"You two all right?" he asked, and tension underlay his normal drawl.

"We're fine," she answered, glancing up at Bolan, leaning on him as she scrambled to her feet. The soldier stood erect, but he kept his automatic pistol in his hand, prepared for anything.

"We're getting by," the Executioner agreed.

THE RADIO HAD TOLD HIM that it was a hundred in the shade, but Enoch Snyder could not find a patch of shade up on the roof of Bud's garage. Some of the other structures lining Main Street might be taller, and they might have offered better cover, but he had been limited in time as well as in mobility. The laundry sack that covered his Garand would not fool anyone, and so he had been forced to scuttle like a pack rat through the alleys, ducking out of sight whenever anybody showed their face along his route. He dared not cross the street to find a better vantage point, with all those hostiles on the prowl. And it struck Old Enoch as poetic justice that the wrath of God should fall upon Bud's killers from the rooftop of his own garage. It just felt *right*.

Before they spotted him, he might have time to crank a whole clip off. Once he was seen, his fate was a foregone conclusion, but they would not take him easily, not like they took his friend. By God, he meant to make them dance before they brought him down, and no mistake.

His sunglasses were old and scratched, providing some protection from the glare but hindering his aim. He took them off and tossed them back across his shoulder, knowing that he would not need them anymore. Old Enoch waited, squinting through his lashes until he had grown accustomed to the light, and then he poked his head above the cornice for a quick look.

Downrange, the hunters were already kicking doors, ransacking shops and homes in search of their elusive prey. Old Enoch didn't know who they were hunting, but he wished the man well. He hoped they never found the poor, doomed bastard, that he got away scot-free and left them running empty circles in the desert. In the meantime, Snyder had a present for them, and he did not plan to keep the sons of bitches waiting any longer.

Scooting forward, so that he could rest his elbows on the cornice of the roof, Old Enoch eased off the M-1's safety and raised it to his shoulder, nestling his cheek against the stock the way a man might rest his head against a woman's shoulder.

Two gunners were emerging from the Laundromat, disgusted after learning that the place contained nothing but dust. They were jawing back and forth, unmindful of the danger they were in, when Enoch sighted quickly, easily, and shot the taller man in the face. You didn't need a fancy telescopic sight to see his forehead blossom scarlet, scalp and brains exploding as if the guy were snorting cherry bombs.

The dead guy's partner did a hasty double-take and dug a pistol from underneath his shirttails. It was far too little, much too late, and Enoch knew the bastard never heard the round that killed him, punching through his chest at more than a thousand feet per second, slamming him against a lamppost, spinning him around to drop down on the pavement.

Two for two, and six rounds left before he needed to reload. He scanned the street, alive with gunners now as they responded to the sound of gunfire. The muffled sound of shots came somewhere from the south, and Enoch wondered if somebody else had found the courage to resist, or if the bastards had begun to murder hostages.

In the long run it didn't affect Snyder's stand. He wasn't going anywhere until they hauled him down, and from his crow's nest, he had ample targets. It was just like a goddamned turkey shoot. Except that this time, all those goddamned turkeys could shoot back, which at least kept the contest interesting.

Lining up another target, Enoch started squeezing off in rapid fire. And watched the bastards dance.

## 17

Luis Rivera pressed his face against the diner's window, shrugging off Camacho's hand as Hector sought to pull him back from the expanse of glass. From outside, the echoes slightly muffled, came another burst of heavy-caliber gunfire. As he watched, one of Rivera's *pistoleros* took a shoulder hit that knocked him sprawling, leaving him to wriggle for the cover of a nearby car like some amphibian deprived of water.

There had been shooting as soon as the sweep had begun. Pistol shots at first, sedately muted, and he had assumed they marked the deaths of the townspeople. Almost immediately, from a different quarter, the reports were followed by a shotgun blast, and he was not so sure. Then came the rifle fire, and he was certain: his forces were under attack.

From where he stood, Rivera could see two bodies lying in the street, as well as the wounded gunner who had made his way to cover. He would have to act on the assumption that there might be other losses, but he dared not falter now, or he would lose momentum, lose it all.

His other guns were under cover now, a few of them returning fire in the direction of a rooftop, somewhere to his left, beyond Rivera's line of sight. No doubt they had already found the sniper's nest, and they would root him out before he could do further damage.

Sudden hope was kindled in Rivera's breast. Suppose the sniper was none other than his quarry, cornered now and fighting for his life? It would make everything so very simple; kill the man, then turn in righteous rage and kill the town that had sheltered him. So easy.

But the sniper had not fired those muffled pistol shots, the shotgun blast had preceded his initial fusillade. Assuming that Rivera's quarry had decided on a last-ditch stand, there still remained a possibility of allies—or of locals acting independently, in the defense of families and homes. If the resistance should begin to spread...

He swiveled, snapping orders at Camacho, satisfied when Hector jumped as if he had been stung and hastened to obey. They must initiate a swift and stunning counterstroke before the enemy could organize and take heart from early victories. If necessary, he would burn the town and grind the ashes under foot before he let the people make a fool of him. In fact, a touch of fire might be the best idea of all.

He caught Camacho halfway to the door and issued further orders, watching Hector's face light up as he imagined Santa Rosa burning to the ground. It was the kind of thing Hector normally enjoyed, and he would have no qualms about destruction of the village, the annihilation of its residents. If anything, he would enjoy the sport.

Rivera moved back from the window, keeping Esteban beside him. The sniper had been spotted, soon he would be rooted out and killed, but there was still no point in taking chances. Any stray round crashing through the picture window might prove fatal, and Rivera had no wish to die—by accident or otherwise. He had too much to live for in Sonora, at the heart of his illicit empire.

Glancing at the waitress, he decided she would have to die with the rest of Santa Rosa. He could kill her now, but there was still an outside chance that he might need a hostage if he had to escape from the village, and together with the grizzled cook, she was the only ace he held. It seemed improbable, a morbid nightmare, but Rivera would not waste his hole card yet, before he had the situation well in hand and Santa Rosa was in flames.

When the town began to burn, its citizens would scatter, screaming, to their shops and homes. They would forget about resistance in their haste to rescue children, pets and prized belongings. They would be completely at his mercy, then, but there would be no mercy for the peasants who had dared to stand against Luis Rivera. Opponents were like insects, to be crushed and then forgotten, thoroughly eradicated. If any one of them survived, his raid on Santa Rosa would have failed, and he would be in grievous jeopardy.

There was no extradition treaty between Mexico and the United States, but the *Americanos* would not have to bring him back to make life difficult. A little diplomatic pressure, if strategically applied, might do the trick, compelling venal *federales* to forget about their bribes for once and launch a real investigation. The annihilation of a town, if traced directly to Rivera, just might be enough to put a temporary clamp on foreign aid, for example, while a case was built against him in Sonoran courts. Rivera would not normally have feared a prosecution—he was strong enough and rich enough to keep the sentence short, and he could run his empire from a cell as well as from his plush *estancia*—but this would be a different sort of prison time. If the United States employed its full resources to "persuade" his native government that stringent measures must be taken, there was ample evidence available to lock him up for life, without parole, in squalid quarters where his cash would do him little good. And it would not be long, if he was jailed, before the hungry sharks would start to circle, snapping pieces from his empire, claiming territories for themselves.

Survival hinged on Santa Rosa, and he could not escape that elementary fact, no matter how he tried. If anyone from Santa Rosa lived, he might be doomed. If two or three of them survived, he was as good as dead. There would not be a second chance, no way to make it up, repair the damage from afar. His life, his empire, everything depended on what happened in the next few hours, on the main street of a town too small to be charted on many road maps. If Rivera lost it here, he lost it all, and there would be no point in going home.

The dealer made up his mind swiftly. If he dared not lose, he would not lose. He would destroy his enemies, and let their dying stand as an example to the world.

He would prevail.

JOHNNY BOLAN SAW THE ROADBLOCK from a mile off, a darker blotch against the heat haze of the far horizon, polished metal glinting in the sun. He pulled the Jimmy over, scrutinized the barricade through his binoculars, and saw that two cars had been parked across the road, their drivers and a third man lounging in the meager shade provided by the vehicles. None of them were in uniform, and none of them were Anglo. Johnny knew instinctively that none of them were lawmen.

They would be Rivera's men, detailed to seal off the town from the north, allowing no one in or out until the dealer's business had been settled, finally, with all concerned. The younger Bolan knew what that might mean, and he could not afford to let the barricade delay him any more than absolutely necessary.

Reaching underneath the driver's seat, he freed the Heckler & Koch VP-70 from its hidden rigging, easing off the safety as he placed it in his lap. The pistol's magazine held eighteen parabellum rounds, with number nineteen in the chamber; it was double-action all the way, and Mack had modified it personally to reduce the normally resistant trigger-pull. At any decent pistol range, it was a killer, and the extra loads would keep him firing when most adversaries had been forced to scramble for a backup magazine. With any luck at all, the piece would be enough. And if his luck ran out...

He pushed the train of thought away. Three men and two machines were standing in the way of a reunion with his brother, and he made his mind up that it would not be enough. With cool deliberation, Johnny put the Jimmy back in gear and rumbled toward the roadblock at a careful forty-five, both hands set firmly on the wheel. He guessed that they would speak to him, at least, and try to turn him back before they opened fire. If they didn't, he would deal with that eventuality when it arose.

The gunners scrambled to a ragged semblance of attention as the Jimmy closed to thirty yards, the leader stepping forward, both hands raised, to flag him down. No hardware was in evidence yet, and Johnny took it as a hopeful sign. If they were forced to start from scratch, the lag time would provide him with a lethal edge that they might never overcome.

He rolled the window down and waited for the leader to approach him, frowning with a simulated curiosity, the VP-70 in hand, poised below the windowsill and out of sight. The spokesman's companions were behind him, taking up positions for triangulated fire if they should be compelled to flash the hardware.

"What's the problem?" Johnny asked.

"We have been forced to quarantine the town, *señor*." The gunner jerked a thumb across his shoulder, indicating Santa Rosa, still invisible beyond the rise. "An accident with chemicals."

"No shit?" He gawked in what he hoped was a convincing imitation of concern. "My brother lives there."

"I understand, *señor*, but no one is allowed to pass."

"Well, rules are rules, I guess."

He raised the VP-70 and shot the gunner squarely through the forehead, blowing him away and tracking on before his two companions could assimilate the fact. The nearest stood his ground, one hand beneath his shirt and digging for his pistol. His partner sought security in motion, fading to the right and weaving while he wrestled with a handgun in the left hip pocket of his slacks.

John shot the nearer gunner first, two parabellum manglers ripping through his chest and lifting him completely off his feet. He was dead before he hit the ground. His sidekick stumbled, going down upon one knee, both hands outflung to break his fall, and it was all the edge that Johnny needed, granting him the time to aim and punch a bullet through the fallen runner's temple. He was quivering as Bolan stepped across his prostrate body, moving toward the cars. The keys were still in both ignitions, and he backed the larger vehicle—a Caddy—over to the shoulder of the road. When he had cleared a lane, he tramped back to the Jimmy and proceeded toward Santa Rosa.

In one respect the roadblock was a hopeful sign. If they were finished with his brother, done with Santa Rosa, they would not have posted guards to close the highway. *Something* must be happening, if nothing more than a mop-up, and he still had time to join the party. There was still a chance for him to bag Rivera before the man could retreat to Mexico. And there was still a chance that he might find his brother. A slender chance that he might find Mack alive.

He would have to be prepared for whatever waited for him in the streets of Santa Rosa. A hundred yards beyond the roadblock, still before he had a glimpse of town, he pulled the Jimmy over once again and walked around the back to choose his weapons. He lifted out the KG-99 and extra magazines, then hesitated, finally choosing the SPAS as well. Between the two, he had power and speed, a lethal combination any way you sliced it. There was still a chance it wouldn't be enough, but he was not intimidated by the odds.

His brother had not come this far by playing safe, and Johnny Bolan knew the odds against him going in. It was a losing game, no matter how you read the stats, with death the only certainty, and Johnny had resigned himself to falling in the cause. But not just yet, if there was any way to put the Reaper off. In lieu of lasting victory, he would accept postponement of the inevitable, another chance to face the savages and drive them back into their burrows, purge them with the cleansing fire.

He knew enough, from following his brother's war, that there would be—could be—no final victory against the cannibals. But he could singe their asses here and now. And he could do a great deal more, if he had come too late for Mack.

Rivera had arrived expecting to annihilate a town. Instead the dealer and his troops might be annihilated if a man had guts enough to stand before the gates of hell. As Bolan dropped the Jimmy into gear, he knew that he had the guts.

"I DIDN'T MEAN to shave it quite that close," Grant Vickers said.

Mack Bolan held the lawman's eyes. "I'm not complaining."

"Reckon you're the fella that Rivera's all revved up about."

"You know his name?" the lady asked.

The constable seemed to pale beneath his desert tan. "We've met," he answered curtly, and he could not seem to meet the woman's gaze.

"But how—"

"We haven't got much time," the soldier interrupted, and he thought the officer looked grateful as he raised his eyes. "Rivera may not notice, but his people on the street will know they didn't fire that shotgun blast."

"I thought of that." The constable was looking Bolan over, closely. "As I recollect, he said that you were wounded. Are you fit to travel?"

"I'll survive. I couldn't say about the girl."

They turned to Dr. Kent, who shrugged dejectedly, still studying the lawman's face. "I've given her a sedative. We'd have to carry her."

"Too risky," Bolan told her. "I'd suggest a suck."

"I beg your pardon?"

"A diversion. Something that will draw the enemy away and keep them busy elsewhere. If we play our cards right, we could lay an ambush, turn it to our own advantage."

"Now you're talkin'," Vickers said, but there was less enthusiasm in his eyes than in his voice.

Before the warrior could elaborate, he heard the sound of rifle fire, immediately answered by the growl of automatic weapons. From the tempo of the gunfire, its direction, Bolan knew the rifleman was not a crony of Rivera's, but a sniper who had brought the raiders under fire.

"We've got some company."

"I'll be goddamned." The constable's amazement was entirely genuine; he had had a passing thought that his constituents might rebel, but he had honestly not expected it. "Who would have thought? I wonder who the hell—"

"Whoever," Bolan cut him off, "they won't hold out for long. We need to put the ball in motion if we plan on walking out of this one."

"Walking out?" The lawman seemed confused. "You mean you think we gotta chance?"

"We're not dead yet."

Grant Vickers seemed about to argue, but he let it go. It struck Mack Bolan that the constable had no intention of surviving through the night. He wondered briefly what had driven Vickers to the point of suicidal heroism, and he let it go. It didn't matter now, and if his first suspicions of the lawman were correct, the answer might be better left alone for now.

"You've got your cruiser?"

Vickers nodded. "Half block down the alley."

"Good. We'll need the lights and siren."

"Say the word."

He turned again to Dr. Kent. "Is there an inside way to reach the roof?"

She nodded. "There's a skylight in the main examination room. You'd need a ladder, though."

"I'll use the furniture."

"Your side—"

"Will have to take its turn. We're out of time."

The lady was about to speak, but kept it to herself. He turned to Vickers. "Give me five, and I'll be looking out for that diversion."

"I'll be there."

The constable was leaving when the lady caught his arm. "Be careful, Grant," she said.

"Hell, yes. You know me, Becky."

As he disengaged, the lawman's eyes met Bolan's, locked there for an instant, and the Executioner saw death, as cold and certain as the print on last night's headlines. Vickers might not let him down, but he had no intention of returning from his mission. He was cashing in, for reasons that the soldier did not have the time or will to contemplate.

"Five minutes."

"I'll be waiting," Bolan promised him.

The lawman grinned, an easy smile this time, and said, "Let's kick some ass."

And he was gone. Before Rebecca Kent could voice her questions, Bolan was in motion, moving toward the main examination room, the skylight that would put him on the roof with a commanding view of Main Street. Given half a chance, he would have opted for a big-game rifle, but the captured submachine gun, his AutoMag and the Beretta 93-R were the best that he could do, and they would have to serve. If used correctly, Bolan knew, they just might be enough.

The lady had begun to follow him, but Bolan turned and froze her with his eyes. "Stay with your patient," he instructed. "Don't come out for anything or anyone, unless I call you or you recognize the state police."

"But what about—"

He handed her the stainless-steel revolver he had lifted from another of Rivera's goons. "Take this," he said, and forced it on her when she hesitated. "If anybody else comes through that door, remember what they've done already, what they mean to do."

"I will," she answered, and the warrior thought she meant it.

For her sake, and for the sake of her sedated patient, Bolan hoped she meant it.

THEY HAD ALREADY SEARCHED the long-deserted Laundromat, and Stancell knew that he would be as safe there, for the moment, as he would be at any place in town. The empty building had a dusty smell about, but the atmosphere was much too dry for mildew, and the place was relatively clean. It was ironic that the usual pests and insects moved away when man departed, following his trail of refuse. There were still a few spiders in the Laundromat, awaiting contact with the few odd roaches that remained, but Rick ignored them. It was his turn now, and he was hunting larger game.

There had been firing up the street; a muffled shotgun blast, and seconds later, rifle fire. The latter was continuing, the raiders firing back with automatic weapons, but Rick could not see the sniper from his place inside the Laundromat. He could see two of the invaders, stretched out on the opposite sidewalk, lying in spreading puddles of their life's blood, and he would give the unseen sniper credit for a sense of style. Whoever he might be, his help was welcome in the crunch.

Rick watched another gunman fall. He had been hit in the shoulder, and started to wriggle toward the cover of a car parked at the curb. His path would bring him into range, and Stancell stepped into the doorway, easing off the safety of the shotgun he had lifted from a dying adversary in the pharmacy. He wasn't a pro at this, but he had sense enough to know that bullets would not pass through glass without some measure of deflection, and he did not wish to waste a single round of precious ammunition. Fortunately, the invaders had already crashed the door, demolishing its lock and knocking out a section of its plate-glass in the process.

Standing in the shadows, Stancell raised his riot gun and sighted through the jagged ruins of the door. He let his target reach the curb, then squeezed the trigger, riding out the mighty recoil as a charge of buckshot drove the wounded gunman back into the street, a rag doll flopping in the desert wind.

He scanned the street immediately, waiting—hoping—for the other gunmen to respond. Across the street and three doors up, a pair of them were crouching in the meager shadow of the grocery store, attempting to escape the sniper's plunging fire. The blast from Stancell's shotgun brought their heads around, and one of them was pointing at him—or at an automatic weapon in the general direction of the laundry, squeezing off a burst that chipped the masonry outside, and then both men were firing for effect. Rick triggered two quick blasts, imagined that he saw one of them stagger as he hit the floor.

A lethal storm broke overhead, with bullets shattering the plate-glass windows, gouging plaster, whining off the pipes that once had been connected to a line of washers on the wall. Rick hugged the floor and crawled through the broken glass to find a vantage point from which he could return fire through the doorway. He had bagged no extra ammunition from the dying gunman, and he knew the shotgun must be almost empty, but he still had pistols, and if he was forced to make his last stand in the Laundromat, they would not find him easy.

Rick poked his head around a corner, found the angle that he wanted, sighted quickly and pulled the trigger. This time there was no doubt: one of the gunners took his blast directly in the chest and toppled backward through a window of the grocery, raining glass and day-old produce around his body. His companion scrambled clear as Stancell worked the shotgun's slide, squeezed the trigger and heard the hammer snap against an empty chamber.

"Shit!"

He tossed the empty gun aside and snagged the automatic from his belt, retreating several feet into the store as some unseen assailant poured another burst through the windows. The crack of rifle fire rang out in counterpoint to the staccato grumbling of automatic weapons.

It was time to cut and run before they trapped him, cut off his last retreat. If he could slip out through the back, he might have a chance to lay another ambush for them, choose another spot to make his final stand. At this rate, hell, they might be chasing him all day.

The thought of victory had never entered Stancell's mind. Survival had seemed so improbable that he had never given it a second thought. But after killing men, and facing death himself, the young man realized how very much he wanted to survive. There was so much to see and do out there, away from Santa Rosa.

Raw survival was the problem, though. He could not count on living through the next five minutes, let alone the afternoon. Evacuation of the Laundromat was a start, but Stancell still had work to do. The enemy was still out there. Waiting. And while any one of *them* survived, Rick knew that he would not be whole, would not be free.

He had a job to do, and it was getting late. He prayed that it was not too late, and took himself away from there. To find the enemy.

## 18

Vickers pulled the safety harness tight across his chest before he started the cruiser's engine. He wasn't concerned with safety—he just didn't want a lucky shot to knock him over, rip his hands off of the steering wheel before he had a chance to show Rivera something special. Glancing at his watch, the lawman saw he had four minutes, thirty seconds left to live, and he was startled to discover he was not afraid.

He put the car in motion, rolling slowly down the alley's length, aware that he had time to spare before the stranger's lethal deadline. It occurred to him that he had never asked the gunman's name, but he supposed it didn't matter. Rivera meant to kill him, kill them all, and any ally in the midst of danger was a welcome hand.

He reached the alley's northern mouth and paused again before he turned the cruiser east toward Main Street. Vickers eased the Python from his holster, placed it on the seat beside him, knowing he would never have an opportunity to use it. It made him feel a damn sight better, having it there, even if that made no sense at all.

He thought that Becky might have figured out his secret toward the end. The stranger knew for certain, somehow; he had seen it clearly, in those graveyard eyes. And yet the man had seemed to pass no judgment on him. Maybe, Vickers thought, the knowledge that he would be dead within five minutes made a difference. Maybe.

But he was relieved that Becky had not challenged him, that there had been no time for her to put the pieces in place. No doubt she would be able to deduce the rest of it, but he would not be there to see the accusation in her eyes, and Vickers hoped the manner of his passing might incline her to spare his soul a kindly thought from time to time.

Three minutes, and he brought the cruiser onto Main Street, idling outside the vacant hulk of what had once been Sundberg's Dry Goods. There was action halfway down the block, and Vickers caught a glimpse of someone on the roof of Stancell's gas station, rising up to take a potshot at Rivera's soldiers with a rifle, ducking down again before they had a chance to return fire. The sniper's profile looked familiar, even from a distance, but he didn't have the time to mull it over. Thankful that some resident of Santa Rosa had come up with guts enough to make a stand, he dropped the squad car into gear and tromped his foot on the accelerator.

Downrange, the gunners saw him coming, heard the squeal of tortured rubber as he powered toward them from a standing start. He hit the switches for the cruiser's lights and siren, letting it unwind as he accelerated past the hardware store, the pharmacy, the clinic where Rebecca and her patient hid. The stranger would be up there, watching from the roof, but Vickers could not see him. He was concentrating on the startled gunners, some of them already scattering, a handful seeming to deduce his target, standing firm and laying down a screen of automatic fire. The cruiser started taking hits, like hail against the fenders, doors and grille. He heard one of the revolving lights explode above him, and he grimaced as a bullet drilled the cruiser's windshield, spilling pebbled safety glass into his lap. He scooped up the Python and thrust it through the vacant window-frame, and he was smiling as he started squeezing off in rapid fire. No time to aim, but at the very least he thought that he could keep the bastards hopping.

Half a block to go, and Vickers swerved his cruiser toward the diner and the cars lined up outside. A flying squad of runners was retreating toward the restaurant and firing as it ran, the bullets drilling bodywork and snapping close beside him in the speeding car. The constable ignored them, as a hunter might ignore the gnats that buzz around his head on an excursion through the forest, concentrating on the sleek Mercedes, which was first in line. It might not be Rivera's private car, although he thought he recognized the dealer's style, but it would do, in any case.

The other winking light exploded overhead, its colored fragments swept away in Vickers's slipstream. He was twenty yards from impact when a white-hot pain shot through his shoulder, knocking him off balance, ripping one hand from the steering wheel. The harness saved him, and he held the cruiser firmly on its course, his boot depressing the accelerator to the floor. He measured out his life in fractions of a second now.

"Kick ass!" he shouted, knowing that the gunners could not hear him, and before the lawman had a chance to lift his good hand off the steering wheel, his world was swallowed up by rolling thunder, tinged with fire.

LYING ON THE CLINIC'S ROOF, Mack Bolan watched the squad car and its driver self-destruct. On impact, both the cruiser and the lead Mercedes were obscured by a rolling fireball, oily smoke ascending, blackening the sky. A lake of fire was spreading underneath the other cars in line, and as he watched, a burning scarecrow staggered out, arms flapping in an agonized, demented parody of flight. It was not Vickers, and he let the runner go, his captured automatic weapon seeking other targets in the street below.

He found them almost instantly. A squad of hardguys had emerged from cover near the diner, darting in and out along the edges of the spreading conflagration, desperate to save the other cars before they all went up in turn. Across the street, from the direction of the service station, Bolan heard another rifle shot and glanced that way in time to see the sniper ducking under cover. He had missed that time, but now his enemies were dodging, seeking cover, hastily abandoning their mission with the convoy.

Bolan chased them with a short, precision burst and cut the legs from under one of them, his human target toppling across the line of fire and twitching as the last three rounds tore through his head and chest. The others scattered, seeking cover in the diner, in the mouth of an adjacent alleyway, or veering off across the empty street toward other shops. The soldier tracked them with his submachine gun, dropped another as the runner gained the opposite sidewalk, his death roll ending with the body crumpled against a standing mailbox.

Sudden automatic fire from an entirely different quarter raked the cornice to his left, and Bolan wriggled backward, out of range. The gunners had divided, probably in answer to the challenge of the sniper at the filling station, and a pair of them were on the street below him, firing skyward, pinning Bolan down.

If he had come prepared with frag grenades, it would have been no contest, but it would be suicide to rise above the cornice, scanning for a target while he posed in silhouette against the sky. There might be more than two below, although at present he could only hear two weapons—one 9 mm, by the sound of it, the other popping .45s—and while he might gain time by shifting his position to another section of the road, he might as easily be killed while on the move. Worse yet, he knew that it would not be long before the gunners tried to reach him through the clinic proper, scouring the rooms for safety's sake, locating Dr. Kent and her sedated patient in the process. It was time to move, unless...

As if in answer to his secret thoughts, the nameless sniper showed himself again, this time directing rapid fire against the gunners moving near the clinic. Bolan could not judge the rifleman's effectiveness, but only one of the assailants answered fire, a ragged burst that drove the sniper under cover once again.

The soldier made his move, already up and running as the scheme took shape. The building next to Santa Rosa's clinic, seemingly a vacant storefront, stood across an alley roughly ten feet wide. In case the scuttling gunner might have missed his move, he fired an aimless burst skyward as he ran, then tucked the stuttergun beneath his arm and leaped across the yawning canyon of the alleyway.

It was an easy jump, all things considered, but the roof of the adjacent building was a good foot taller than the clinic's, with a higher cornice, and the soldier lost his footing, going down on hands and knees to catch himself, the submachine gun clattering beside him. Thankful that the roof was flat, instead of canted at an angle, Bolan spent a heartbeat breathing deeply, mindful of the sudden, spastic pain that emanated from his wound as sutures tugged against the tender flesh. Below him, angry shouts and a halfhearted burst of autofire informed the soldier that his shift had not been overlooked.

With any luck, they would pursue him, leaving Dr. Kent and Amy Schultz in peace for now. If nothing else, the Executioner could try to buy them time, a chance to cut and run, but he was not primarily concerned with holding actions. It was not by accident that he was closing on the diner, where the greatest concentration of Rivera's gunners seemed to be. The palace guard would stand its ground around *el jefe*, and if Bolan did not miss his guess, Rivera would be inside the restaurant.

Grant Vickers had succeeded in annihilating the Mercedes tank. The other cars in line were burning furiously, on the verge of secondary detonations as their fuel tanks were licked by flames. As they exploded, one behind the other, it was like a string of giant fireworks, spewing jagged shrapnel, spouts of oil and gasoline like fiery streamers in the air. A Cadillac, parked close behind the long Mercedes, was the first to blow, its broad hood airborne, like a piece of cardboard riding on a desert whirlwind. Next in line, a dusty squad car—captured somewhere, somehow, from the Border Patrol—erupted in a ball of greasy flame. A secondary blast destroyed the cruiser, broke its back, and left it squatting like a blackened toad on melting tires. The others blew in turn, their detonations culminating in a blast that ripped the stolen ambulance apart, emergency supplies and rolls of bandages erupting, all in flames. A tank of oxygen exploded, with the echo of a giant's fowling piece, and then the battleground fell relatively silent, save for the devouring crackle of the flames.

It was an artificial peace, and swiftly broken as Rivera's gunners scrambled out from under cover, gawking at the ruined vehicles that were their only transport home. They would discover other cars and trucks in Santa Rosa, given time, but it was Bolan's task to keep them jumping, whittling the ranks, so that they never found the necessary time to mount a search. He raised his captured weapon, rattled off a 3-round burst, and heard the hammer fall upon an empty chamber. Feeding in his solitary backup magazine, he was prepared to spray the street again when hostile fire erupted on his flank and drove him back to cover.

Bolan realized that he was cornered. He could not retreat in the direction of the clinic, nor could he advance to the diner from where he was. His only avenue of exit was the alley in back, assuming that the gunners did not flank him first, and in the absence of a ladder he would have to jump.

Procrastination was a fatal flaw in combat situations, and the soldier did not hesitate once he had weighed the narrow range of his alternatives. He popped up, fired a burst in the direction of the diner, then pivoted to bring the gunners near the clinic under fire. Before they could react, he was already moving out, across the dusty roof and toward the alleyway that ran behind the buildings fronting Main Street, separating them from stucco homes that faced the desert to the west.

A glance in each direction, verifying that the enemy had not surrounded him completely, and the Executioner was looking for the best way down when something hit the roof behind him, heavily, and started rolling. Bolan spun around and saw the frag grenade as it began to wobble toward him. He could hear the doomsday numbers falling as the lethal egg rolled closer, and he did not need to calculate trajectories to know that he was in deep trouble. Escape was mandatory, and it could not be postponed.

He leaped, free-falling, and the shock wave struck him in midair. He was a tumbling straw man, trapped and buffeted inside a smoky thunder clap, with angry hornets buzzing past him, plucking at his clothing. Then the ground was rushing up to meet him, and there was not even time to break his fall.

RIVERA CAME OUT of his hiding place behind the counter, and he saw the line of cars outside reduced to twisted, smoking hulks. They were on foot now, but he knew that other vehicles would be available. It was not the destruction of machines that worried him, but rather the realization of *who* had destroyed them.

The constable had turned against him with a vengeance, overriding years of purchased loyalty to sacrifice his life for the town, choosing fiery death above allegiance to Rivera. It was not a typical reaction, and the dealer was disturbed. If he could not control his underlings, if one whom he considered bought and paid for could betray him thus, what might the other citizens of Santa Rosa do? What might they risk to save their miserable pest hole of a town?

The nameless rooftop sniper had apparently been joined by yet another, this one with an automatic weapon. Betting the percentages, Rivera recognized the odds against a local citizen possessing a machine gun, and he knew that in all probability the weapon had been captured from a member of his own crew. That meant another casualty, and he was stricken by the rapid decimation of his forces, conscious of the fact that they could not hold out for long inside the diner, if the town should rise against them.

Moving closer to the windows, scanning through the smoke, he searched the street for a sign of Hector. Shadows darted in and out amid the drifting, oily clouds, but he could not pick out their faces or identify the men beyond a general knowledge that they were his men, his troops. They held the street, but they were fighting desperately to keep it, and Rivera wondered if it might be a losing battle. Should the other citizens of Santa Rosa be prepared to sacrifice themselves as Vickers had, Rivera's gunners could not hope to stand before them. They had been outnumbered from the start, and blind fanaticism neutralized the opening advantage of their weapons, their professional experience.

It struck the dealer that he might be marked to die in Santa Rosa, but he pushed the thought away. He had survived too many close encounters with the Reaper to be daunted now, and he would persevere, no matter what should happen on the street outside. His honor was at stake. Rivera had not worked so long and hard to give it up without a fight. He had not killed so many men to be intimidated by a village full of peasants in rebellion. If he could not wipe them out entirely, he could make the bastards pay a ghastly price for their resistance. Even if the peasants should defeat him somehow, in the end they would remember him in grief and rue the day when they had raised their hands against Luis Rivera.

The cars were burning out, except for their upholstery and carpeting, but now there seemed to be more smoke outside than previously. Glancing to the south, Rivera saw a tongue of flame, extruded from the shattered windows of an empty shop. Beside it, yet another store was burning, and he saw Camacho now, with several other *pistoleros* racing from a third shop as the smoke began to billow on their heels.

Camacho was obeying orders, under fire, and thus far he had been successful. If another shop or two was set ablaze, the rest might catch spontaneously, from their neighbors, and the arson team could cross to work the other side of Main Street. Soon enough, the town would lie in ashes, and if that was not enough to smother the resistance by its occupants, Rivera's gunners would have little problem mopping up amid the ruins. Provided that they had not been overpowered in the meantime.

Reaching underneath the jacket of his leisure suit, Rivera pulled the nickel-plated automatic from its shoulder rigging, drawing back the slide to verify a live round in the firing chamber. He would not go quietly, whatever happened. If the peasants overran his troops, they would be forced to face Rivera last of all, and some of them, at least, would not survive the confrontation. He would make them pay for their impertinence, and if his life was forfeit, he would not go down alone.

If all else failed, he had the hostages. The cook was old and weather-beaten, but the waitress was young and succulent. A sniper might think twice before he cut the woman down, and any hesitation by the enemy could be converted to a positive advantage, with sufficient skill and daring. Confident that he possessed both qualities, Rivera slipped his side arm back into its armpit holster, moving back to the rear of the restaurant.

From somewhere to the north, he heard the muffled blast of a grenade, immediately followed by the sound of automatic weapons. That would have to be his strike force; in the worst scenario, he could not let himself believe the peasants had explosives on their side. His men were rooting out the snipers, running them to earth, and once the opposition had been stifled, if indeed it could be localized, they would be free to finish with the town, escaping in such vehicles as they might pick up off the street.

The stolen cars might be a problem, if they tried to cross the border in a convoy, but Rivera knew that there were ways around the difficulty. They could find another town, patch through a phone call to his home, and have vehicles meet them on the highway. And if worse came to worst, he carried cash enough to buy a car or two, with title in his name, before they headed south again.

A crafty businessman, Rivera took great pains to be prepared for any given situation. He had let his guard down once too often here in Santa Rosa, but he would not make the same mistake again. The unexpected treason of Grant Vickers might work out to his advantage, inasmuch as it prepared him for the worst and made him conscious of the fact that he was not invincible. It never hurt to be reminded of one's own mortality, as long as the reminder was not fatal in itself.

"Esteban!"

The gunner moved to stand before him, almost at attention. Even under pressure, he took care to show Rivera the respect that he deserved. *"Sí, jefe?"*

"When Camacho and the others start to burn the buildings on this side, we must be ready to depart." He nodded toward the hostages and said, "These gringos will be coming with us, for security."

Esteban smiled approval of the plan. *"Sí, jefe.* As you say."

"Be ready when I give the order."

*"Sí."*

Rivera turned back to the windows and the street beyond, a gesture of dismissal that Esteban took in stride. The gunner moved away and left Rivera with his thoughts of life and death, defeat and victory.

He could prevail against the peasants, if his luck had not gone sour. He was not a superstitious man, but he had seen enough of life to know that even preparation might not always be sufficient to ensure success. There was an element of chance, or risk, in every human undertaking, and the odds grew worse as each new person was involved, each wild card added to the deck. Within established limits, it was possible to stack the deck somewhat, but you could never totally eliminate the element of chance. Dumb luck might cause the best of plans to go awry, and he was looking at a situation now where Fate had seemingly stepped in to lend a hand.

But if Rivera was not superstitious, neither had he ever been a man of faith. Predestination was a concept foreign to his thinking; he did not believe in a supreme intelligence or guiding hand behind the workings of the universe. Raised in poverty and filth, he put no stock in gods or idols, carrying a lifelong grudge against the notion of a great Creator who would leave the world in such a state. Within the limitations set by chance, coincidence and pure dumb luck, man was the captain of his fate, achievements limited by individual intelligence, initiative and drive.

Rivera knew that he possessed those qualities, and he had every confidence that they would help him to survive. If not, God help the peasants who were sent to bring him down.

**19**

As he approached Santa Rosa, Johnny Bolan realized the town was burning. Smoky columns rose above the crossroads, staining what had been a pristine sky. He was downwind and driving with his window open; half a mile from town he caught the stench of burning gasoline and rubber.

Cars. But buildings were involved, as well. However it had started, Santa Rosa was in flames, and Johnny saw no evidence of anyone attempting to control the conflagration. Standing on the gas, he powered through the outskirts, passing ancient mobile homes, a vacant stucco dwelling gone to ruin in the baking desert heat. He entered Santa Rosa from the north and found himself inside a combat zone.

Downrange, a line of cars were smoldering against the curb outside a diner. Just across the street several shops were burning furiously, pouring smoke into the street and sky. He caught a glimpse of figures moving through the smoke in furtive rushes, scuttling back and forth without apparent destinations. Closer to his own position, on the roof of a garage a half block down, he saw a wiry figure with a rifle rise out of concealment, snap off three quick rounds in the direction of the running men, and duck back under cover.

Mack would be somewhere in the middle of that chaos, whether he was still alive or not. The younger Bolan sat for several seconds, watching Santa Rosa die, a passing thought to the images of Dante as the smoke curled toward him, driven on the desert wind. That wind would also be propelling flames, and in a few more moments half the shops in town would be on fire.

It would be suicidal, Johnny knew, to drive his Jimmy through the heart of town, attracting hostile fire from every side. He dropped the vehicle into reverse and powered backward, cranking on the wheel and gunning back into a narrow alleyway between two vacant shops. It would be safe enough, until the fire was close at hand, and he would be back well before that time. If he was coming back at all.

He slung the SPAS across his shoulder, grabbed the KG-99 and stuffed the extra magazines inside his belt. He locked the driver's door and set the tamperproof defense against intruders. If a car thief tried to break the lock, a loud alarm would sound; if he succeeded, it would blow up in his face, with force enough to flatten anyone or anything inside a radius of thirty yards.

He hit the street and homed in on the sound of automatic weapons. Santa Rosa was a tiny town, and he could see from one end to the other, barring interference from the smoke, but now the racket raised by autofire was coming from *behind* the shops that lined the west side of the street, as though a portion of the battle had moved on, retreating toward the desert. Johnny was about to follow, hoping for a chance encounter with his brother, when another portion of the war erupted in his face.

Above him, and to Johnny's left, the filling station's rooftop sniper sprang erect to bring his adversaries under fire once more. No sooner had he showed himself than a half dozen gunners broke from cover in a shop across the street, advancing at a run and firing as they came. They were Hispanic, dressed like street thugs, and it took no giant intellect to realize that they must be Rivera's men.

The sniper saw them coming, swiveling to drop the pointman in his tracks and ducking out of sight again before they started scouring the roof with autofire. One of them hesitated, stooped to check for vitals on his friend, and Johnny blew the gunner's face off with a well-placed parabellum round. The others scattered, laying down a screen of cover fire and racing for the sanctuary of surrounding shops, but Johnny bagged another on the run, the impact of a bullet in the spine propelling him against a lamppost with concussive force. The dying gunner slumped into a kneeling position, slowly toppled toward the street and finally lay still.

Not his three companions. They were bobbing in and out of cover, potting rounds at Johnny as well as the rooftop where the sniper had been seen. The younger Bolan knew they could not reach him where he was, but neither could he find his brother while they pinned him down. A change of strategy was called for, and he slipped the KG-99 across his shoulder on its sling before he snapped the safety off his SPAS.

In military parlance, the weapon was a Special Purpose Assault Shotgun, and it was something of an engineering wonder, capable of switching back and forth from semi-auto fire to slide action at the press of a button. Johnny's SPAS was set for semi-auto now, with seven rounds of double-ought inside the magazine and one more in the chamber. He did not unfold the weapon's stock, but rather used the tension of its sling to hold it steady as he peeked around the corner, marking targets, making ready for his move.

He let the gunners throw a few wild rounds his way and then erupted from his hiding place, the awesome shotgun tracking, seeking a target. The nearest gunner was sequestered in a doorway, on his own side of the street, and Johnny triggered off a blast that struck the alcove like a whirlwind. Sweeping on, without a backward glance, he caught the second *pistolero* just emerging from his place behind a pickup truck, his weapon poised to fire, and Johnny took his head off with a quick, reflexive blast.

The third man up was opting for the better part of valor, taking to his heels, when Johnny swung the SPAS around and helped him with a charge of shot that riddled him from neck to knees. The impact lifted him completely off his feet and pitched him forward, facedown on the faded center stripe of Main Street.

Awkward, clumping movement sounded on his flank, and Johnny pivoted to find the gunner from the blasted doorway lurching into view. He had been hit, more than once, but he was walking on his own and very capable of using the revolver that he carried. Bolan hit a combat crouch and squeezed the trigger of his riot gun, a stunning double-punch that blew the shooter backward through the doorway where he had been previously concealed.

He was about to turn away when movement on the rooftop of the service station froze him in his tracks. The sniper had emerged from cover once again, and he was sighting down the barrel of an M-1 rifle, straight at Johnny's face. The younger Bolan brought his shotgun up, his finger tensing on the trigger, wondering if there was any chance at all for him to drop the rifleman before a bullet cut him down. He didn't think so.

Suddenly the sniper lifted off his stance, the M-1's muzzle veering skyward. With a grin, the wiry figure thrust one fist at Johnny, thumb extended in a high-sign of congratulation. Bolan gave him back the same, and watched the sniper drop from sight again, prepared to wait for other enemies to show themselves.

It was a luxury Johnny Bolan could not well afford. If he stood still and waited for the enemy to find him, he would forfeit any chance he might still have of finding Mack alive. Such a chance existed, he deduced from the continued sound of automatic weapons hammering away behind the storefronts on the far side of the street. The warrior headed in that direction, moving out to find the sole surviving member of his family. Failing that, he was prepared to find the fires of hell, and carry them against his enemies, until no trace of them remained.

CAMACHO SNAPPED OFF two quick rounds, then ducked back quickly, diving behind the garbage Dumpster as a bullet sliced the air above his head. He cursed the gringo's aim, his obvious proficiency with firearms, and a sudden thought intruded on Camacho's mind: he wondered if they might have found the bastard they were hunting.

He had not seen the gringo clearly; just a glimpse of denim clothing, which was not the garb their enemy had worn last night. He could have changed, of course, but when they glimpsed him, he had not been moving like a wounded man already at death's door. He had been sprinting like an athlete, running serpentine to spoil their aim, and when he turned to face them, there was thunder in his hands.

Two of Camacho's men had fallen in the first exchange of fire. That left him only two, and they were staying safely under cover now, reluctant to expose themselves and tempt the gringo. Scowling at their cowardice, Rivera's crew chief risked a hasty glance around the Dumpster, scanning for his enemy, retreating quickly as a flicker of movement at the far end of the alley caught his eye. He waited for incoming rounds, then crouch-walked backward to the Dumpster's other end, abruptly popping up with pistol leveled to surprise the gunman.

Nothing.

The top flaps of a cardboard box were fanning in the arid breeze where he had imagined human movement seconds earlier. Camacho scowled, aware that he had almost wasted precious ammunition on a paper target while his enemy was safely hidden, waiting for the sound and muzzle-flash to offer him a target. Ducking back, Camacho knew that he would have to break the stalemate soon or risk disaster in the form of a surprise attack by other townspeople.

Behind him, from the general direction of the street, he could hear heavy firing, concentrated near the diner where Rivera would be waiting for him to report. Unless the other troops were emptying their guns at shadows, they must be meeting stiff resistance, and he wondered how much longer it would be before the angry citizens of Santa Rosa found him in the alleyway, cut off, with only two men to assist him. What had seemed a simple hunting party at the outset had degenerated into something desperate, something deadly, and Camacho had begun to wonder if he would survive.

It was the first time he had questioned the pronouncements of Luis Rivera, and the first time in at least decade that Camacho had been doubtful of his own ability to do a job. It had been simple: find the gunman, capture him and take him home for questioning at the *estancia*. As time went by, and they encountered marginal resistance, he had drawn another relatively simple job: burn down the town. But now, instead of herding frightened peons to their deaths like sheep to slaughter, he was pinned down in an alley, smelling garbage, fighting for his life. Camacho wondered, briefly, where he had gone wrong, and gave it up at once in favor of considering a different strategy against his enemy.

He snapped his fingers twice, attracting the attention of his two surviving gunners, who cowered on the far side of the alley. They were less than twenty feet away, but now they squinted at him, as if he were standing on the far side of a giant chasm. He directed them to rush the enemy's position, root him out. Camacho would be right behind them, bringing up the rear. He would be present at the kill.

They gawked at each other, whispering, and then they shook their heads in unison, a negative response for which Camacho was completely unprepared. He felt the color rising in his cheeks, restrained himself from shrieking at them with an effort. In the place of angry words, he raised his automatic pistol, trained it on their faces and repeated his instructions in a somber tone. The pistol's cold, unblinking stare left them in no confusion as to the alternative should they defy his orders.

Hector kept his finger on the trigger as they tottered to their feet, aware that they might turn on him, trusting in the strength of two-on-one to save their lives. He was prepared to kill them, if he had to, but it would not solve his problem. Rather, it would leave him all alone to face his adversary, and that was precisely what Hector wanted to avoid.

His men were cowards, anxious to retreat and save themselves. Camacho, on the other hand, was simply exercising the prerogatives of his command, employing solid logic. Two-on-one might take the gringo, although it was doubtful when Camacho thought about his swift response to five-on-one a moment earlier. If nothing else, the rush would force him to reveal himself, and when he rose from hiding to annihilate the others, Hector would be waiting for him, safely under cover, with his pistol primed and ready for the kill.

It was a simple plan, and therefore nearly foolproof. Any latitude for failure would be interjected by the sorry soldiers under his command. He waited, gestured with his pistol when they hesitated in the starting gate, then watched with satisfaction as they set out, one behind the other, running awkwardly, crouched, shouting, firing blindly toward the far end of the alleyway. A pair of Dumpsters stood together there, and Hector's enemy was bound to be behind them, certainly, unless...

No time for supposition now, as Hector stood erect, his pistol braced in both hands, elbows locked and resting on the hard edge of the garbage bin. He sighted down the automatic's slide with both eyes open, ready for minute adjustments when the gringo showed himself, prepared to empty out the whole damned clip in rapid fire and send his adversary off to hell without a face to call his own.

He waited, smiling, knowing that his time had come to shine.

THE WOUND IN BOLAN'S SIDE had opened when he landed on his hands and knees in the alleyway, but he was scarcely conscious of the pain as he waited for the enemy to rush him, finish off the job. He had exhausted the supply of ammunition for his captured automatic weapon, and he had discarded it before the hunting party overtook him in the alley, firing wildly, closing fast. It had been luck as much as skill when had Bolan dropped a pair of them with hasty rounds designed to frighten more than kill, and now he waited for the final rush, a pistol in each hand, fresh blood like sticky perspiration soaking through his denim shirt.

He heard them coming, knew that they were making for the Dumpsters, counting on him to be there, relying on the greater cover to conceal their enemy. They would not spare a second glance for ancient, battered trash cans farther down the alley, where the Executioner sat, his back against a picket fence that bordered brown, withered grass, the small backyard of a deserted mobile home.

He pushed forward and stood, tracking with the Beretta in his left hand and Big Thunder in his right. Two men, already closing fast at twenty yards, were about to realize their last mistake too late, as Bolan's furtive movement brought their eyes and guns around toward unexpected target acquisition. They had bet their lives that he was behind the Dumpsters, and it was the soldier's moment to collect, in full.

He lightly stroked the 93-R's trigger, ripping off a 3-round burst that caught the foremost gunner in the chest and knocked him backward, off his stride and off his feet. He jerked and twitched for a moment, like a viper with a severed head, and then lay still. His partner, meantime, leaped across the new obstruction, desperate to stay in motion, counting on the Dumpsters for his own protection. He pegged a shot at Bolan, missing him by yards, undoubtedly aware that he could never make it, that his life was measured out in fractions of a heartbeat.

Bolan put a 3-round cluster through the runner's throat and nearly took the man's head off in the process, the lethal impact spinning his assailant right around and hurling him against the wall of an adjacent shop. Rebounding, Bolan's late opponent left wet traces of himself behind, like abstract artwork on the dusty stucco, drying quickly in the desert heat.

Four down, but there had been another, and before the thought had time to form, he was aware of subtle movement there, behind another Dumpster, halfway down the alley's length. A head and shoulders were revealed, hands interlocked around a pistol aimed at Bolan from a range of fifty feet. He squeezed the trigger of his AutoMag three times in swift succession, heard the heavy boattails clang against the siding of the Dumpster, drilling through, and then the silhouette of his assailant seemed to sag, collapsing, disappearing by degrees. The hands veered skyward, swinging up the pistol into close alignment on the sun, while head and shoulders kept on sinking, out of sight. Another moment passed, and the lifeless hands had disappeared as well.

He didn't bother checking on the guy. If his target was not dead or dying, he was out of it, so far as any action was concerned. Whatever happened to him now, the Executioner had business elsewhere, and Rivera's goon would have to look out for himself, if he was still alive.

Beyond the roofline of adjacent buildings, Bolan saw the rising smoke of shops on fire and knew the town was dying while he watched. Its death might be a swifter one, more merciful than lingering extinction brought on by neglect, but he could not escape a pang of guilt. If not for him, Rivera would have shown no interest in Santa Rosa, and the blight of Bolan's private war would not have fallen on so many other lives.

But there was no time to wallow in self-condemnation now that it was done. Survival was the top priority, for Bolan, for the citizens of Santa Rosa. Some of them, at least, were standing tall against the enemy; continued firing from the Main Street battleground informed him that Rivera's men had not found it easy going. He thought about Grant Vickers, the elusive sniper on the roof of the garage, and wondered if there might be others, fighting even now to save the town that was their home.

He hoped so, realizing that the only hope for Santa Rosa lay within her people. If they cared enough to stand and fight, there might still be a chance. If they did not, then the town and all had been long dead before Rivera ever showed his face and called for Bolan's blood on Main Street.

Concentrating on Rivera, the soldier knew his best and
only chance of ringing down the curtain on the dealer's
game was through a confrontation with the man himself—
a confrontation in which only one of them would walk
away.

There might still be a chance to keep Rivera from annihilating everyone in Santa Rosa, if the Executioner was swift
enough and sure enough about his tactics. He would have to
find a way inside the diner, first of all, or force the dealer to
emerge . . . but, then again, the latter course of action might
not be the problem that it seemed. Rivera had already been
deprived of transportation, and the town was burning down
around him. He would have to find some wheels, unless he
meant to hang around and fry, or wait for the eventual ar-
rival of the state police. But to acquire another car, or cars,
it would be necessary to dispatch his gunners, singly or in
teams. And if they failed to reappear . . .

Rivera would be forced to do it himself.

It was a plan, but Bolan knew that his success in pulling
off the scheme was far from guaranteed. He might yet fail,
and failing, he would lose it all: his war against Rivera's
filthy empire, his crusade against the broader evil of the
savages. He knew that death had been inevitable from day
one, but the reality was something else entirely. Bolan was
not ready to surrender by any means, but it was time to face
the fact that he was not immortal, that he might not make
it out of Santa Rosa.

He might die here, and with the town in flames, Rivera's
troopers on the prowl, there was a chance his death might
never be officially discovered. Johnny would suspect, of
course, suspicion growing into certainty with time, and he
would pass the word to Hal and the team at Stony Man. It
did not matter to the Executioner that he might die un-

heralded, unnoticed by the world; what bothered Bolan was the thought that he might die in vain.

If he allowed Rivera to escape, resume his dirty trade from the Sonoran rancho, then he would have failed. It would not matter if he killed off half the dealer's troops and left the others scattered in the desert. The viper's lethal head might still survive, unless he crushed it totally, without remorse.

And that brought Bolan back to penetration of the diner, or a suck play that would draw Rivera into the open. There appeared to be no third alternative available within the time remaining.

He was conscious of the seeping blood inside his shirt, the denim sticking to his ribs and underneath his arm. He would not bleed to death before he finished with his work, but it was a distraction, and it weakened him by slow degrees.

No time to waste, then. If he meant to do it right, he had to do it *now*. The soldier turned to face the alley's southern mouth...and froze. His eyes were riveted upon the muzzle of an automatic pistol, aimed directly at his face from fifteen feet away.

## 20

"You're not one of them," Rick Stancell said.

"You got that right," the stranger answered, seeming to relax a bit.

Rick kept the big man covered, anyway, uncertain of himself now that another player had been dropped into the game. His father's death was proof enough that no one could be trusted absolutely. Granted that this man was not with the invaders—and he must not be, for Rick had watched him kill a number of them in the alley—he was obviously dangerous, for all of that. An unknown quantity at present, he might prove to be another enemy.

"Who are you?"

"I'm the one they're looking for."

"That doesn't tell me anything." Rick held the captured automatic steady, leveled at the stranger's face.

The big man thought about his answer for a moment, as if cooking up a lie inside his mind, but when he spoke again, Rick thought his words rang true enough. "My name is Bolan. I've been working to eliminate Rivera's operation in Sonora. He's the leader of this gang, the one who made the speech on Main Street."

"I was there."

The stranger nodded solemnly. "I saw you. I'm sorry about your father... and the girl."

Rick stared, dumbfounded, at the older man. How could he know? Instead of asking, Stancell simply said, "Her name is Amy."

Bolan nodded. "She's all right, for the moment. It's important that Rivera's men don't get a chance to check out the clinic."

"I understand."

"How are you with that thing?" the tall man asked. His eyes were on the automatic pistol.

"Fair. I've killed four of them, maybe five."

The man called Bolan looked surprised, but there was something else—could it be sadness?—in his eyes. "I'd say you've done enough."

"Not yet." He let the automatic's muzzle dip a fraction. It was pointed at the stranger's navel, now, but Stancell did not plan to use it. Not unless the man proved to be an enemy. "How did you now about my father?"

"I was at the clinic when you brought him in."

"I didn't see you."

Bolan shrugged. "You weren't supposed to. I was hiding."

"From this guy Rivera?" Bolan nodded, and for the first time Rick noticed that a crimson stain was spreading underneath his arm. "You're hurt."

"It looks worse than it is."

"You ought to let the doctor—"

"There's no time, Rick."

Stancell found that he was not amazed to hear the stranger speak his name. If Bolan had been hiding in the clinic when he brought his father in, he would have heard it there.

"What can I do to help?" he asked.

The tall man shook his head. "I don't want your blood on my hands."

"They're killing everybody," Rick informed him. "I won't stand around and watch it happen. If I can't help you, I'll face them on my own."

"They'll kill you, Rick."

"So far it's been the other way around. Besides, I don't much care."

"Okay." The stranger shrugged. "But what about Amy? She's lost her family already. If she loses you, what's left?"

Rick turned it over in his mind. So far his only thoughts of Amy had been inspirational, propelling him to seek revenge against the animals who had abused her, killed her parents and his father. Now, with Bolan's words in mind, he saw her in a different light, as someone who required protection. Still, if the invaders were not killed or driven out of town, it would not matter. They would all be dead.

"I've still got work to do," he said. "If we don't stop these bastards, there won't be a thing that I can do for Amy."

It took the big man half a dozen heartbeats to decide. "Rivera's in the diner. He's already lost his wheels, and now he'll have to find replacements. It's our job to cut him off before he does."

"Why don't we just go in and get him?"

"Hostages. If they're alive, I'd like to see them stay that way."

"That means we have to wait for him to show himself."

"It won't be long. And waiting doesn't have to be the same as standing still."

"All right," he said. "Just tell me what to do."

"For starters, you could drop the gun."

The voice was strange, originating from behind him. Stancell turned—but carefully—and saw a young man with a futuristic-looking shotgun pointed at his face. He seemed to read Rick's mind.

"Don't even think about it, kid," he said.

"IT'S OKAY, JOHNNY. He's with me."

The younger Bolan glanced at Mack, took in his haggard face, the bloodstain spreading underneath his arm. Reluctantly, he swung the SPAS off target, saw the kid relax a fraction, but he could react with swift and lethal force to any sudden, hostile move the boy might make. A rapid scan informed him that the youth was carrying another pistol, tucked inside his belt, beneath the cover of his shirttail. Despite his age, John marked the boy as being dangerous.

"What's happening?" he asked.

"We're working on a way to flush Rivera from the diner," Mack replied.

"I'm in."

"Okay. He has to find himself some wheels. I want you out there, waiting, when he sends his people shopping."

"Do you think he'll tag along to keep them company?"

The warrior shook his head. "He'll save the personal appearance as a last resort. Right now he's holding hostages. He feels secure."

"But not for long?" John didn't know precisely what his brother had in mind, but he could hear the mental wheels in motion.

"He's already set the town on fire," Mack answered. "Who knows what might happen if we had a shift in wind direction."

"Right."

The boy was nodding earnestly. "I know just how to do it," he declared. "The air-conditioner's around back, and all I have to do is—"

"I was hoping you'd be out in front with Johnny," Mack responded, trying to be tactful. "We'll need someone who can recognize the locals when it comes to spotting hostages."

The boy was glancing back and forth between them, finally nodding. "That makes sense, I guess."

"We don't want any accidents."

"All right."

"Be careful on the way," Mack cautioned. "There's a sniper on the service station's roof."

"We've met," John answered.

"That's Old Enoch Snyder," said the boy. "He used to spend a lot of time around the station . . . with my dad. He was some kind of hero during World War Two. I guess the war's not over yet."

"You're right again," Mack said. "I'll give you five to get in place, and then I start to smoke Rivera out."

"We'll be there," Johnny promised him. The boy was moving out already, toward the nearest access onto Main Street. Hanging back a moment, Johnny stood beside his brother on the killing ground. "You want the KG-99?" he asked.

"No, thanks. You'll need the extra punch out front. I'm getting by with what I have."

"Be careful."

"You the same."

Their eyes locked for an instant, and the younger Bolan knew that there was nothing more to say. He set off, following the boy, and overtook him at the entrance of a narrow alley opening on Main, between two vacant stores.

"The diner's four doors down, this side," the boy explained, and Johnny let him talk. "To cover it, I think we need to cross the street."

"I'd say you're right. You ready?"

"As I'll ever be."

"Okay." He swept the sidewalk with a glance in each direction, spotting no apparent ambush. Then again, it was the ones you didn't see that killed you. "On three."

He started counting down, hit "three," and then they both exploded out of cover, charging for the far side of the street. A stuttering report of automatic fire erupted on their right, from the direction of the diner and the burning cars, immediately answered by a crack of rifle fire from Johnny's left. The service-station sniper was providing cover, pinning down the opposition, and they made it to the grocery store intact, burst through the open doorway, weapons scanning for a sign of hostile gunners, finding none.

A stray round cracked the grocery's plate-glass window, and they went to ground behind a broad display of produce. The diner was across the street and clearly visible behind a line of burned-out cars.

"What now?" the boy asked, sounding very young for one who had already seen so much of death.

"We wait," he said. And he wondered if they might be waiting for an opportunity to die.

ATOP THE SERVICE STATION, Enoch Snyder fed his hot M-1 another clip and brought an ought-six round into the firing chamber. All around him cartridge cases littered the flat, dusty roof, and half a dozen bodies littering the street below were silent testimony to his marksmanship. The bastards would be running out of reinforcements soon, unless he missed his guess, but Enoch wondered if it would be soon enough.

They were inside the station, even now. They had been smart enough to force him to keep his head down, raking automatic fire along the cornice every time he showed himself until a team had worked its way across the street and slipped inside. It wouldn't help them, he reflected, since there was no inside access to the roof, but there were other tricks that they might try to force him down.

He wished them luck. All bad. He had survived the beach at Tarawa, but he did not intend to see the sun go down this day. Before he even climbed the ladder, pulled it up behind him, he had known the odds against survival and accepted them. Old Enoch was not looking for a medal this time; he was looking for revenge, a chance to even up the score for Bud, the others who were murdered or abused by the invaders. So far he had done all right, but he was definitely running out of time.

The ammunition would not be a problem. He had better than a thousand rounds left, after all the firing he had done, and with a bit of luck, he just might drop a few more of the bastards yet before they brought him down. He was encouraged by the fact that there were others in the game now. Vickers, with his suicidal banzai charge that left the sons of bitches minus transportation, or the stranger with the fancy hardware who had shown up on the street a short while earlier. God knows where *he* had come from, but he wasn't taking any shit from the invaders, and it had been good to see a real, live fighting man in action.

Enoch risked a peek above the cornice, just in time to see Rick Stancell and the stranger break from cover down below, both of them sprinting for the grocery like the hounds of hell were snapping at their heels. An automatic weapon started spitting at them from the doorway of the diner, and Old Enoch snapped his rifle up, unmindful of the danger to himself. He cranked off one quick round to spoil the gunner's aim, then started firing for effect, his bullets chipping masonry and bringing down the diner's plate-glass window in a frosty avalanche. The gunner staggered, wounded, going down, and Snyder nailed him with the last round in his clip, rewarded by a spray of blood that streaked the diner's wall.

The empty clip ejected automatically, and he was fishing for another in his pocket when he caught a hint of movement at the edge of sight, a figure stepping into view below him, to his right. He knew at once that it was trouble, that it could be nothing else, and he was reeling backward, seeking cover, when the bullet ripped into his side, beneath his arm. The impact drove him backward, saved him from other rounds that crackled overhead, but one could do the job, and Snyder knew that he was badly wounded. Sudden difficulty with his breathing told the combat veteran his lung was punctured, and he felt the telltale pressure of internal bleeding. He could not locate an exit wound, and that was something to be thankful for, reducing blood loss to a single hole instead of two, but mounting dizziness informed him that the wound was serious enough.

Old Enoch managed to reload his rifle, chambering a round, and he was crawling slowly, painfully, in the direction of the cornice when he smelled the smoke. He had been smelling smoke all afternoon—the burning cars, at first, and later from the shops downrange—but this was different. Closer. Pausing, taking time to test the air, he realized that it was coming from beneath him, rising from the garage.

The bastards meant to smoke him out or fry him where he lay, but Enoch wasn't having any of it. Even with a bullet rattling around inside him, he would not lie back and wait for death like some poor invalid who couldn't lift a finger to defend himself. Whatever happened, he would go out fighting, and the men who took him down would know, by God, that he had been alive and kicking to the bitter end.

They could not stay inside the station after setting it afire. He knew that much, and realized that it could work to his advantage. Enoch used his rifle as a crutch, aware that he was losing blood as he staggered to his feet. In a few more moments, he would not be needing any blood at all.

He stepped up to the roof's edge, paused with one foot resting on the cornice. Down below, the gunner saw him coming, raised his submachine gun for the killing burst, and toppled over backward with a bullet in his face. Old Enoch had not even bothered aiming; it had been that easy.

Frightened voices babbled in Spanish from the doorway just below him. It was getting hot in there, with wisps of smoke already snaking from the doors and windows. He could picture them inside the smoky cave of the garage, beginning to believe they might be trapped. He laid the rifle down, removed the old Colt automatic from a pocket of his coveralls, and thumbed the hammer back. A sudden hush below informed him that the enemy had come to a decision.

Standing on the cornice, Old Enoch was amazed at just how easily he kept his balance. Anyone could pick him off but they wouldn't. Snyder had a job to do.

Number one erupted from the doorway of the station, gagging on the smoke, immediately followed by another gunman and another. Enoch smiled, and fell upon them like the wrath of God.

LUIS RIVERA SMELLED THE SMOKE before Esteban called his name and pointed to the ceiling vents. He had not seen Camacho or the others recently, had no idea if they were still alive, but somehow sparks had crossed the street and kindled on the diner's roof. Rivera thought he recognized the stench of burning shingles, insulation, and he knew that they would all be trapped like rats if he did not take some decisive action soon.

Four gunners remained inside the small diner. For all Rivera knew, the others might have been annihilated on the street. Four men would have to do. If they followed orders, acted ruthlessly and with courage, he believed that four should be enough.

He barked at Esteban and the others, ordered them to leave the cover of the restaurant and find some means of transportation, of escape. The *pistoleros* hesitated, whispering among themselves, until he turned his steely gaze upon them, cowing them with the force of his personality. They might have overpowered him with little difficulty, but they were accustomed to obeying his instructions, witnessing the fate of others who defied him, and they dared not turn against him now. Outside, their fate might be uncertain, but inside the diner, with Rivera, there could be no doubt about their fear.

They clustered at the doorway, crouching, glancing this and that way, up and down the street. There was sudden gunfire from the direction of the service station, punctuated by the screams of frightened, dying men. Another moment, and the sounds were lost, devoured and swept away by the relentless desert wind.

Esteban was the first to move. The others followed in a rush, and for a moment, in the stillness of the street, Rivera thought that they might make it. Sudden gunfire changed his mind—a pistol, joined by automatic weapons and a shotgun—and Rivera knew that he would never see his men alive again.

He drew the nickel-plated automatic from his shoulder rigging and crossed the narrow room with long, determined strides. The waitress saw him coming, whispered something to the fry cook as Rivera closed the gap. He stared at them in silence for a moment, then reached out to grasp the woman's arm and pull her toward him. When his arm was wrapped around her waist and she was firmly in his grasp, he raised his weapon, sighted down its slide and shot the old man in the face.

Two hostages would be unmanageable in his present situation, but a single woman, terrified and sobbing for her life, should fit his needs precisely. There was still a chance that someone on the street might fire on him, sacrifice the waitress to eliminate the last of their surviving enemies, but such an action would require the ruthless daring of a battle-hardened warrior. Peasants were conditioned to protect their women and their offspring, even at the cost of life itself. He would be stunned if anyone should risk a shot while he retained the woman as a shield, but if they found the nerve, he would at least enjoy the satisfaction of returning fire and watching one more peon die before they cut him down.

Rivera dragged his sobbing, human burden toward the doorway, coughing as the smoke began to swirl around them, growing thicker by the moment. Santa Rosa, thus far, had been a disaster for him. He had gambled to regain his honor, save face, and he had lost. The best that he could hope for now was survival, but there was still an outside chance that he could make it home to Mexico.

And what would he find waiting for him there? His other troops would be dismayed to learn of what had happened in the tiny hamlet. Some of them might leave him, if he gave them time to think, to reason out their doubts and fears. It would be necessary for him to react, now more than ever, after suffering an even greater loss of face. Whatever might be left of Santa Rosa must be razed, as an example to his enemies . . . and there was still the matter of the gringo who had dared invade his home.

Rivera felt as if a century had passed since he'd laid eyes on Santa Rosa, since the hellish siege began. The time might have been measured out in hours, but it had been a lifetime for his troops, and for an unknown number of the locals. They had managed to surprise him this time, but Rivera had them locked into his memory forever, waiting for the day when retribution would be his.

There would be some delay, of course, while the police investigated, took photographs and made their empty statements to the press. Aside from the elusive gringo, Vickers was the only man in Santa Rosa who had known Rivera's name, and he would not be making any statements to the state police. In that respect, the lawman's fiery suicide had been fortuitous, for all the havoc it had wreaked upon Rivera's transportation.

If he could make it out of Santa Rosa, back across the border to Sonora, he was safe. The burned-out vehicles would be no problem; fire had taken care of any fingerprints. As for the men that he would leave behind, they all had prison records for assorted violent crimes, and none of them would cause a ripple by their passing. If police in Mexico suspected some of them were on Rivera's payroll, extra bribes should keep the matter quiet—just as long as he, himself, was not accused by law-enforcement officers in the United States. Without the threat of diplomatic pressure from the north, the *federales* would have nothing to concern themselves about.

If he could just escape...

He held the woman closer, concentrating on her cheap perfume and trying to ignore the smoke. If he allowed it to grow thicker, offering him better cover, the gunmen on the street might not detect his hostage soon enough to stay their hands. If he was going, it had best be done at once.

"This way, *chiquita*." Nudging one plump breast with the muzzle of his automatic, he propelled the waitress toward the door of the diner.

MACK BOLAN SLID the 93-R back into its shoulder rigging, hefting the big .44 in his fist. The trash fire he had built beside the air-conditioner was burning down, but it had done its job; from where he stood, the Executioner could see smoke curling from the windows of what seemed to be a rest room, and he knew the atmosphere inside the diner would be getting thick by now.

He tried the back door, found that it had not been locked, and entered in a combat crouch, ignoring spastic pain that emanated from his wounded side. The smoke was sharp inside his nostrils, and it burned his eyes, but Bolan took his time, maneuvering along a narrow corridor that linked the exit and employee rest rooms with the kitchen and the diner proper. Probing with the AutoMag, allowing it to lead him, ready to respond in case of any challenge from the enemy, he sought Rivera in the dealer's own command post.

He had heard the burst of firing moments earlier, on Main Street, followed swiftly by a single shot inside the diner. It had been the latter that propelled him into motion, worried that Rivera would begin to sacrifice his hostages in desperation. Bolan had no firm idea of the employee head count for the diner, but he estimated that there must be two or three, at least. One shot, so far, meant hope of rescuing survivors.

As he edged into the diner, Bolan made out figures moving through the smoke. A man and woman, from the look of it, and if he was not very much mistaken, that must be—

"Rivera!"

At the sound of his name, the dealer whirled, a woman clutched in front of him to form a human shield. Rivera held an automatic pressed against her cheek, the hammer back, his finger on the trigger.

"So." There was a note of triumph in Rivera's voice. "I knew you were alive."

The soldier came erect, advancing slowly through the smoke. "That's one of us."

"You have embarrassed me," the dealer said.

"It was the least that I could do."

"I have no choice but to kill you."

"You've been trying that all day."

"This time I will succeed."

"The woman has no part in this."

Rivera smiled, a canine grimace. "But we mean so much to each other."

"Let her go."

"Not yet. I have to ask you something, gringo."

"Ask."

"Who sent you after me? Who pays you?"

"No one paid me. It's a freebie."

"All of this, you do without a hope of payment? Have I harmed you in some way?"

"That's right."

"What have I done to you that you should take such risks?"

"You breathe. You walk the earth with human beings. You infest the planet."

"You are an idealist?"

"A realist," the soldier told him flatly. "I don't start a job unless I have a decent chance of getting through it."

"You have failed."

"I'd say you need to look around."

"You cannot hold me here."

"I don't intend to hold you anywhere."

"You are—how is it called?—a vigilante?"

"I'm a soldier. You're the enemy. It's simple."

"So. And there is nothing more to say?"

"I can't think of a thing."

Rivera's move was sudden, swift, but Bolan had been waiting for it. As the dealer shoved the waitress out in front of him, retreating toward the door, he raised his shiny automatic, snapping off two rounds at Bolan through the smoke. By that time, though, the warrior had already gone to ground; he felt the slugs slice air above him as the AutoMag responded, bucking once in hard, reflexive fire.

The heavy slug ripped through Rivera's shoulder, nearly severing his arm. The impact drove him backward, through the open door and out onto the sidewalk. Somehow he regained his balance, staying on his feet and staggering away, his limp, left arm in bloody tatters while the right one fought to bring his pistol into target acquisition. Lurching off into the smoke, he fired three more quick rounds at Bolan through the vacant windowframe. And he was gone.

The Executioner was on his feet and moving toward the door when hell broke loose outside. A pistol started cracking out in rapid fire, immediately answered by Rivera's automatic, both side arms eclipsed and silenced by the roaring of a 12-gauge, semi-automatic shotgun. Bolan froze, relaxed, aware that there was no more hurry, that Rivera wasn't going anywhere.

He stooped to help up the waitress, aware of panic in her eyes. "It's all right, now," he told her softly, and he meant it.

It was very nearly finished for the Executioner in Santa Rosa.

## EPILOGUE

"See to it that he gets some proper rest this time," Rebecca Kent told Johnny Bolan sternly. Turning toward the Executioner as she began to stow her instruments, she softened slightly. "Doctor's orders."

"How can I refuse?"

The younger Bolan cleared his throat. "I'll get the Jimmy."

"Fine."

When he was gone, Mack Bolan faced the doctor with a solemn smile. "I owe you one," he said.

"You owe me nothing. It's my job."

"Okay." He hesitated, and the silence stretched between them like a frail suspension bridge. "About the girl...we've got a CB, and I'll send the cavalry first thing, soon as we're clear."

The doctor nodded thoughtfully. "Those things I said before, about the way you live..."

"Forget it, Doc. You called it right. I lead a miserable life."

"I don't believe that anymore. You help. You stand with people when they seem too weak to stand alone."

"You do a decent job of standing up yourself."

She blushed. "I haven't got your courage. I couldn't do...the things you do."

"The world needs healers, too," he said.

"About Grant Vickers...was he...I mean..."

"Brave?" the soldier finished for her, knowing it was not precisely what the lady had in mind. "I'd say he qualified. Whatever else he may have been or done, the guy came out a winner."

"Thank you."

Bolan heard the Jimmy grumble to a stop out front. "That must be me," he said.

"I don't suppose..."

He saw the question in her eyes, and knew the only answer that would serve. "I shouldn't think so."

"No."

The lady did not follow Bolan to the door, and it was just as well. The world had need of healers *and* of warriors, but they were different breeds. The healers settled, found themselves a home and served their neighbors with the skills they had learned, the talent God had granted them. A warrior, on the other hand, must be forever moving, seeking out his enemy, another killing ground.

The enemy was waiting for Mack Bolan, and he did not have to ask about the setting of his next campaign.

The goddamned war was everywhere.

**Mack Bolan's**

**by Dick Stivers**

Action writhes in the reader's own streets
as Able Team's Carl "Ironman" Lyons,
Pol Blancanales and Gadgets Schwarz
make triple trouble in blazing war. Join
Dick Stivers's Able Team as it returns to
the United States to become the country's
finest tactical neutralization squad in an
era of urban terror and unbridled crime.

"Able Team will go anywhere, do anything,
in order to complete their mission. Plenty
of action! Recommended!"
—*West Coast Review of Books*

Able Team titles are available
wherever paperbacks are sold.

AT-1

# TAKE 'EM FREE
## 4 action-packed novels plus a mystery bonus

## NO RISK
## NO OBLIGATION TO BUY

---